JACK
HAPPY LIVING

JACK
HAPPY LIVING
A Novel

JAMES H. LEET

authorHOUSE®

AuthorHouse™
1663 Liberty Drive
Bloomington, IN 47403
www.authorhouse.com
Phone: 1-800-839-8640

Published by AuthorHouse   03/15/2013

ISBN: 978-1-4817-8703-1 (sc)
ISBN: 978-1-4817-8704-8 (hc)
ISBN: 978-1-4817-8705-5 (e)

CONTENTS

FOREWORD

This is the story of a young boy who grows into a special kind of man. But then we are all special in our own way, the choices we make in our journey through life dictate that. Our young boy has a cheek that gets him through some scrapes and a sense of humour too. He has a sensitive side that will touch you sometimes and an arrogance that will make you cringe at other times. He is a hero and a villain, a lover and a fighter, but above all else he is a risk taker and a survivor. Despite some of the foreword suggesting it, this is not a book about sales, but it does suggest that we all have to survive and win, we sometimes have to sell ourselves to the world and more often than not to ourselves at the same time.

"SALESMEN"

What does that word conjure up in your mind? Images of annoying, slimy individuals with slick back hair and cheap suits? Horribly smooth or worse, inaudible voices reciting a sales pitch over the telephone at tea time? Ever so dodgy and definitely not to be 100% trusted. Stereotypes of Arthur Daley and Frank Butcher type characters, operating from a world of double-glazing and selling vacuum cleaners to old ladies. I'm right aren't I! That's what you're thinking and you're horrified at the thought of being trapped by one of them.

But the real horror hits you when you realise that you are one of them! We all are! All of us young and old, male and female, we have all sold something, every day of our lives! It might not be a second hand car, half of Bearings Bank or even a piece of rotting fruit from a market stall with some clever banter. But think about it honestly, you will have convinced somebody somewhere, even if it's just yourself, to do something or buy into something that they were not planning on or bargaining for that day.

Congratulations! YOU are in sales now!

It's the only profession where you can't get a qualification! But there is training; Oh there is training, because some of us realise that to do it better than the rest, can just get us that bit more. If there's something you really, really want, that something that just seems so out of reach, so unobtainable, there may be no way that you could ever buy it, but selling your ass off might just win it for you! Interested now?

So what is this book about? Is it a sales manual? There are already too many of those promising all and returning nothing! Is it a just a novel? (a saucy one in places) A comedy? A tragedy? A biography? Well that depends on your needs right now.

Lesson 1 "The buyer has needs, fulfil those needs but remember to convince them that what they need is not necessarily what they think they want!"

So what do you want this book to be Hmmm? Because experiencing this book is something we do together. The best things happen "with people" not "to people". What does it have to offer? It will make you laugh! It will scare you death when you recognise yourself! Then you'll laugh again, nervously this time. It will make you think! It will make you want to read it again, in a different light! But the key word here is light, not gloom but light.

Life is not measured by the number of breaths we take, but by the moments that take our breath away. Open your mind and read on. This book is for you! So be careful what you wish for! It might just happen!

This book is based very loosely on events that have actually happened and therefore the lessons learned through life become more meaningful as you read through the storyline. It is however, a work of fiction and the characters have been made to fit the storyline. If you recognise yourself in one of these characters I will have achieved my aim of making a connection with you. Who is William? Whoever you want him to be. Did he really do all those things? Naaahmaybe . . .

If you want to live a William like existence (which thankfully is not for everyone) simply operate on this principal:

It's better to regret something you have done, than something you haven't.

JACK

Jack is the affectionate tag given to sailors who serve in the Royal Navy. It is the shortened version of Jolly Jack Tar and derives its origins when during the 17th and 18th centuries, the technique of using ship's tar to keep the hair tidy and safely out of the way was widely employed. The practice gave rise to the familiar blue, oversized square collar becoming part of the uniform that is now used by most of the world's Navies, making military sailors from all cultures, instantly recognizable. Originally this collar was a simple rag keeping the tar from spoiling the serge uniform, but Jack likes to be a bit smarter than that.

Royal Navy ratings are still, to a man, known as Jack. Jack is often referred to in the third person and the references typify the spirit and character required to make up the special kind of person who can spend months at sea in close proximity to a mass of human beings all under pressure, while coping with doing a tough job in cramped conditions with often very little sleep, on a moving living thing that is built not for comfort but for speed and agility. Jack manages to do this and remain chipper about it, that takes a special kind of tolerance and because of that, Jack has a few unique and special qualities.

Jack is tolerant yes, but he is also cheeky and mischievous. Jack the lad. Jack can't resist finding humour in anything, even at other's expense, especially in some cases. But Jack also loves it when he is the target, he can take it too. Jack is crafty, clever, can find the good in most situations and exaggerate the bad when it suits him (just as well there is no such thing as Jack Flu . . .)

Jack is loyal to his friends and to what he believes in. If you are friends with Jack, then you truly have a "bezzy Oppo". Jack is not easily impressed with much, but will take it if it's a "gizzit".

Jack is unique and yet there are thousands of him just the same (well almost). We are lucky to have him.

So next time you find yourself fancying a rum, or a gin, or a port, or anything that you feel appropriate (Jack won't mind) take a quiet moment to salute Jack, he (and she nowadays) does you proud!

Up spirits Jack!

AUTHORS NOTE

It is not for me to tell you how to read this, or any, book. I hope you enjoy reading it for the novel that it is, and I also know that some people have and will get some inspiration from the top tips, quotes and content. The top tips are something that I wanted to do in order to add value to the read. They are all proven techniques or methods that I have used successfully as a professional trainer and coach or in my own personal life. Some of them you may recognise from developmental programs you may have engaged with yourself. If reading this novel brings them back into focus and helps you, then I will have achieved one of my little mini goals for this project.

The play list is an idea that came to me as I was around halfway through the writing process, and some of you will notice that there are slight continuity errors. The music buffs will notice that at certain points, William was listening to music that had yet to be released, however it was certainly around the time and I have shamelessly bent the truth to make it fit with the storyline and the emotions felt by him at the time. What I hope the playlist does do is to bring back a few happy memories for some of you, and to help others get a feel for what was happening in the UK during that period. I know I always remember the year of certain songs by remembering what I was doing at the time, and nostalgic memories nearly always come flooding back and produce smiles, and sometimes the odd cringe.

The Quotes have all been influential and or inspirational to me, and one of my objectives was to contextualise some of my favourite quotes, I hope I have achieved that in part for you. If I have misquoted anyone, then I apologise humbly, however, what I would say is, the misquotes have helped many people I know personality through a number of situations, so I thank you for at least giving some context by providing the basis of the wisdom in the first place.

Please bear in mind that the social politics of the time do not reflect the more responsible society of today, however I have tried to remain faithful to the culture of the 70's and early 80's and the people that lived it. I hope some of you will smile, cringe at the accuracy and others will wonder how we survived it.

I want to thank all those people who gave me their candid feedback throughout the process of getting this book to print. What started out as a bit of fun became a journey of self-doubt to total belief and that belief was fuelled by honesty from those of you that I trusted along the way. I would like to say a special thank you to Shelley Costello, author of Holiday Road, who convinced me that I really should publish the book. My dialogue with Shelley gave the whole project a massive shove forward as a result.

My original plan was for a book that spanned William's whole life, but it soon became clear that I could never cram it all into one volume, so hopefully you will want to engage with William in later volumes, where if the appetite of the reader demands it, he will have many adventures.

The one caveat I will apply is that while the top tips I can confidently commend to everyone, William is a fiction and the scenarios and the way he approaches and overcomes the scrapes he gets into may not work in the real world, so kids, please don't try this at home would be good advice to heed.

All that remains is for me to wish you a happy read and I really hope you enjoy it.

CHAPTER 1

THE INNOCENCE OF THE VERY YOUNG

The boy's heart was pounding! The feeling in his stomach was sickening. At the age of seven he couldn't possibly describe the feelings of anxiety or the worry of what was to come, and nor was he interested, he was seven, he knew what he knew. What he didn't know, and would not realise for many years yet, was that he was about to pull off this week's "sale of the century".

William James Dole had been born in the sixties, to a well off, middle class family. A good looking, stocky little lad, with an innocent but cheeky face, that beamed under a mop of light brown hair. The type that almost turned blonde in the summer. He was the youngest of four children, Simon, David, Elizabeth and of course William, they had a dedicated full time Mother in Mary, and their Father Jack was a self-made man. As a businessman, William's father's success was down to a combination of three main elements.

One, he was a hard worker. A real grafter who would work all the hours God sent to ensure that his family had food on the table. In the early years of marriage he had had to do just that. He was a technical man, good with his hands and a time served apprentice, but he was also the type of person to whom most things came naturally. He was physically very strong, a bear of a man, and had used his National Service years as a way to better himself all round, rather than see them as a necessary evil as most did. He was a handsome man, his wavy blonde hair, natural strong features were the symbol of classically good looks in that time, and popular with his comrades despite his slightly different approach and work ethic. He had worked hard all his life, from humble beginnings as a farm labourer's son, always a hand full but always coming good by being bright, strong and full of life. He earned himself an apprenticeship at a carpenters shop and took to it well. After National Service he applied his tradesman's skills and began to climb the ladder toward an almost inevitable management position, taking extra jobs in the evenings as a handy man even at one stage signing on as a retained Fireman for the extra little bit along the way. Until finally he set up his own business and again through much hard work and long hours started to reap the financial rewards.

Two, He was nobody's fool. A shrewd judge of character with a good head for a business deal, rarely did he leave himself on the wrong side of a situation. And with that, came an intimidating confidence that ensured very few tried to put him there. Those that did, rarely came back for a second bight of the cherry. His leadership skills were naturally outstanding, always focussed on the getting the job done, he ensured his team worked together and individuals pulled their weight and got their just deserts as a result. He had a gift for getting the best out of people, the shop stewards never really found a way of getting to grips with his style, and maybe just didn't want to for a confusing variety of reasons. In other words he was clever with people, not quite Nelson or Monty maybe, but this was a man to be admired.

Three, when cornered he was a ruthless bastard. Always fair, kind and charitable when the situation warranted it, but what ever you had coming from this man, you could be sure you would get it without compromise, malice or favour. This was another trait of his good leadership. He was consistent in his praise and his admonishment. His workers knew it, his suppliers knew it, and his management team knew it, in a way that is only understood by those who have had the privilege to work with, or for such men, they even loved him for it. But above all his children knew it.

In short this was not a man to be messed with.

When you were bringing up a family in the decades immediately after the War, and held such values as these, there were a number of behavioural deterrents, which were considered not just acceptable, but almost a blessing to any child's development.

It was 1973, and William was the last of the brood. Why change now, the others have turned out great? If you were seven in 1973 with a proud father such as this, who you loved, admired and feared with all your heart, you just knew that every "negative result" that your actions had brought to the world, was going to have a painful consequence, and no arguments. Those were the rules. Arguments, or far worse, lies would just result in double the pain.

So William had a bit of thinking to do.

And he had to do it fast. He couldn't lie, his father hated lying. Lying was not the way forward! And his father always seemed to know the truth about everything, that blackbird with the yellow beak was apparently the source of most of his information, he always told Dad stuff. How did it do that? So many unanswered questions, that so far in his life only had the answer "because I say so!"

Only last night and this morning he had seen the results of not being truthful, when his brother David had lied to his father. David had been out as usual, he had told his mother that it was a college study night and that he would be home late.

"No later than 10 o'clock David I don't want you waking the house up again do you hear me?" had been his mother's reply.

"OK whatever Mum"

"No, not "whatever", 10 o'clock!" was the shout from the kitchen, but that shout was never heard as David had slipped out and was through the back gate which clanged loudly into position again after being returned by its heavy spring.

Now David *was* going to the college grounds, that was true, as this was a very convenient meeting place for his college mates. But any study they would be doing was purely around that of the effects hops and barley might have, if when fermented, you drank large quantities of it. And in particular, David's party piece of a four-pint jug of the stuff, consumed in around 17 seconds.

David was six feet and six inches, and like his father, of very stocky build. For a seventeen year old, who easily passed for twenty, he took his ale very well indeed. So he thought he could get away with sneaking home each night and no one would be any the wiser. But of course he wasn't fooling anyone. The stink of his bedroom was enough without the thumping and bumping as he undressed after a session.

His parents tolerated it to a point, but the line had been crossed and although he had no idea at this point, tonight would be a benchmark.

Despite last minute reservations from his mother, the door was locked at one minute past ten, and they went to bed. It was January, David was too proud to wear a "proper" coat, he was a teenager in 1973 he had an image to think of. His mother lay awake for what seemed like hours, worrying and crying. His father lay next to her engrossed in a novel while waiting for the familiar clang of the gate.

At half past eleven there it was "CLANG", at this, his father stopped worrying and turned off his bedside light after setting an alarm for half past midnight and rolled over for an hours sleep. His mother at this point was distraught but went along with the charade.

The door was locked and bolted, and after five minutes of frustrated effort it was clear that there was no way in. Fuelled by beer, the anger was welling up inside David, but there was something else as well, an anxiety that was confused somewhere in the back of his drunk brain.

He circled the house for the next fifteen minutes looking for an entry point, of which there were none. This then just gave way to rage, as he battered the door and shouted through the letterbox. The problem was of course that normally he would have drunk 4 pints of water by now (his normal routine) and gone to bed comatose, as it was the alcohol was starting to take hold of him and surge through his system and the cold was slowing down his senses still further.

His father on the other hand was just rousing himself and completely chilled. As he plodded down the stairs he was calculating his responses to all possible case scenarios that might confront him. He was actually counting on the fact that David would now be at the height of his drunkenness, and in a state of confused anger. In his extensive experience, cold calculation always defeated blind rage, whether physically or psychologically.

David was back outside the back door, huddled in the corner arms wrapped around himself, trembling with a combination of cold, anger and if he was totally honest a little bit of fear. As he heard the key in the lock, he jumped up and made a move to barge through the opening door, only to find his way completely blocked by his father. His heart sank, he had really hoped it was his mother having snuck down to let him in but that was just too much to hope for, he was going to have to confront his dad.

With teenage, masculine, drunk pride running through him, he drew himself up to his full height and held his fathers steely gaze for what seemed an eternity.

"Where have you been?"

"College with the . . . ."

"WHERE have you been? Last chance, do not lie!"

He was past the stage of back peddling in his own stubborn mind, "College!"

In one lightning swift movement, the flat of one enormous hand connected squarely with the side of David's head. It was a stinging blow! Very painful and rendering temporary disorientation, this simple technique was a favourite among such people as professional doormen, special forces personnel and genuinely hard men who needed a result one way or the other. By the time David was able to see and think straight again, the door was again locked, this time there was a blanket on the floor outside it with an envelope laid on top. The envelope contained a key; the key in turn displayed a label that was simply titled SHED. It was to be a long, cold night of reflection, something that his father had of course budgeted on. In the morning the matter would be closed.

So if his father could see through David in this way, who was after all a man in William's eyes and indeed somewhat of a revered character, what chance did a boy stand? No he could not lie.

The problem David faced was linked to the fact that his father didn't particularly enjoy gardening. It was considered a chore. He was however a perfectionist, and often invited business clients and colleagues around to entertain them. He therefore insisted that the gardens were kept immaculate. It was fine to play on the lawn and have toys laying about the place, as long as everything was cleared up before the grass needed mowing. But the flowerbeds and borders were off limits. He would not be pleased at the fact that not only was one of the beds all neatly weeded and dug over ready for the spring in a few weeks, completely stomped on. But the fence that in bordered was now badly damaged after William had got slightly carried away while killing imaginary Germans with a garden fork he had found in the now unlocked but usually out of bounds, garden shed(those Sunday afternoon war films were inspirational).

As he was slowly trudging his way up the long garden toward the back of the house, William thought of many things, all of them problems in the form of what punishments would befall him, and none of the thoughts were answers to his problems. His young mind could only focus on the fear that his instincts provided him with. The French doors were open and the sound of the wireless playing brought the lyrics floating toward William that he had always found a little sinister yet compelling ". . . one day these boots are gonna walk all over you!" it felt almost like a portent to oncoming doom.

It was at this point that he heard the familiar low growl that was the distinctive noise of his father's car. There was no mistaking it, William didn't know that the car was a Jenson Interceptor III, or why it attracted so much attention from passers by, or why it was all some people talked about when they came around. Why all his brothers' friends were always peering through the windows at the dashboard was beyond him. He just knew that the back seats were just right for him to be on his own in the back, that the smell of leather was like nothing else and that the noise it made was most definitely different from any other car he had ever heard, by a long way.

One minute later the clang of the back gate signalled his father's arrival, and sure enough, whistling away to himself, his father emerged around the corner of the house toward the back door.

At the moment William saw his father, dressed in his business suit, jacket slung over one shoulder, brief case gripped in the other hand highlighting the enormous forearms that appeared from the crisp short sleeved air force blue shirt, tie slightly loosened, and that imposing gait that intimidated so many people, all the emotion welled up inside William and he simply burst into tears, the twisted knot in his stomach filling his senses with fear, how strange that this feeling would become so exciting in his future life.

On seeing William, his father stopped whistling.

"What's up boy?"

But William couldn't talk. He tried but all that would come out were breathless, panting sobs. A sort of "Hu, bu, bu, bu, ba" as he tried to catch his breath.

Firmly but with compassion, his father squatted down and held William by the shoulders.

"Now calm down, and tell me what's the matter"

"I, I, I . . . ."

In a moment of inspiration maybe or whatever you have when your seven, William said exactly the right thing.

"I need your help Dad!"

William's father relaxed and stood up. More interested that worried now, after all what problems could a seven year old have that he couldn't resolve or at least put into perspective. But more importantly his sub conscious mind had triggered human kinds' nature to help the underdog.

Most people when asked for help have an uncontrollable urge to respond positively. If a complete stranger asks, then suspicion is aroused, but they nearly always want to investigate a bit more before saying no. The usual response is "I will if I can". This is one of the things that has made the human race so successful. They exist through co-operation and collaboration, if nobody had ever helped anybody else, we would never have invented the wheel or discovered fire, and insects would be running things by now.

Now add all that to a close family tie, especially when there's offspring involved and automatically your attitude toward a set of circumstances is changed for you. This is called a paradigm shift. A paradigm is a map of how you see things. If you try to change your attitude toward something the process requires a lot of effort and is almost impossible to sustain for extended periods. However if you change the way you view something your attitude is simply changed for you as a result, with no effort.

For example, somebody barges into you, really quite hard, and for apparently no reason. Understandably, your attitude toward them becomes very hostile. When you challenge them you find out that they have just a new prosthetic leg fitted. They are in a lot of pain and are clearly having problems getting used to it. Suddenly, because you now see the situation very differently your attitude has completely reversed as a result, and you haven't had to work on it at all. Now rather than thump the person, you are desperate to help them without giving offence. What a powerful piece of psychology that is.

Now his son was crying and asking for help, William's father wanted to do just that. His attitude was just ready to buy into whatever came next. Now he was in a primed and ready position for William to make his sale.

"What do you want help with son?"

"I've spoiled the garden and I want to put it right but I don't know how and I know I'm in trouble and I'll probably get smacked but I just want to mend it and I promise I won't do it again and . . ."

"All right, all right, stop, calm down and show me!"

As they walked down the garden, all sorts of horror stories were flooding through the mind of William's father. What would he find? What could be so bad as to provoke his son to tears?

When he saw the bit if trampled earth that he had weeded in readiness for the bulbs to come through in spring, he almost laughed.

"Is that it Will? Is that what all the fuss is about? Look you know you shouldn't be on there but there is no harm done it would have settled down in the rain any way!"

"But Dad I've ruined it, I've let you down and I'm so sorry!"

William couldn't understand how the rain would have settled the earth down anyway, and the slats in the fence that were now broken and hanging on by their nails had been rotten for years.

William's father on the other hand was feeling an overwhelming sense of pride that his youngest boy had the courage to face up to his problem and was working hard to remain as serious as he could, so that he could empathise with his son.

"How have you let me down son?"

"It's broken!"

"It's all right it's just the bulb bed, your mother might be cross if you walk in the house with those boots on though!"

"But what about the fence?"

William's father hadn't noticed the fence. The truth was that the fence was a real heath robinson effort anyway, and desperately needed replacing, but wanting to turn this to his advantage he stood and thought for a while.

"Well I'm disappointed about the fence William!"

William had started to become a little bit more comfortable with his father's warm approach and had even dared to thing he had gotten away with it. But with those words the twisting feeling in his gut returned.

"What do you propose to do about it?"

"I don't know Dad"

"Right well instead of playing this weekend you can put up a new fence. I'll help you, but you don't get to do anything else until the job's done."

William couldn't believe his luck, this was great, he was going to be allowed to build a fence. He didn't have the first clue on how to go about it, but what an opportunity. He was always building dens in the bit of waste-land at the very bottom of the garden, out of sight from the rest of the world behind the trees. But this was something real and very important.

What William didn't realise is that his father was just as keen to spend a bit of quality time with his boy, this was the perfect solution, the fence needed fixing anyway.

The deal was over. The result was a win-win, the best kind.

In these early years, growing up in a busy, bustling household, with people coming and going all the time, William learned the first and most important sales lesson of all. This was to build relationships with people quickly if you wanted to get in on the action.

William loved being centre of attention, and of course hated being left out. The trouble was he was at the bottom of the pecking order in this house full of strong personalities. He hated being left out, at the same time feared his brothers' admonishment if he pushed in and annoyed them in front of friends and girlfriends.

But one thing he noticed and latched onto straight away, is that the girlfriends, for a while at least, thought he was cute, and were open with their affection toward him (a buying signal).

So he watched and learned, observed the responses that certain phrases, mannerisms and routines got, and started to filter the bad stuff, while building on the good stuff. First impressions got him a bit of airtime, then he milked his audience.

The real beauty was that the audience was wide, varied and constant. A stream of his brothers' mates, girlfriends, girlfriend's friends, baby sitters, baby sitter's friends, Aunties, Uncles and business associates, flooded through the house day in day out.

During these first very few but seemingly endless years, William had sold everything from his milk teeth including the jar he kept them in (it had a picture of George Best on which added to the value), pictures he'd knock up as soon as he heard the gate clang (usually to Aunties, they were always a good buyer of those types of product) right through to unwittingly closing a huge business deal for his Father.

His Father was great believer in entertaining his clients, but did not wish to spend too much time away from his family. He saw little enough of them as it was with his busy schedule. So he would do much of his entertaining at home, when of course the whole house would be under strict instructions as to how to behave. Simon and David would usually take this opportunity to slip out, Elisabeth would relish the opportunity to play hostess with her Mother and William was supposed to be seen and not heard.

On one such occasion, William, who had been through the ritual of introductions several times and knew the script, had seen an opportunity to steal the laugh that his Father had always seemed to get.

William was not looking forward to his evening. A large stern looking Scotsman had been introduced to his Mother who had scurried of to prepare him a drink, then his brothers who had immediately made their excuses had gone out. The man looked really scary, with his big purple nose, big bushy eyebrows and very piercing stare. Tonight was going to be horrible, just to sit quietly till bedtime while this horrible man talked to Dad about boring stuff.

Then the man was introduced to his sister Elisabeth, who was clearly nervous as well. But this big Scotsman, was a long way from home and had daughters of his own, his whole being seemed to change as he began to tease William's teenage sister. As he kissed Elisabeth's hand in a very formal and overblown gesture, she giggled and he smiled.

He smiled! Williams buying signal and his window of opportunity, just as William's Mother came back into the reception room with a tray of drinks, William made his move. He stepped forward, put out his hand as he had seen his Father do many times and said "Hello, I'm William, I'm the best mistake he ever made in his life!"

Just as the tray hit the floor, the man's smile broke into an uncontrollable belly laugh that lasted for minutes and became so infectious that the whole household could not stop. William had no idea why it was so funny, but suddenly this big scary man didn't look so scary at all.

After the initial commotion petered out, and the businessman was engaged in a routine of practiced tricks, which made Elisabeth laugh still further, his Father ruffled William's hair and whispered "I shall have to be careful what I say in front of you in future young man!"

It had turned out that the man was notoriously difficult to do business with, and never dropped his guard. William's father had tried everything to build a relationship with this man, so he might find a way to get his business, but without success. That evening was to be his last attempt to win the deal and find some kind of common ground that would break the deadlock.

William had pressed the right button with is opening line. And rule 1 had been executed effectively.

Top Tip - Build a relationship, quickly!

In order for any kind of transaction to take place, a relationship, no matter how fragile, must exist. If a relationship does not exist, communication cannot take place. If communication cannot take place, needs cannot be established. If a need cannot be established, there is no transaction! Two things have just happened. The needy person still has a problem. The person with a solution still has something they don't necessarily need. This happens all the time because people don't communicate properly or are too fearful of starting a relationship.

To get past the first hurdle we need to make a relationship and make it fast before the window of opportunity disappears.

First impressions do count!

Cold relationship forming, is psychologically difficult for most people, until they realise that a relationship can be as simple as good eye contact! Eye contact starts every good relationship. Conversation then follows. Anyone who has ever found love across a crowded room knows that. It's the same at any level.

Dogs can't talk, but they are "man's best friend". What they do to invite us to stroke them (thus satisfying their need), is simply wag their tails. Humans don't have tails, but we do have very expressive faces. A genuine, warm smile is as good as any tail wagging. The fact is, if you smile at someone and mean it, they will generally smile back, and bingo! You have a relationship! Try it, it works, and because there are now two people in the world that are smiling, it feels a better place for a second.

So those first few seconds are crucial, and are nothing to do with what you have to say. It's about eye contact and body language! Our eyes face forward, we are hunting animals, so we must be careful to not make other people feel like prey, or they will run. There are of course, those undesirables who do indeed regard people as prey. That's why we are nervous around strangers. It's part instinct, part experience. So use good eye contact and positive not aggressive body language to let people know we are friendly, then they will be less wary and more curious. When a person is curious they are receptive, when they are receptive we can then put our case forward. It sounds simple and it is, but it's a practice that must be sincere if it is to be sustainable.

So, we still haven't said a word, but we have a relationship, albeit seconds old. The other person is curious, what we say next will either create further interest, or end the relationship. Think carefully about that, but be natural not scripted, but above all be interesting. Everybody can spot a script, from a corny chat up line in a bar to a telephone sales person reading from a card. Be yourself, be honest be sincere. If your nervous because this is alien to you, don't try to hide it too much, you might get the sympathy vote by being honest and natural.

The fact is we need people! Society is reliant upon co-operation between people. If everybody over night became insular and selfish to the extreme the world would end. Fact!

Don't be nervous of meeting new people, we should love meeting new people! There are approximately six and a half billion people on the planet, the more of those people we know, the more chance we have of buying or selling with them, or gaining the ultimate prize;

Knowledge.

CHAPTER 2

BIG SCHOOL

Primary school for William had been a reasonably happy experience. He was popular with the other kids, and while he didn't realise it at the time he was fairly popular with his teachers. He had a character which was cheeky, but a value system which stopped him from going too far. This was an endearing combination that would allow William to push a few boundaries in later life.

Academically he was one of those children that always frustrated teachers. Often his reports would say, "William is a bright pupil who would do so much better if he worked harder" or "William has a quick mind but is slow to apply it!". William always seemed to come up with all the right things at the right time, so as to satisfy the system, but his teachers knew there was more.

This level of intelligence meant that he was never destined to be a rocket scientist or a surgeon, and to be successful at anything at the very top level he had to work extremely hard. As a result, William's strength became his weakness. He was clever enough to do well without having to work too hard, this left him the energy to play just as hard. He preferred to play!

The purist educational minds would say that this was a terrible waste, and that someone like this should be forced to see it right through to university and beyond, thus eradicating all the natural character which provides for mischief. The other side of that argument is that in learning to interact with risk at all levels, from school bully to head teacher, provides an excellent training ground for a successful business executive. In William's case it would have been a tragic loss to the world if he were to never venture outside of the school walls, and would later go on to have the opinion that teachers should be forced to have a "real job" in the "real world" before being allowed to influence young minds.

So by the last year of his primary education, William had become a confident, popular, and ever so slightly cocky young man. He wasn't what you would call a naturally gifted sportsman, but he loved his sport, and so, because he enjoyed it, he worked hard at becoming good at certain sports. He loved cricket and swimming, and had pursued these activities outside of school, so he was well ahead of his peers in these two activities. He was not keen on football, as most of the other boys' were, but his ball co-ordination and fitness allowed him to compete, he was much happier playing bulldog, where physically and tactically he had the edge over most of the other boys. He was yet to discover rugby but his bulldog days would come in useful in a few years.

Something else was beginning to fascinate William during this last year at primary school. He was now eleven years old and had started to notice that the girls, while still terribly annoying and always seemed to have private jokes that he just didn't get, were also mysteriously attractive. This was confusing, sort of, because he didn't like them, but he did like the look of them. Especially the older girls like his brothers had brought home, or his sisters friends, and some of his younger teachers for that matter. In fact, William was becoming quite a lecherous eleven year old, something that would get him into trouble for many years to come. William however didn't regard this as trouble, and never would. To William it was sheer opportunistic delight.

The first time he fell foul of this was in the pursuit of one of his sporting passions, swimming. The swimming baths at the primary school were outdoor and therefore usually cold, but that never stopped William from taking every opportunity to use them. He could not understand why some of his friends were always looking for excuses to get out of swimming sessions. He'd been in much colder water with his father on holidays and weekends at the coast, and once you were in you hardly noticed it. But one thing William was just beginning to notice was the that girls looked different in swimming costumes, and the effect that the cold water seemed to have, changed the way they appeared to William, it was a strange but fascinating feeling. He needed to know more.

The changing rooms were a single wooden structure that resembled a Scandinavian style sauna room. The girls were designated one side and the boys the other with individual access to each but a simple partition wall separating them. There were cracks in the wall where the wood had moved over the years of condensation and heat variation. A plan was forming in William's mind. For once he was actually looking forward to getting out of the pool and into the changing rooms.

Generally William was a dawdler when it came to getting changed. He hated getting dry and into his clothes, and would much rather mess about, playing tricks on his friends, flicking towels and hiding other peoples pants and socks. So he was always the last one to be out of the changing rooms. Unbeknown to William, he would be the first one out today, but not necessarily as he might have thought.

As usual, getting out of the wet swimming trunks took about 30 seconds after entering the changing rooms. Then the usual bout of messing about, a bit of towel flicking action between William and his usual sparring partners filled a few minutes. The boys often got away with more than the girls as it was Miss Plum who took them for swimming this year. Not that Miss Plum wasn't strict, quite the opposite in fact, as the Deputy Head, she had a fearsome reputation and was not to be crossed. She was however, reluctant to enter the boys changing rooms at this age group, unless there was a real fuss going on. Usually a good bang on the door and a curt "hurry up" was more than enough to chivvy the boys along, the girls of course being no trouble as she would supervise them from their changing room, a detail the boys were not aware of.

So the boys had a little false sense of security for which William was going to suffer the consequences.

After a few minutes of boyish larks Williams attention turned to the job in hand, the mission he had been planning since the start of the swim session.

"Let's have a peep into the girls'" suggested William boldly.

"How?" one of the others boys questioned

"There's a big crack in the boards over here! Come on Mark, move your stuff!" As he made this statement William shoved Mark and all his neatly placed clothing along the bench that ran all along the walls of the changing room. Mark was about to protest when William loaded his towel into the flick position and to everyone's delight Mark squealed and retreated into the corner.

"Somebody give me a pencil" said William with his faced pushed right up against the 2" vertical hairline crack running between two of the planks that made up the wall. He could make out the light that came through but not much else. He needed to make a bigger gap.

"Here you go" his best friend Michael had placed a pencil in William's hand. William grasped it without looking round and moving his head back a few inches began work by pushing the pencil into the crack and wiggling.

Inevitably the pencil point snapped in the gap and rather than make a bigger hole, the largest part of the crack was now full of pencil.

"Bugger it!" cursed William "anybody got a compass?"

"Mark has!" shouted Michael

"No I haven't" cried Mark, who was less than enthusiastic about being implicated in this venture.

"Let's have it!" Michael said as he grabbed Mark's bag.

"NO!" screamed Mark, and a scuffle commenced as the boy's wrestled over the bag on the wet floor of the changing room, much to the delight of the rest of the class, who whooped and laughed and goaded the two boys on with the chant "Fight, Fight, Fight".

William in the mean time was completely focussed on getting the pencil point out of the crack. Working at it with his fingernails, softened from half an hour in the pool. Finally he was able to hook a nail under a small part of the scarred wood, and out it came, the whole lump of pencil and a bit of the wall beside.

William could not believe his luck. He could now see quite clearly a large section of the girls changing room. The girls were all giggling and appearing to be listening at the wall as well. One of the girls who had started to develop early breasts was virtually opposite William on the other side of the thin partition.

William hadn't heard Miss Plum banging on the door, not just because of the noise the fight was making but also as he was completely consumed in the image that was in front of him.

The fraction of a second it took for his brain to comprehend that the whole room had gone deathly quiet, was too much to stop the words as they flowed excitedly from his mouth "I can see Sally Rendall's tits!"

The next sensation William felt was the sting on his naked backside, which was beautifully presented to Miss Plum by being stuck up in the air as William knelt on the bench. Miss Plum momentarily had lost her temper when upon coming into the room to quell the riot that had failed to cease when she had banged on the door, she was greeted by the image of this "disgusting little peeping tom" before her, and reacted with a sound slap on the right buttock.

The surprise was almost as painful as the blow. William found himself snapped back into the boys changing room, and a very angry looking Miss Plum glaring straight at him. This was to be his first learning experience around how the fairer sex, have a slightly different tolerance to this kind of behaviour than the male of the species.

"William Dole, get outside now!"

"But ..."

"Don't but me, if you think it's ok to go peeping at people you can jolly well get changed outside so that they can peep at you!"

So, humiliated by being chastised and beaten in front of his friends, William trudged outside with his things and began to dry himself quickly before getting dressed.

At this point all the girls and some of the boys for that matter were standing on the benches inside the changing rooms trying to peer out of the high windows which allowed some light into the gloomy rooms. Sniggering and pointing at William the girls were whipping themselves up into an excited frenzy, laughing at William's humiliation.

William however, had found himself once again the centre of attention. If this was supposed to be his real punishment, it was a result for William. Far from being embarrassed, William was actually quite comfortable with his nakedness and was more interested now in milking his moment. So he began to dance while he dressed causing even more raucous excitement from the girls and bellows of laughter from the boys. He had turned a very poor situation into a great opportunity for building a fan base, to William it didn't matter how popularity came, this was all part of building his legend.

1977 was a big year in Britain. It was the Queen's Silver Jubilee, Virginia Wade won Wimbledon and William was about to leave Primary School and start at the bottom of the heap again, it was a daunting prospect. Up until this point, William had never really thought about his actual academic ability, he had done what was asked of him, no more and no less. He had recently taken his first formal examination without really considering what it was all about. He hadn't found it particularly difficult and consequently had forgotten all about it.

This state of mind was about to change with events that unfolded one early summers day toward the end of his last term at Primary. A trip had been arranged to visit the secondary school that William was to attend after the summer holidays. Up until now, William only ever attended one school, which was centred in a relatively close-knit society. His primary school was a mixed school. The children had all come from a similar background where moral values were high and behaviour generally good. This was simply due to the schools catchment being in a reasonably affluent area, where parents had generally worked very hard to enjoy some of the finer things in life, and therefore tried to instil these high ethical values into their children.

William was about to be introduced to King William's Boys' School. The obvious name association had captured William's interest, but he was unprepared for what he was about to experience.

Considering that it was school exclusively for boys, King William's was huge with something close to 1,500 pupils which included a small upper & lower sixth form. There was also a King William's Girls' School located at the opposite side of town.

At assembly that morning there was a buzz among the pupils of Class 1, William's class, as they anticipated the trip that lay ahead, and rather than the usual file back to the class room, Class 1 was escorted out into two waiting buses. One bus had been arranged for the Boys, the other one for the Girls. The usual gestures were exchanged between the two groups as they boarded their transport. The odd raspberry was blown and a lot of the Girls simply made that "stick your tongue out" face with the wrinkled nose, that only girls can really master.

After a ten minute bus ride, which seemed to last forever, the bus pulled into the school entrance. The boys craned their necks for the first view of what was to become their next school, which for most of the boys, would see them through to working adulthood. The building was imposing. It was massive in comparison to what they were used to. The school had been built in the early 1920's and you could feel the history as you walked through the main entrance at the top of three very large stone steps which appeared to wrap themselves around the double doors.

As the boys stood in the impressive reception area, they took in these new surroundings. There seemed to be enough dark wood in the construction of floors, panelled walls and beams, to make an 18th century ship of the line. The floors were wooden tiles, heavily waxed over the years and hard as concrete. The smell of old wood, wax polish and age was almost nostalgic.

As if to break the spell that was falling over everyone, the booming voice of the Headmaster of King William's Boys' School, echoed across the large reception hall.

"Welcome to King William's Boys' School. Please follow me and refrain from talking."

It was a voice that naturally commanded respect without shouting. It was almost a beautiful voice. It projected and resonated and would not have been out of place reciting Hamlet to a packed theatre. To these boys, it was something to be intimidated by. This was a very new experience and fear started to grip a few of the less confident ones. Nervous whisperings and murmurings began between some of the boys. This provoked what was a planned response from the Headmaster.

"Clearly you do not understand the meaning of the word REFRAIN!" He boomed "To REFRAIN, to keep oneself from doing! In this case the verb in question is to talk. Your learning experience at this school has begun. Do not test me on this particular subject again." His eyes bored into the petrified boys for just long enough, before the Headmaster turned and lead on once more, quietly smiling to himself for once again pulling off his yearly ritual. He had been an RAF Officer during the war and loved discipline, proper discipline, not complete dominance through fear but the winning of hearts and minds through setting rules and building respect and admiration. A little fear helped that process, he was sure about that, it was justified, they loved it really.

The class now noiseless, hardly daring to breath, followed the Headmaster into an enormous assembly hall, at the end of which was a huge stage. The stage was unlike the one they were used to in that this one was fully kitted out with all the theatrical trimmings, including three sets of curtains positioned at three different levels of the stage, a full lighting kit, set into the ceiling of the hall, these looked strangely out of place being high tech in such an old fashioned style room. The centre piece of the stage was a lectern with microphone, large speakers were arranged all around the hall, the boys could not imagine what the Headmasters voice would sound like coming out of those.

Once again the smell of old polished wood was very evident, and a sense of school history embodied itself in this room. There were honours boards, sepia photographs from a bygone age of cricket teams and soccer teams, display cabinets full of trophies, some tarnished by age, some gleaming and new. These things were all around the walls of this great hall.

At the end of the hall, in front of the stage, a few chairs had been neatly arranged. The Headmaster indicated that the boys were to sit on these seats. There were exactly enough for one chair per boy. Not benches or the floor, but a chair each! In the assembly hall! This was so totally different from anything the boys' were used to. This was "Big School".

Then the other shock came. William hadn't considered how many pupils from other schools would be converging in one year, and that these boys would all be streamed into classes by ability, and that for the first time this would actually give William an idea of where he featured in the scheme of things. The headmaster outlined how the class structure worked. The first number designated the year followed by the letter T and another number from one to nine which designated the class. Therefore 1T1 would be the cleverest class on paper in the first year and 1T9 was for the "retards", this was 1977. Now it was time for the moment of truth, the names would be read out in alphabetical order and the class designation along with it. The headmaster read without emotion through the list of names. William was astounded when he heard "William Dole, 1T1". It had never occurred to him that this would be possible. As the earlier names were read out he naturally began to grade himself and hoped he would be in 1T3 with his best friend Michael. The thought of being in the top just hadn't figured anywhere in his thoughts.

As they filed out of the hall, William was drawn to a board on the wall which displayed the results of the form competition that ran each year. There were years of history displayed on that board with coloured dots representing awe inspiring house names such as Romans, Grecians, Trojans and Spartans. William immediately wanted to be a Spartan, which meant being disloyal to his favourite colour blue but the name Spartan conjured images of warlike courage and mystery, he was experiencing his first emotions of belonging to a team and what it meant to have an identity that gave him a sense of pride and belonging. He hoped he would be a Spartan despite the red house colour.

The intimidation that he had felt as they entered the school had now disappeared and was replaced by a feeling of anticipation and almost nostalgia provoked by these snapshots of history. He wondered what houses his brothers had been in many years before.

It was strange in the bus on the way back, most of the boys were now quiet, lost in their own thoughts, already the segregation was kicking in and the classes were starting to group together and sneer at each end of the scale for very different reasons depending on where you sat. William couldn't be bothered by all that, and sat alone with his own thoughts.

That night, he rushed home from school for a change, normally he would dawdle along the footpath stopping at the usual places hidden from view to play the odd prank on unsuspecting victims and was usually the first to enter the hedge lined gravel path that ran for about 400 yards from the bottom of the playing field to the road his house was on, and was the last out. Today he ran home, he didn't know why but he was desperate to tell his parents the news. He wanted his Dad to know.

It seemed an age before the rumble of the Jensen in the drive made its way through the house. One minute later the "clang" of the gate and Dad was walking through the back door. William was there, beaming as the big hand ruffled hair that was now closer to the man's chest, the boy was growing up.

"Alright Will?"

"Yeh Dad, I'm in 1T1" the words were blurted out so quickly, William's father didn't really register it.

"Are you? Good. What's for tea Mother?"

William's mother gave him *the look!*

"What?"

She inclined her head toward a hovering William, with her eyebrows raised and eyes that only women can do that urgently required action.

"So Will, what's this all about?"

"I'm in 1T1 Dad" said William this time with a slight timber to his voice that if he had been born twenty years later would have translated as a sarcastic "Duuuuh"

Williams dad was looking to his wife for inspiration but she was enjoying watching his usual control under threat and gave nothing away.

"What's that son?"

"My new class Dad, 1T1 is the best class in the year, I am in the top class Dad, there are nine classes and I am in the top one."

William's father's heart swelled with pride, but he could not show it, he had to maintain his consistency.

"Well you will need to work hard then won't you son, don't let yourself down."

This was about as close to praise as it got from William's father. If ever William or any of the other kids did anything, they craved their fathers approval, what they invariably got was advice on how to make it better. So this level of praise was high indeed. It was acceptance of his achievement, that was enough for William.

Top Tip – Give Honest Feedback

While it's great to be positive and see the smiles on faces as you issue praise for an OK job, it's also taking an easy short term win over a much more productive long term improvement strategy. People benefit from good, honest, and consistent feedback. It helps them to improve and grow as individuals and gives credibility to the mentor who is offering feedback.

Feedback, should never be criticism, but should be constructive help and advice.

Feedback should be given in two ways:

- Positive feedback

    o   What you particularly liked
    o   What you want to see more of
    o   What impressed you most

- Formative feedback

    o   What could be improve upon
    o   What would work there
    o   What should be omitted

To really drill this home, the feedback must be underpinned with evidence. Giving feedback is hard, receiving it is just as difficult. People need evidence in order to believe. For example, next time you wish to give some feedback to somebody try doing it this way:

"I noticed last week that you stayed behind to finish that job, thank you for that, I appreciate it!" The fact that you noticed brings power to the feedback, it shows that you notice things, it also cannot be denied because the evidence is within the statement.

All forms of feedback are good if they are handled with skill and empathy and underpinned with evidence. The trick is to ask yourself what you want to achieve from offering feedback. Think of the motivational and de-motivational consequences of offering feedback to the person concerned.

Sometimes of course in the interest of safety or for the good of your organisation, feedback must be harsh and immediate, at other times you can gain more by being tactful.

The worst thing you can do is nothing. What is the point of moaning about some-ones performance if you are not prepared or brave enough to talk to them about it. People want to know what is expected of them and they want to know how they stack up against that level of expectation.

The ability to give great feedback is a real skill and a valuable leadership tool. If you're people are not performing ask yourself "Do they know what's expected of them? Am I consistent with my levels of expectation? Am I being a mentor or a monster?"

CHAPTER 3

PUBERTY

William spent that summer reading through past editions of the school magazine, planning how he could aspire to be as good as some of the people that had made features and articles. Creating a fantasy of how good he would be because he was in 1T1. His next door neighbour, Patrick Moyles, was also moving up next term and he had only managed 1T2. This was not something that William was particularly interested in but it clearly bothered Patrick as he was expecting to be in 1T1 and couldn't believe that William had "nicked his place". The truth is that Patrick was the kind of kid that had delusions of grandeur and only a few friends of his own. William tolerated him because he was next door and he did have some cool stuff, in fact he was spoilt. Patrick had introduced William to cricket and then got the hump when William took to it with a real passion and some natural talent, whereas Patrick ran in to bowl like a baby giraffe. Consequently William had found his first love and Patrick had once more lost his edge.

William and Patrick lived opposite the town cricket club and spent hours in the long summer days over the field exploring the dykes and hedges that surrounded the pitch, of course during the week there was little sign of life, the club professional, Harry Larchwood, lived in the pavilion and was usually around to say hello. William was quietly smug that it was him that Harry spoke to not Patrick.

During one of these days another breakthrough moment came as Patrick was boasting about his tracking ability because he had a badge from Scouts. Just as well for Patrick that William really didn't fancy the idea of scouting, it just all seemed a bit "nancy boy" to him, wearing a scarf and that toggelly woggelly thingy. But a little signpost was planted in William's unconscious brain, he liked the idea of tracking and field-craft, but not at scouts.

It was just as well the signpost was planted because this day would end the tenuous friendship forever. As Patrick was trying to recruit William into the scouts, William just got fed up and said "look mate, it's for poufs I don't want to go, now drop it."

"You might as well join then" was the response.

William had to have a comeback, so he hit with the main thing he had on his mind at the moment "well at least I'm not a bloody thicko like you, you tosser!"

Something happened in Patricks eyes that William had never seen before. He had wounded him to the core. For almost half his life William had over shadowed Patrick and the only advantage Patrick thought he had, had just been ripped away from him.

It took a while for William to register the pain of what happened next. Patrick had brought with him a six foot long fishing rod, and as William had turned his back he swung it with all his might across William's back. At first the sensation was one of sting as the blow fell followed immediately by nothing, then as the second blow came the burning bite of the first welt made his back feel on fire. William looked round at Patrick, not really understanding the rage he saw. He felt confused, hurt, but strangely he didn't feel fear. He did feel an instinct to survive and as the next two blows rained down on him William stopped trying to avoid them and started moving toward Patrick. His back was on fire his arm had absorbed a blow too but he had to get this weapon away from Patrick.

As Patrick recognised what was happening, he began to show the fear that had somehow had by-past his adversary. His rage had melted and the realisation of what he had done had started to kick it. William instinctively sensed a hesitation in the next coil of

Patricks arm, and he lunged forward and for the first time in his life punched someone with all his strength. His brothers had taught him how, spending endless hours in front of the springboard punch bag with a football tied to the top, that if you got your aim wrong you missed the ball and took the skin off your knuckles on the hard plastic base. The lessons came back to him as his right arm extended, fist bunched and at the last minute a twist of the wrist to add timing and pressure to the moment of contact when the first two knuckles of his fist hit their target. Patrick's nose seemed to explode across his face, blood suddenly pouring from both nostrils and smearing across his face as the force of the blow continued on and through.

William didn't stop to gloat or to follow up on it, he had achieved what he wanted. The whipping had stopped. The fishing rod now lay on the floor, he stooped to pick it up and ran home, in more pain than he had ever felt in his life, not caring about his friend . . . ex-friend.

As he got home, the adrenaline began to wear off and the shock began to kick in. He had been in control, albeit in autopilot somehow, it was bizarre, almost slow motion and yet as he stood here now, bewildered, his sister looked at him and her face looked like she had seen a ghost, her eyes wide like a terrified horse, she squealed "oh my god, Muuuuuuuuuum!"

William didn't know why, but he then suddenly felt the fear he should have had before and burst into tears and begun to shake uncontrollably.

The rod had not broken the skin, but it had produced some very impressive angry red stripes, the one that his sister had seen was diagonal up his neck and onto his face. As his mother gingerly pealed his shirt off, she revealed a criss cross pattern of angry welts that were now raised and reddening as the blood surged through his system. The next time his back would look like this would be for very different and much more pleasurable reasons and in many years time.

The incident had shaken William more than he realised. He had a natural ability to move on and not worry about things, and while he had resolved that his friendship had most definitely ended and that should be a finish to it, he was now genuinely nervous about getting into fights at the new school. He didn't want to be a coward, but he felt like one. He didn't want another fight ever again, he had to find a way to escape them somehow with credibility. It nagged at him and suddenly the looming school term did not seem quite so attractive.

School came and the excitement soon settled down into routine. The myths about new boy's heads being flushed down the toilets by 5th years and being rolled round in dust bins were exactly that, myths. It was rough, there were fights and William tried to steer clear of all of it. He was still terrified of getting into a fight. Strange then that every time a game of bulldog, which was banned by the teachers, was whispered about the large yard which was full of boys at break time and lunch time, William was always up for it. He was nearly always in the last few rounds. The game was easy to start with, as a few boys, less than ten, would stand in the middle of the large asphalt yard, bigger than a football pitch, and then the masses would charge from one end to the other. Anyone who was upended by the few "catchers" would then become a catcher themselves thus increasing the odds of people getting caught in the next wave. By the time the game came to an end there were usually less than ten boys facing hundreds with no chance of getting past, yet the challenge to William was almost hypnotic, despite the grazes and the rips in clothing that usually resulted from the contact with the tarmac.

The early rounds needed different tactics, all you needed was a sense of awareness, and some decent speed. The awareness allowed you to put people between you and the catcher, to melt into the crowd and not get singled out. The rest was about timing, speed and grace. If a catcher had you in his sights, you simply timed your spurt to leave him or fended him off with a hand. William was twelve years old and hadn't really thought about it but people his own age bounced off him when he ran with pace, he was turning into a bit of "a unit". He loved Bulldog.

It was during one of these games that a turning point in his life occurred. William was in the last twenty or so of a massive game, there must have been three hundred boys playing and already a few pints of blood had been collectively spilt. The teachers were on the rampage to stop the next round as the cry went up "BULLDOG", this was the signal, half the boys ran straight into the waiting masses, William also made his jog out but was looking for a gap to get as far as he could before the game was killed or he was. Strangely, he never felt fear at this, but the thought of a fight where he would probably fare better with the odds still made him feel sick. The power of the distracted unconscious mind.

As William jagged and swerved other boys were being tackled and slammed to the floor. William saw a gap and head down flew for it, he didn't see the 2nd year coming from the side and suddenly "SLAM" he was on the floor. In a heart-beat there were a dozen boys grabbing him to hurl him into the air and shout "Bulldog". As he lay on the floor with a few scrapes and bruises about to appear the fierce voice of Mr. Tucker came through the mêlée, boys scattered both from fear and from Mr. Tucker flinging them aside, his cane was out and he would wield it. Mr. Tucker had a fantastic technique with the cane, he would have the length of it hidden up the sleeve of his suit jacket and it would suddenly whip into his hand in a flash, like a magician producing a bunch of paper flowers. It was something to enjoy watching so long as you weren't the one in the way. William on this occasion was the boy in the middle of a pile of arms and legs, and the one that Mr. Tucker wanted to protect. William didn't think the teachers had really grasped the rules of bulldog. He wanted to run the gauntlet he wasn't forced to. Mr. Tucker grabbed the 2nd year who had so very efficiently taken William out from the side. He had him by the side burn and was yanking him off the floor so that the boy was standing on his tip toes, squealing with as much credibility as he could around his peers.

"Is this hideous creature bullying you boy?" the teacher's eyes bored into William as he asked the question.

"No Sir, he was just after my autograph!" William had built a new defence mechanism, it was humour, and he was good with it. With comic timing he had changed the whole dynamic of this exchange and won himself some credibility points with those boys watching within earshot.

Mr Tucker grabbed William's side burn with the other hand and now held both boys suspended, their toes only touching the ground, faces contorted and mouths open, "Comedian 'ey?"

"No sir, 1st year, I know nothing Sir, I am but a slug in the scheme of things, thank you for hurting me sir!"

By now two other teachers had broken the surrounding boys up and were listening with interest to the exchange. One began to snigger at Williams jive with Mr Tucker, who did have a fearsome reputation with both pupils and in the staff room. Mr. Tucker usually taught the boys of 1T9 and never really came across the brighter boys.

"Give me one good reason why I shouldn't whack you both"

"I'm too young to die sir, my parents would miss me!"

The other teachers lost it and held onto each other as they tried in vain to suppress their giggles. Mr Tucker glared at his colleagues as he let both boys go with a slap to the back of the head, that frankly was a relief to the burning sensation of side burn suffrage.

As the teachers drifted away, Mr. Tucker clearly not happy with his colleagues' lack of solidarity, William and the other boy began to empathise with each other.

"You're alright for a 1st year" said William's tackler, a solid lad who stood a good three inches taller than William and had a thick mop of black, slightly greasy hair that was unusual in that while the fringe was full and low on the brow, the style was very old fashioned short back and sides, it stood out as very different among the fashionable shoulder length locks of that majority of the boys.

"You're a bloody hard tackler, I never saw you coming." Said William rubbing his side burn.

"What class you in?"

"1T1!"

"Oh bloody hell, a bloody girly swot!"

"Hardly, I'm bottom of the class, what class are you in then?"

"2T3"

"Top stream then, what's the difference?"

"Nothing really, what clubs are you in?"

"I didn't know there were any?"

"Not here, after school! I'm in Sea Cadets, you should come!".

Now in these days the uniformed cadet services were considered really quite cool. Almost an extension to the armed forces themselves. William suddenly thought back to that day in the cricket field with Patrick and thought to himself "yeh, bollocks to the Scouts"

"When is it?

"Tuesday is for the Sea Cadets and Fridays the GN's come too"

"The what?"

"The GN's they are the girls, some of them are well fit, and they have to wear uniform too, it's brilliant."

William's imagination started to run wild and he was interested in joining this organisation. He had played at being in the army for years, now to wear a proper uniform, learn stuff and to have a whole new audience, yes he was up for that.

The first night was a Tuesday, and his new friend Andy (Bruno) Brown, the boy who had tackled him so well and who had since got him interested was picking him up. His uniform was so smart, the classic look of the British Sailor, blue collar, brilliant white cap, shirt and lanyard, shiny boots. William was impressed. Bruno had a certain swagger about himself in his "rig". As they walked into the unit a smell of polish and old rope hit William and it felt great. Bruno explained that there was a boring bit called colours at the start where they had to do drill and put the flags up after which they would go off into different groups and learn all sorts of skills. The thought of drill did not sound boring to William but he kept that to himself.

William, as a new entry was told to stand in a squad of 10 boys at the back and given basic instruction on how to come to attention and stand at ease. Then the ceremonial side of the evening began and William was utterly hooked. The bells, the whistles (bosun's calls, as they were known) the salutes and formalities, William thought to himself "if this is boring how good will the rest be?" He was hooked.

Friday's were different again. William had not really been in too much contact with girls for the best part of six months and he had matured a lot in that time. With a different outlook on life, suddenly this was an environment where it seemed ok to like them. In fact the older boys, who William had come to revere, had extra credibility if they were able to "get off" with a GN, which William now knew was the term for a member of the GNTC or Girls' Nautical Training Corps. William was popular with the GN's he was young and innocent and had a cheekiness about him that the older girls liked. He was milking it, finding the game different from that of appeasing potential bullies or teachers. At the age of twelve, William suddenly had the realisation that he had missed the company of girls since beginning secondary school, but there was something else, a different feeling, a new and exciting yet strangely dangerous feeling. William was entering a new period in his life, and consequently a new chapter in his sales career. His customer base would need a lot of research and his product needed some work, but there was a strange and very real desire to get into this market. William had entered the world of puberty, where sales and marketing become real. Building a brand, getting a buy in, selling change, unconscious incompetence, we have heard these phrases in board rooms for years. But it's in the world of the pubescent novice that these things become a stark reality. William was about to walk into his apprenticeship, but there were no workshops or training for this one, he was going to learn the best way of all and get stuck in.

Top Tips – Signposting

What is a signpost?

Something that lets you know when you have arrived at a decision or destination and something that points you in the right direction at that stage. It's also something that confirms you have arrived, something that you look out for when you are expecting it. Signposts let us know that we are on the right track.

So if you can put signposts in place for people that you are trying to influence, you will help them to confirm their journey is going in the right direction.

Whether you are mentoring, counselling, training or selling to someone, if you plant a signpost early in the conversation, when they reach that signpost they will feel safe that they are on track and confirm for themselves that this is the way.

For example;

The sales person opens with something like "I am going to show you something today that is perfect for your business, I saw it and thought of you guys so I have brought it to you first, I know you are going to want to use it in your business." The customer is expecting to see a new product and slightly intrigued about what it is, later when the sales person brings it into the meeting, the customer thinks "Ah this is the time I get to hear about this new product!" They have seen the signpost and they know the next direction is to investigate, you have already achieved a buy in to the idea at least.

Another example is if you are mentoring someone you might say "When you get to X in the process, things will seem impossible, but don't worry that's normal, you just need to . . ." In this way when the person reaches the stage of panic they will recognise the signpost and know their next course of action.

Signposting really adds a sense of safety to people's decision making, and people buy safety. If you want to have the ability to get other people to do willingly and happily the things they might otherwise choose not to, put some sign posts in place.

Signposts, show people the way.

CHAPTER 4

IDENTITY

School became routine. After a couple of terms it was clear that William was not enjoying the culture of 1T1. He was clever enough, but really did not fit in with the diligent pupils that just didn't want to have any kind of laugh. The egg heads taunted him a bit, but this didn't bother William in the slightest, he was of the opinion that worrying about things that were beyond his own influence was an absolute waste of emotional and physical energy. This sometimes came across as a lack of care in the boy, but it was a trait that would help him through life, as it is of course, a fact.

The way the days were divided meant that registration was taken in his form class, which was run by Mr Huggins. The old house system of Spartans and Romans etc. had been dropped in favour of what was called a Pastoral system. The idea was that all boys from all class levels could intermingle at the beginning of the day. The other benefit of this system was that Mr Huggins would be the boys' mentor for their entire time at the school and he would thereby learn to spot any potential issues and deal with them with knowledge and empathy. William had been slightly disappointed at not having the opportunity to become a Spartan, but Mr Huggins had explained that there was still a competition between pastoral classes and that these competitions could be opened across year groups too. This thought was enough to satisfy William's open and trusting mind.

Mr. Huggins liked William and had observed that while he was intelligent enough he didn't fit in with the other boys of 1T1. The fact was that William found more empathy with some of his friends in the form than he did with his 1T1 class mates, and Mr. Huggins could see that when they trailed off to class, his other three 1T1 boys, in their optional blazers and brief cases, never waited for William who was always using the last few moments of the registration session to plan some kind of sport during the long lunch hour with his other friends and inevitably would run out at the last minute to make his lesson, dragging his blue and white Adidas bag, scuffed and battered from various games having acted as either a wicket or a weapon sometimes even an improvised curling stone, behind him. He would get to his classroom and do the minimum necessary to get through the lessons. William always had an eye on the clock, waiting for the next break, he lived for the breaks.

Break times were filled with sport. In the last term of the academic year this meant cricket. William was far ahead of his year in cricket but not as it happened in his form class. In a twist of fate Mr. Huggins could not have imagined possible, he had inherited some very fine cricketers, two of which went on to play first class cricket in their later years. There was an open cricket competition each year and Mr. Huggins form won every year, beating the 5th years even while being 1st years. This may seem unlikely, but eight of the boys had been coached at the town club by Harry the professional who had played several seasons for Middlesex, and they were already playing club cricket. The rest of the school were no match.

Mr. Huggins was to become a very positive influence in William's life. He had taken an interest in the boy when he had learned about his involvement with the Sea Cadets. As an ex Royal Navy officer and a sportsman himself, William ticked many of his boxes as a boy to take under his wing. He enjoyed mentoring his boys and every so often a special one would come along that was an absolute joy to have a positive influence over. The rapport they had built over the first two terms of the academic year had been mutually rewarding. William had already put a couple of trophies in the form's cabinet at the swimming gala, and William had found in Mr. Huggins a teacher who actually had a genuine interest in some of the activities that he was into outside of school. William felt that he could talk to Mr. Huggins without fear of ridicule or judgement. He respected Mr. Huggins as an ex Royal Naval Officer and someone who had achieved things similar to those that he himself aspired to do. William had a respect for all teachers. It was part of his value system that his father had skilfully woven into his make-up. However he was beginning to form an opinion that the best teachers were those that had been and done something in the real world then come back into teaching, rather than going straight from school to college, then on to University and straight back into school having never seen any other kind of environment. Who were they to tell pupils about the real world? They had never seen it.

Mr. Huggins, though he was careful not to mention it in the staff room, had a very similar opinion to that of William. He was constantly frustrated by the narrow minded views of some of the career teachers that did nothing but take pride in berating the boys and were borderline militant about their profession. To Mr. Huggins teaching was a joy, to make a difference to a young person's life, to inspire and enthuse them toward improving their chances in life while encouraging the playful mischief of teenage youth and working to channel that energy toward something productive. He believed passionately that people learned better when they were relaxed and open, that humour had its place in the learning cycle. He was no push over, he had a fierce side that the boys all knew about, and he knew all the tricks. However he administered punishment in a very considered way, even managing to insert some humour to the deterrents at his disposal. Mr Huggins, like many teachers of the period, accepted corporal punishment as part of the job and believed that if used correctly as a deterrent, it worked. He was also of the oppinion that the cane should be kept as a hallowed weapon to be wielded only by head teachers or heads of year thus creating another level of severity in any potential deviants mind. He did however have a whole tool kit of his own full of torture devices such as his skull and cross bones slipper that would leave a jolly roger mark in chalk on the boy's bottom after contact, "the cricket bat of woe" which he would use to dramatically practice his cut shots with the added torture of telling the boy that he would make 6 swipes at the target area (the maximum allowed under the law), but he may well choose not to land them all. This was particularly good as a punishment as he sometimes chose not to land any, but the anticipation of the blow was often more painful than the sting itself and boys were often quivering and in tears by the fifth swipe without having felt the physical pain of the beating. One boy had even shouted once "for fucks sake hit me with it will you?" which Mr Huggins delighted in obliging with immediately with a solid smack square on, qualified with "Don't swear boy!" much to the delight of the rest of the class. His favourite tool was his pride and joy, in was known throughout the school even by boys who had never been taught by him as the "Huggy Bear" because it growled and it hurt. It was a simple but brilliant invention of three wooden 12 inch rulers sellotaped together so that it made a whirring noise through the air (the growl) and clattered into the target area with added bite as the three pieces of wood worked together, he had also split the wood of the bottom ruler so that it nipped the skin slightly on contact. This was particularly effective on the palm of a hand. Rarely did it ever need to be deployed, often just the sight of it, coupled with the myth surround the Huggy Bear, was enough to quell any hint of misbehaviour. Many of the boys had older brothers who had handed down the information and added their own dramatic twist, the historical tales spread like mystical wildfire. He was always careful to calculate the potential outcome of his punishments, and therefore his results were good. The pupils liked him and he got results from them, but he was no push over.

Some of the other teachers resented this approach and they believed that you just had to punish behaviour, and the future had no bearing on the past. Mr Huggins divorced himself from these people and their ivory towers built around the elitism of academia. He knew in his mind that these individuals would never survive outside of their own comfort zone and that many of the boys they taught now would be able to eat them for breakfast in a few years. Mr Huggins believed that his job was to give the boys some all round life skills as well as a few O Level's, what was the point of an O Level if you can't come over confidently at the interview? This was why he loved to be a form tutor, many of the other teachers saw it as an inconvenience at the start of the day, having to take the register while they could be having a cup of tea while finalising the lesson plans they should have done the previous night but the pub had seemed such a good idea at the time.

Today Mr. Huggins had finally decided that William would be better suited in a different class than 1T1, but he certainly needed to be in the top stream. 1T1 - 1T3 were top stream and boys within that stream could qualify for a scholarship to the Grammar School which would commence from the 3rd year. Mr. Huggins wanted to make sure that William had a chance at that but also wanted him to get the most out of his all round schooling, he wanted to talk to William and sell him the concept of moving down a class and begin to build relationships with some equally intelligent boys that had more in common.

He had decided to talk to him about this and wanted to approach it from a casual angle that would put William at ease from the start. That meant talking to William on his turf. At lunch time, he set off to find William in the massive complex of the school grounds. There was only one place to look, out to the sports field which had a large and complicated circumference of one mile. William knew all the nooks and crannies around the perimeter of the playing field. He hated cross country running, he couldn't see the point in getting out of breath for no purpose other than following somebody round a field it was just a waste of effort and boring at that. Often during games the PE teacher would simply tell the boys to do two laps of the field and effectively give themselves half an hour off while the boys ran. William soon worked out that if he ran off at a fast pace with the front runners, he could get half way round the circuit and nip down into the dyke which was out of view in one of the spurs of the complicated shaped field that bordered onto industrial land. He could then sit and wait for fifteen minutes or so till those same front runners would come round on their second lap, then he would jump out and fall in behind them, effectively halving the amount of running while getting a breather in the middle. Genius! Today, Mr. Huggins would simply scan the big field and look for a game of cricket that looked semi organised and he was sure he would find William in there somewhere.

Sure enough, there was a game on the go under a tree at one side of the field. The trunk of the big oak tree providing the perfect set of stumps with the first branches so high up, typical of oak. Mr Hughes recognised William's battered Adidas bag acting as the stumps at the bowlers end, and headed over. During the two hundred yard walk he watched the game unfold as he drew nearer and began to slow his walk, enjoying the skills being displayed and the uncompromising effort that was going into the game. As if his life depended on it William was steaming in to bowl with the tennis ball, mimicking the long run of Bob Willis, his right arm, holding the ball, extended out to the side and in time with his curved run working like an old fashioned water pump handle. With a hugely exaggerated bound William then delivered the ball as fast as he could toward the cowering batsman at the other end. The batsman took evasive action and fell onto his bottom much to the delight of the rest of the group especially William who "whoop whooped" during his follow through.

Now as Mr. Huggins got nearer he could hear the boys' dialogue and one of the fielders urged William on "Come on Wills, get him out he's been in ages".

William turned back to his mark, the carefully stepped out 12 pace run up. Went a further 4 paces beyond and instinctively started his run, knowing that his right foot had landed exactly on the mark he had scuffed into the ground earlier. This time there was no mimicking of famous heroes, this was William's run and William's action, and he was concentration on getting his man. He had a naturally beautiful bowling action and Mr. Huggins unconsciously stopped in his tracks to watch it. The few controlled short steps the start that then steadily accelerated into a build up of momentum after hitting the mark. With six paces to go the run settled into perfect rhythm and William appeared to glide over the ground. His wrist was cocked and loose and as he gathered for the bound his left arm curled up so that he was looking directly at the target over his left shoulder, then in a burst of power and timing, the most unnatural of bodily movements was turned into a thing of beauty as William uncurled his body to release the ball from his right hand. The first two fingers were lightly holding on to the ball, he wished it were a cricket ball then he could have moved the seam and set the shiny side for an away swinger that his natural action was suited to. Some bowlers, even at test level were all bustle and effort, but William had the ability to gracefully glide up to the wicket and let the wrist do the work, like a medieval trebuchet at the point of hurling a rock at the castle walls, Williams wrist flicked the ball at the optimum point of release, the fingers adding to the leverage and with pinpoint accuracy and control the ball was now hurtling toward the batsman at a better pace than the fourteen year old was capable of playing. William had also judged the length well and as the boy's bat came down a fraction to late, the ball ducked underneath it, the perfect Yorker, and hit the tree behind with a distinctive "puck" noise that a tennis ball makes.

"That boy is good!" Mr Huggins smiled to himself "He's very good!"

"Dole, when you have stopped showing off to your elders and betters, a word please" Mr Huggins knew that the veiled compliment would work on William and he duly came trotting over with a beam on his face like an adoring Labrador to his master.

"You like your sport don't you lad"

"Yes sir, I love it sir."

"Why don't you play some with your classmates at lunch times?"

"Pah, they would rather go to chess club sir"

"You play chess don't you?"

"Well, yes sir but why would you want to when the sun's shining sir? Chess is for winter and wanke . . . . , sorry sir" Williams face turned meek as he pulled out of the last word almost in time.

Mr Huggins suppressed a smile and pretended he hadn't noticed. "You know, you are a bright lad and you should make the most of that brain of yours."

William was beginning to become uncomfortable with where this was potentially heading.

"Sir?"

"You should be able to play sport and have intelligent banter with your classmates"

"But sir, they are all a bit stiff sir."

"So get some more classmates."

"Yeh right, ... I Don't get it"

"Well if you had a class that was full of intelligent boys, that could potentially go to Grammar, but who also enjoyed cricket and rugby, what would that be?"

"A bloody miracle sir, sorry sir"

"No, not a bloody miracle Dole it would be 1T2"

Silence while this idea was planted, another signpost was taking root.

"What are you saying sir? That I am too thick for 1T1"

"No boy, I am suggesting that you could have you cake and eat it if you could swallow some of that pride. Think about it, you can go from bottom of one class to the top half of another, the difference being that you have friends in that one and you would still be in the top stream, it makes sense."

"I don't know sir . . ." William went off into quiet thought, his face contorted and his body language uncertain.

Mr. Huggins detected the internal wrestle that was going on, and recognised that William was suffering a dilemma. The last thing he wanted to do was to impose any pressure, so he decided to end the conversation powerfully and leave William to make the right decision for himself. He used a tool that broke through the boundaries, he used William's Christian name

"Look, William . . ." this provoked William's head to snap round and look directly at Mr. Huggins, "If you want to stay where you are that's fine, if you want to move I can make it happen. I won't make you mind up for you but have think about what you really want out of class." Then it dawned on Mr Huggins that the emotion William was wrestling with was pride. Why had he not thought of that? How could he be so stupid as to miss the obvious? It wasn't about getting William to swallow his pride, he needed somehow to massage it.

"To be honest, there is probably more in 1T2 that you can get involved with. They are just as competitive, just with a slightly different focus. There's more of your kind of activity going on and more of your kind of people doing it. It wouldn't be like going down a class, more like changing the way you can be in the top set."

William was warming to the idea, he noticed the shift in body language, it was time to leave the seed to germinate.

"Your call William, let me know when you're ready. Good lad, it looks like you're needed to bat, off you go."

"Thank you sir." Mind immediately back in the game, William would now proceed to bat till the end of lunch, already starting to warm to the idea of a new challenge in a new class, and was forming his sales pitch to his father. He then realised that his real concern was not moving class, but disappointing his father by being downgraded. He was grateful to Huggo for helping him with a bloody good line to spin. He beamed as he grabbed the bat, his unconscious mind would work on the problem, already settled on the outcome.

Top Tips - Find a mentor

Successful people are generally in control of their own state of mind. They don't get dragged down by other people's negativity or by other people's circumstances. They are driven by their own set of principals and unconscious objectives. Feed off these people, tap into their strength and if you are lucky enough to find council from one of these people, consider it a gift. You don't have to follow the advice or even agree with it, but a good mentor will light a path up for you to follow, the path may have many stopping points and spurs but as long as the general direction is sound you won't go far wrong.

You can find a mentor at any stage of life and in any circumstances. As a child the obvious mentors we find ourselves following are of course parents, close family members, teachers and youth leaders. As we grow through the teenage years, we tend to err toward people outside of school or home because a true mentor is someone we follow out of volition not a sense of duty or out of discipline. As adults, especially when we are in the state of mind that focuses us on attainable outcomes, we fix on people we admire at work or even in some cases we seek professional mentors.

The message is to avoid being too proud to seek solace from a mentor. We all have our moments of self doubt, we all need a crutch to lean on sometimes. You should view a mentor like a map; factual, accurate, something that shows you the way, but you get to choose which route you take and if you get lost, refer to the map again. But remember the map is not the territory only the two dimensional guide.

CHAPTER 5

THE FIRST KISS

And so it was that William did indeed find himself in a different class. He saw the end of the first year out in 1T1, and it was confirmed, after parents evening, in which Mr Huggins had done a great job with his parents, that William would go into 2T2 the following term. The summer holidays were approaching, and his life began to take on a very different and exciting outlook, some of the pressure shifting. Gone were the shackles of academic focus, he would now have classmates that enjoyed fun as much as he did. His work would become much improved, not that he really had any consciousness of that, but his teachers did. The fact was that he was relaxed and following his own value system. His father had noticed the change too. A new and sometimes frustrating confidence had begun to become part of William's persona. On balance, William's father approved and felt a swell of pride as he watched his son take on the world and all its challenges with enthusiasm and gusto.

Unbeknown to William, he was establishing himself as a product, a brand, and his market was opening up. He had a voracious appetite for the market too, and looked to open it up with several routes to the market. He had become passionate about the Sea Cadets and took incredible pride from wearing *"the finest uniform the world had ever seen"* as he had heard one inspirational officer describe it at a parade.

Throughout the summer holidays of 1978, William threw himself into as much activity as the days would stand. If he were not at the cricket club, he would be helping on the boats on the river with cadets, or organising a gang of friends to play bulldog over the field. The Cadets organised lots of water borne activity during summer, and William embraced them all, pulling or rowing as it is known outside of the Navy, kayaking, sailing, power boating, swimming all were good. Plus he had been introduced to another activity which sparked his interest, camping and field craft. This was the real deal in Williams mind, not ging gang gooley scouting, but proper military field craft, he was a sponge for the information and enjoyed the feeling of outdoor living. Waking up to the sound of rain on canvas was somehow great, despite the fact that the military style 12 by 12 mess tents didn't have sewn-in ground sheets and a river would often flow through and catch out the less prepared sleeper. The lessons of the day, around camouflage and concealment were like little pearls of magic, and they worked. William felt invincible in his camouflage pattern, army issue uniform, two sizes too big for him, but issued from stores for the duration of the camps. He was amazed at how invisible you could become simply by laying still and blending in with the terrain, having the confidence to know that you could not been seen if you stuck to your guns and committed to being still. It gave him a great sense of satisfaction when instructors walked past him a few feet away in the dark, oblivious of his presence during escape and evasion exercises. He had listened to all the advice and had total belief in the principles and in himself. The mantra ran through his head "in the trees? Freeze! In open ground? Get down!" He loved it all. Yes it was a busy summer.

There was one other draw on William's attention this year too, one that wasn't present at school, but one that had began to consume his thoughts and dreams.

Girls!

He'd had his first experience of the feelings they could provoke at a Cadet disco. It thrilled him to the core and he wanted more. Sea Cadet, DIY disco's were something that the Cadets organised themselves with permission of the staff who were gracious enough to offer only the minimum of supervision, preferring to slip off into the adult bar area of the unit for their own entertainment, leaving the policing of the event to the older, senior "more sensible" Cadets.

The format was simple, there was a record player set up in one room with the speakers run out onto the "main-deck" area of the unit (the layout of any unit was like that of a ship or Naval shore establishment, the main-deck being the biggest common area). The records would be brought along by all the cadets and someone would take on the job of loading up the drop down system with four or five of the vinyl discs before going out to join the throng. The temptation to load up too many would invariably mean going back to the record deck and reloading after the first drop was hampered because the weight of the stack would bring the lot down at once, prompting boo's and moans from those who had specifically requested their choices to come on.

There was always a discussion going on around the piles of records carefully separated into individual ownership. Records, record sleeves and album covers were a real talking point, especially if someone had brought the latest picture discs along. William only had two records that he owned, the first one being a brand new compilation idea called "Action Replay", this was to be the forerunner of a new spin off called Action Trax which would spur a craze in the 80's of Now albums. Action Replay had opened Williams eyes to music, it contained an impressive list of tracks, opened on side one with the Boomtown Rat's "Rat Trap" and track two had driven him to buy his second album. He had coveted the copy of the Blondie album "Eat to the Beat" since he had owned it, his favourite sound from Action Replay being Blondie's "Hanging on the telephone". When he made the investment, it had been a real wrench parting with so much money all at once, on just one band. He got it home and carefully opened each layer of the album, pouring over the cover and the contents, the cover being not just packaging but an integral part of the experience, very different from the simple cover of the compilation.

As he stood here now and looked at the extensive collections of the other cadet's he felt both in awe and in wonder as to how they could afford so many records. He actively engaged in the hubbub of comparing collections and impressing each other with knowledge. The usual rivalry existed between Queen fans and Status Quo fans, heavy metal and pop and more recently the new craze of Ska that was creeping into fashion, a sound that bands like The Specials. This new, two step sound, was intoxicating to William, the reggae beat mixed with an edginess that you couldn't quite define and it was upbeat and fun, not the mindless noise of screaming heavy bands with head banging fans. William hated the head banging scene, it just seemed crazy.

Most of William's music was taped from the radio on a hand held recorder, or from top of the pops, the microphone picking up all the coughs and noises from the room, despite all efforts to keep people quiet while carefully holding the microphone near the speaker of the television or radio. Over the next few years, he would become particularly proud of his collection of Madness picture discs and the only LP's he would buy would be compilation albums the first of which would be but for now he was in love with the album cover from "Eat to the Beat". Debbie Harry just looked so desirable and he actually resented the lustful looks of the other band members on the cover, he was genuinely jealous of the way they were allowed to touch her and the easy way she appeared to lean on them in the pictures while looking out at him, almost as a personal taunt as if to suggest *"bet you wish it was you!"* and he did, but it was a strange and somehow scary feeling, A private feeling that he dare not share with his mates. It was as if he had two lives, the public one where his brand with his peer group was developing nicely and his private one where he was beginning to get such strong feelings that were starting to drive him in such a strange, inexplicable way. It was out of his control and therefore made him feel anxious but in an exciting way. The knots in his stomach when he saw these images of Debbie Harry and other equally alluring celebrity images were publicly something to consider as soppy, but privately he ached for something but did not really know what.

The only evidence he had to support that these things were wrong and "girly" came from observing his elder sister. Many times he had seen her crying over David Cassidy records, while looking at photographs of boys that had once come into the house and teased William, but disappointingly never returned after their first few visits. When he had asked things like "when is Barry coming round again?" she had just burst into tears or gone into a violent rant which just baffled William. It was such a stupid way to be, no way would he ever want to be like that in his boys' world, just so soppy.

The big hit at the cinema that year had been Grease, and as a result a lot of the chart hits of the summer had come from the score. The record player had a few of these singles loaded, and as Grease Lightning finished, the needle arm returned automatically to its cradle and in doing so triggered the next record on the stalk to drop down onto the previous and begin to play. It was Olivia Newton John, "Hopelessly devoted". At that point, before the song had got past the introductory bars, the music abruptly stopped as someone had gone onto change all the records on the stack. Provoked it seemed by the record that they had stopped, which it looked like was going on the bottom of the new stack.

It was then that he was approached by Tracy. Tracy was two years older than William and respected by the girls in the same way that William respected some of the senior boys who out-ranked him, he would obey them without question, partly because that was the hierarchy of rank, but also because they had knowledge and confidence that he wanted too.

Tracy looked at William and came straight out with it, "Silvie wants to dance with you!"

"What?"

"Silvia, Silvie, she wants to dance with you, I think you should, she's nice and she likes you."

"But this slow one is on now."

Tracy burst out laughing, "You saddo, you don't get it do you."

William flushed red with hurt and anger, she was taunting him and he felt out of control again. He hated being in this position and had to recover face somehow, but there was a knowing look of power in Tracy's eyes that made the knot in his stomach grow bigger.

"'course I get it, I just don't know what music is coming on that we can dance to." He said grasping for some kind of control in the conversation he had a feeling he was missing.

Tracy burst out laughing again and it was like a stinging slap to William's ego. She saw it land and immediately stopped laughing. They were alone in the corner of the room and she came closer to William and with kindness in her eyes genuinely asked the question, "Will, have you ever kissed someone?"

Defensively the reply came back "yes!"

"properly?"

With a shrug of his shoulders and shoving his hands into the tight pockets of his burgundy stay pressed, "loads of times" it was unconvincing but Tracy wasn't out to score points, she was helping her younger friend and of course growing her own little following by taking the role of matriarch, fearless and all knowing on such matters of the heart.

"Ok Will, that's good then. Look, Silvie really likes you and I think you should dance with her now while the slowies are on. Yeah?" The "yeah" had an inflection of confirmation in the tone, checking that William had got the meaning. He hadn't!

"You get it?"

Suddenly the penny dropped. The older cadets did tend to take over the floor a bit when the slow records were played and smooch together for ages. Normally it was a part of the night that William had found boring, and had been admonished in the past for changing the records for something more upbeat, quickly rectifying the mistake when the 16 year olds came blustering into the record room hurling abuse.

He was being asked for a smooch!

Tracy saw the information hit home and nodded as she left him with his thoughts.

Suddenly William felt very nervous indeed, what would his mates think? How was he going to justify this? What would he say? At no point however, did his thought process entertain the idea of not dancing. This was different, exciting, scary. Pride was at stake, but excitement, thrill and a certain amount of instinct was driving him forward.

For the next twenty minutes or so, none of William's friends could understand why he was so quiet. They left him to it as he sat in the corner with a numb look on his face that reflected his thoughts. He was looking across the main deck at Silvie, noticing things about her that he had never seen before. She was slight and a bit short, but now under scrutiny she was also slightly shapely too, not like Debbie Harry, but showing the early signs of approaching womanhood. She was pretty too, her thin features almost made her look elf like especially with her vivid green eyes. She had long, silky brown hair that would normally be tightly wrapped in a bun on a Cadet night. Now it was down it framed her face and made her look older somehow, yet shy and demure. Silvie was cute.

Silvia hated her given name, it sounded so old and unusual, nobody was called Silvia these days, unless they were 102 or something, and it meant that she was not at all confident around boys, yet like so many girls she was far more aware and mature than her male counterparts, so she preferred Silvie. She had been trying to pluck up the courage to ask William out for ages, she adored him. She had shared this information with her friends, as girls do, and finally Tracy had taken control and made something happen.

From time to time she glanced over at William, and for a second they held eye contact before both breaking off in embarrassment. But soon their eyes met again, and again, growing in confidence and both of them could feel their hearts racing in anticipation, completely lost in their focus on the next act, they were oblivious to the world around them.

It was an awkward moment when the dance music stopped while the records were being changed to a Medley of slow records. A signpost to tell them they were about to have their moment, and the nervous tension tightened in on them both like knots under pressure. William heard one of his friends voices project over to him "com'on Wills, let's go down to the canteen while this slow stuff is on"

William temporarily snapped out of the surreal world his head was swimming in to utter back "no you're alright, I'm staying here."

"What? Ooooooh" in a mocking inflection, was the taunt that came back, but they quickly retreated when William glared and they just ran off giggling among themselves, a little gang of two or three, William couldn't be sure and didn't much care. The moment was nearly here, as he walked over towards Silvie and they stood awkwardly next to each other, neither happy to say anything, just waiting for the music to start.

As the opening bars of Hopelessly Devoted by Olivia Newton John broke the moment of awkward silence, and the lights were turned out by the closing of the door to the record room once more, William felt the sudden shock of proximity as Silvie melted into his arm and laid her head on his chest, just as the older cadets were doing. William consciously put his arms around her and all his senses tingled as he felt hers slip around him, awkwardly at first, then finding a comfortable place to rest, her elbows at his sides and her forearms extended up his back, hands splayed and in full contact with his back and pressed themselves hard into the muscle of his upper back, toned spongy hard by his swimming, pulling herself onto him as if he had saved her life. He was shocked by the sudden full on contact, the warmth and movement of her body against his felt alien yet somehow nice.

Silvie didn't know what else to do as she flung herself at William, she had longed for this moment for ages and unlike William had discussed the whole thing with her friends as they giggled about such things at school. She idolised William, she had been longing for this contact and dreamed about copying the movie stars that seemed so hopelessly in love when they dramatically threw themselves together. Her heart was beating so fast she thought that William must surely feel it against him and was terrified that he might laugh his confident laugh and break off, so she clung to him, desperate for the moment to never end and fearful of the shame should he decide he didn't like her. This was a pivotal moment in her life, a massive leap into young womanhood, a conscious decision to fall in to the arms of a boy.

William felt the urgency of the embrace from Silvie and didn't really know what to make of it. It was kind of nice but restricted movements. He looked around to see the others just swaying from foot to foot in time with the music, and so he began to do the same, attempting to pick up the rhythm. As Silvie clung to him almost rigidly, he began to let his senses pick up the new feelings, she was wearing a satin blue top that was so shiny and smooth, he let his hands stroke her back, feeling the bra strap underneath, the sensations brand new and unusual to hands that were far more comfortable with a cricket bat in them. He felt her shudder as his hands ran lightly over Silvie's back and wondered if he had done something wrong, but Silvie seemed to push even further into him so he figured he would carry on.

Silvie was smiling against his chest. The feeling of his hands stroking her back was a signal to her that he had accepted her and that the dream of being William's girl friend had come true. She let him move her with the music, giving herself over to his control completely. There were strange warm feelings building inside her. Butterflies in her stomach were being replaced with something more intense, not scary but somehow still a little like being scared, was it guilt? No not quite, while they were in this bubble it didn't matter what it felt like, she just didn't want it to end.

William was enjoying the feeling of her soft blouse under his hands and began to enjoy making her shudder when he stroked her. He let his hand drift up to the top of her collar and brushed his fingers along her hairline at the back of her neck, and he thought he heard her groan, but couldn't be sure over the music. He let his fingers play there for a while and she responded by copying him, each encouraging the other unconsciously. William wasn't quite as keen, it tickled him a bit and shuffled his head to one side. As he did so he looked around him to see the older teenagers dancing, looking far more comfortable with the slow dance format. Most of the lads were fixed on their own mission of trying to subtly drift their wandering hands down toward their dancing partners buttocks, some were having more success than others with this mission. The girls were well aware of what the boys were attempting and enjoyed the game, but many would wait until the last moment before reaching behind themselves and placing these wandering hands back up for the whole charade to begin again. Other couples were kissing while dancing, eyes closed and lips welded together, to William it looked like many of them were trying to wrestle a gobstopper out of each others' mouths, and he stifled a laugh as this thought intruded for a brief moment before he felt Silvie squash into him again and his focus returned to his dance.

As the first song finished, Silvie held on and for a funny moment they continued to sway to the beat of the song until another record had dropped down into place and the needle engaged. Another hit from Grease began, and as John Travolta was declaring his desperate love for Sandy, William and Silvie settled into the new beat and continued the heady moment. William wondered if Silvie would move his hand back up if he put it on her bottom. Slowly he began to slide his hand down, his heart beating fast with the anticipation. He was surprised how quickly his hand reached the top of her skirt, he hadn't been expecting that, girls waists were higher that boys and he only had his own frame of reference to work from. The sudden shock of being at that point put some doubt in his mind and he hesitated before going lower.

Silvie was oblivious to William's plans, as far as she was concerned this was it, bliss, lost in her own dreams she was relishing every moment. This was all she wanted, all she needed. She felt safe and accepted, the insecurities all forgotten.

William was plucking up the courage to let his hand go further down. Then he decided to go for it and just like he would on the sports field he went for the strike. In a swift decisive movement he suddenly placed his hand on Silvie's bottom, grabbing her cheek in his strong palm, and was horrified when she screamed.

She hadn't been expecting that, it shocked her and she wasn't quite ready for the sensation that his intruding hand had provoked. Her squeal was an unconscious release that she immediately regretted, she didn't want the dance to stop, she didn't want to let go of William but she wasn't ready for that stuff either.

The older couples turned and laughed for a moment before returning to their own dances and William stood for a moment like a rabbit in headlights, not knowing what to do. Tracy was looking over from the side of the room, not having a partner herself, and gestured with an encouraging and exaggerating movement of the head, while mouthing the words "go on". He opened his arms and once more Silvie melted into them, somewhat cautiously, but relaxed once William's hands once more began to stroke her back.

He let his hand drift back up to her neck again, she had seemed to like that before. He was enjoying learning about her responses, if a little scared at the same time. He let the back of his hand brush the side of her neck and touched her jawbone for an instant. He was a few inches taller than her and while she ducked her head down and laid it on his chest it was comfortable. William had lifted his head to accommodate this and was beginning to feel a little uncomfortable, so he let his head drop slightly and his chin touched her temple. This was a new skin to skin contact that made his heart race once more.

Silvie wanted to kiss him, she had never kissed anyone before and she wanted her first kiss to come from the boy she idolised. She hoped he would try, she was desperate for him to try. She was almost whimpering in her own head "please kiss me, pleeease kiss me."

William, wanted to kiss her too, but was still reeling from the knock back of his attempted grope, and was treading very carefully over this new ground. His heart was racing again, and he hoped the music would keep going and going, but the record was nearly finished. There had to be more surely, they would have loaded up at least four wouldn't they? They had.

The break in music had allowed William to move position slightly and now his chin had moved down to almost the side of Silvie's eye. The warmth of her skin on his face was almost paralysing and he left it there, wondering how on earth he was going to make the kiss happen, he let his hands continue to stroke her back while pondering his next move.

Silvie was desperate to turn her head up towards him and let him kiss her, but she too was paralysed with uncertainty and fear as to what to do. Would it push him away? What did he think of her already after squealing like that? Oh what a feeling, she was almost feeling sick with all the confusing messages being sent round her naive brain.

As William moved his hand up again to Silvie's neck, he once more let his fingers move to her jaw line and gently stroked, each time he stroked he pushed ever so slightly to encourage her head up toward his. The first movement was a slide of skin against skin that was so delicious that both of them squeezed a bit tighter with their arms, feeling the jolt as chemicals were being released around their young systems. They slid further, now cheek to cheek, both wanting so much to finalise the movement but neither willing to risk the potential eye contact that might break the spell.

In an act of desperation Silvie was the one to make the move and she lifted her head up, her eyes tightly closed and waited for the feeling of his lips on hers. She didn't have to wait long, as the feeling of his lips touching hers registered, her heart nearly stopped. He was gentle, so soft, his moist lips felt like fire on hers and she opened her mouth slightly as Tracy had told her to, and was prepared for the invasion that she had been warned about, but it didn't come. Instead she felt the gentle flick of Williams tongue gently touch her bottom lip. It was like static electricity being released and she relaxed what she now realised was a very tense mouth.

William took her upturned head as the invitation it had been intended as, and he allowed his mouth to fall on hers. Still a little uncertain after his early mistake, he wanted to know what it was to "taste a girl's lips" he had heard this phrase so many times and it had always been put in the context of pleasure, so he wanted to know what the fuss was about. He licked his lips involuntarily, and the moisture on them allowed them to slide over hers as they made contact. It felt so intense, so good, William liked kissing from that moment of first contact and would like it for the rest of his life. He was soaking up the sensation and he was surprised as to how hard her lips were, as if they were thin and tense, which was not the image he had in his head of her lovely mouth. He felt her open her mouth slightly and he let his lips slide further onto her kiss and he tentatively let his tongue touch her lips to taste them. No taste at all, none, just a wonderful sensation that was thrilling and spine tingling. As his tongue touched her lip the hardness of her mouth melted into something soft and spongy, he loved the feeling of their lips sliding softly against each other, the soft resistance sending shivers down his spine. He was in rapture, loving the sensation, happy for this to be his experience.

It was like an electric shock when it happened. The jolt he felt as her tongue gently touched his would change his life forever. Those first tentative touches were so nervous, yet so tender that they were exquisite.

Silvie wanted to let William know that she liked his tongue there, so she touched hers to his, and for a moment regretted the move when she felt the recoil of his tongue, only to once more feel the relief she had so many other times tonight when his tongue almost immediately returned to gently spar with her own. It was nothing like the invasion that she had been warned about. They were just touching tongues like Eskimos rubbing noses, yet somehow it was just so lovely, so right.

William was totally lost in this moment, he couldn't define the feeling he had, it was like nothing else he had experienced. He liked it, but what he really liked about it was that Silvie seemed to like it too. This was exciting. To think that doing this to someone could make them feel like he was feeling too. So far his pleasure had always come from winning, from beating the opposition. His world had been turned upside down, now he could win by creating pleasure for someone else. Not only that, but he was thrilled by the thought. So how come it turned his belly to mush?

As the slow music came to a final end, (how many songs had it been?) they were both slowly drawn from the spell and Silvie appeared to want to break away from William as she was moving her body away from him, yet confusingly it was obvious that she wanted to continue with the kiss. These mixed messages were confusing William and the magic was dissolving, then finally broken by a teasing adult voice jeering "break it up you two, you won't eat you're supper". They both jumped away from each other and retreated back into their own personas once more.

William flushed with embarrassment at the snipe and the wry smile on the instructors face, then realised with further embarrassment the potential source of Silvie's concern while she was trying to wriggle away. Due to a redistribution of blood, his Burgundy Stay Press were now much tighter than ever.

The bright lights came on and snapped everything back into reality once more. The order and discipline of the cadet unit flooded back into the large room and the fantasy and romance of the dance floor seemed a million miles away.

"Com'on you lot, there are parents waiting outside, let's go!" boomed the instructor's voice as people were gathering records and coats and saying their goodbyes, making plans and laughing with one another. Like the teenagers they were, they just kept going at their own pace despite the robust encouragement.

William was smiling his big broad grin. His friends had returned to find him and immediately saw what looked like a 28 tooth smile plastered on his face. "What's up with you Wills?"

"Absolutely nothing" then almost to himself he uttered "that was fantastic"

"what?"

"Oh, never mind, com'on let's go" He felt older than his friends all of a sudden, somehow more in touch with the senior cadets he had observed smooching as if it were all perfectly normal to them. He felt like he had moved up into their world. As he walked out of the unit with his friends, his chin up and chest inflated, he was the pack leader once more.

He didn't see her, but she had been waiting for him, much to the annoyance of her parents. As he stepped out of the door, she was there and his heart jumped not for the first time that night. She simply said "I'll see you next Friday Will" then after a brief moment of eye contact, she smiled and ran off to the open back door of her father's car, and she was gone.

"Bloody hell, what was all that about Will?"

"Nothing, just meeting Silvie next Friday at Cadets I s'pose."

"Oh brilliant" with a big inflection on sarcasm "what about going to the fair next Friday after Cadets like you said."

William turned with a big grin still on his face and said "Don't worry fellas, nothing's changed!"

But things would never be the same again.

Top Tips - Live a little

There is a wonderful saying that goes like this:

"Life is not measured by the number of breaths we take, but by the moments that take our breath away."

The pivotal moments in life, that make our heart beat and shape our future are often the most profound memories that we store. As we grow older and supposedly wiser we become more risk averse and sometimes avoid these highly charged and wonderfully heart stopping moments.

Just like a theme park ride, the fear that precedes the first peak as the truck slowly clacks it's way to the top, builds and builds making us wonder why on earth we got on in the first place, yet by getting in and strapping in we have committed. Then the ride takes over and as we release all of those thrill seeking chemicals that make us squeal with delight we hear ourselves shouting "again, again".

There are many reasons why we should not do something, usually attached to a risk, but don't forget that the nature of risk usually comes with some kind of trade off, if the potential benefits outweigh the risk, then maybe you should commit and go for it. Let yourself live a little and when the time comes to look back and reflect, those memories will be the ones that make you smile.

But what if?

Why not change that question to "and what if?" see what a difference that makes to your decision, for it is your decision alone . . .

CHAPTER 6

NEW, CONFUSING, FEELINGS

The next morning started, for William, like most other Saturday mornings with the smell of bacon and his Mother's voice calling him down for breakfast. William looked at the clock, his head still full of confused dreams and muffled thoughts of the previous night, thoughts that had been contorted throughout his dreams. William had spent the night drifting in and out of sleep, reliving the kiss and the feel of Silvia in his arms. During the moments that he had awoken, struggling to fall into the deep, teenage sleep that normally consumed him totally and would last well into the afternoons of weekends if he were left, he had tried to play the movie forward to what might happen next. He tried to imagine the scenario of Silvy consenting to all his teenage lust, but the dream would blur and drift away into obscurity as he once more fell into fitful slumber.

It was 10am, and he was awake now. The pit of his stomach was churning with the thoughts that had taken over his mind since the events on the main-deck at the Cadet disco. Normally he would roll over and grab a few more precious moments before his Mother would physically drag him out of bed by pulling back the covers and threatening to throw a pan of cold water over him. It was a ritual that they had played out many times usually ending with his

Mother putting the always empty pan on the bottom of William's feet to make him jump out of bed.

Today however he got up, left his bedroom and padded down the long landing to the bathroom. He felt funny. Not quite sick, not nervous or even scared, but similar to those kinds of feelings, his stomach had that kind of knot in it that you might get before a big swimming race or facing a fast bowler for the first time, excited at the challenge but wary of the potential failure. And yet there was something else to this feeling, something more powerful yet somehow less defined, and it was out of his control.

He stood at the toilet and relieved himself, almost hypnotised by the stream he was creating, ensuring his aim was true, William even turned this most basic of human functions into a competitive sport, subconsciously scoring himself with a percentage of how much he could get directly into the water. Normally, his mind would create a game and any of his stream that hit the bowl instead of the water would alert the guards of the toilet empire to his presence and result in certain death, whereas if he successfully struck at the heart of their empire they would suffer that fate instead. Of course the rules would always change in his favour if things went wrong.

Today however, was different. Nothing could pull his mind out of the fog that was invading his thoughts and churning his stomach. He moved to the sink and turned on the cold tap, the sudden gush splashing his bare chest. He didn't mind the feeling of cold water on him, he had become very used to diving into cold water or falling out of kayaks into freezing rivers, capsizing sailing boats and washing in cold water while camping, and so he cupped his hands under the stream and just watched the water for a while as it violently moved in eddies in his hands and spilled over the sides into the sink and away. He breathed in and suddenly splashed a whole double handful of the cold water onto his face, breathing out as he did so with an audible flubber as the water refreshed and cleansed the last of his sleep from his brain. He rubbed his hands up and down over his face and repeated the process, allowing the water to wet the fringe of his hair.

He felt better, but that feeling was still in his stomach, nagging away as he dried his face and hands on the warm towel that hung from the heated pipes in the old fashioned bathroom. As he hung the towel back the thick pipes gurgled and popped, his father would be up to bleed the air from the system later as was the weekend ritual, one of a list of many jobs that his father did every weekend.

William ran back to his room, bowling an imaginary cricket ball as he did so, half way down the landing, he imagined removing the off stump of Viv Richards's protected wicket, sending the ash pole tumbling end over end as Richards slouched off in his Caribbean lope while Ian Botham and Bob Willis came rushing over to congratulate William on his first test wicket, "and the crowd go wild as this new promising youngster bursts into the England team" the commentary added for good effect. He quickly darted into his bedroom, momentarily self conscious in case anyone should have heard his little self adulation, feeling slightly silly. He pulled on a tea shirt and jeans that lay crumpled at the bottom of the bed and made his way downstairs.

"Wow, what's this? Have you wet the bed? Has there been a fire? Is there an intruder in the house?" William's mother said with as much drama as she could muster as she stood at the stove with her flour dusted pinafore covering her flowery dress, a spatula in hand moving yet another batch of bacon around in the pan. Having already fed William's brothers and sister with triple-decker bacon sandwiches, she had been planning to have the next batch for herself before dragging William down, but it looked like she would now have to wait once more. It was just as well William's uncle was a butcher, she reflected to herself as she went back to the fridge for yet more of the bacon that had seemed to disappear quicker that it took to cook in the first place.

"ha ha, very funny" said William ironically.

"Do you want sauce in your sandwiches?"

Suddenly William really didn't want anything to eat, the feeling he had was very slightly nauseating. "No thanks, I'm not really hungry Mum"

The spatula went down on the side and his mother turned to face him with barely concealed shock on her face, "Are you alright Will?"

"Yeh" William said, a little too defensively, now his sister was interested too. "I just don't fancy any brecky thanks, that's all."

"That's not like you Will, are you sure you're OK?" with slight concern in her voice now rather than the irony of before, William's mother looked through from the kitchen to view her son in the dining room that adjoined and was the main meeting place for the family during the day.

His sister was now fully alert for an opportunity to have a snipe "Must be love sickness, I bet you have been with the girls haven't you, you little scumbag."

"Get stuffed you cow!" how could she know???

"William! I will not have you talk like that! What on earth makes you think you can in this house?" his mother admonished, now in a serious tone.

"Well she just always has a go Mum, and she just hacks me off"

"That's because you're a dirty little pervert." Elizabeth was on a roll and wanted to score against her brother, who she believed was the spoiled one and deserved everything he got.

The truth was that great efforts were made to ensure all the children had equal levels of treatment, but with such age ranges and gender differences it was difficult of not impossible to achieve the kind of parity that would negate any inter sibling jealousy. So, the relationships were built like so many close families, on a deep routed love that often was displayed in a less than affectionate way. In other words William and his sister Elisabeth, fought like cat and dog and genuinely thought that they hated each other. The truth of the matter was that they loved each other very much but refused to admit it. They certainly understood each other enough to know exactly how to press each others' buttons, much to the despair of their mother who often had to pick up the pieces. What they didn't often do was act responsibly with that understanding, not yet anyway, teenage understanding doesn't work like that.

Elisabeth was on the moral high ground at the moment, still playing the role of the victim after a series of events that had happened two weeks previously. It was a week that Elisabeth would remember as one of the worst in her life.

It began in the garden with her love of all creatures. Elisabeth had a real affinity with animals, she loved them. On this day she had spent hours just sitting as still as she could surrounded by bread crumbs, waiting for the bold little birds to come closer and closer as they became more trusting in grabbing little morsels of bread before fluttering off into nearby trees to swallow the food down in safety. The boldest bird so far had been the resident robin, who Elisabeth called Rufus. The inquisitive creature would respond to Elisabeth's warbling mimic of a robins call, like all robins it was nosey and territorial, he wanted to know what all the noise was and would come to investigate, once perched in the bush near to this new strange whistle, he would then be stimulated by the presence of an opportunistic feast and the fact that a slow human was near posed no real threat so he would swoop down grab bread and take it back to the bush where he would flip his head back allowing the bread to fall into his crop, then chirp defiantly before swooping again.

Elisabeth took delight in watching this, convinced that the bird interacting with her and had become her true friend. Once the robin had enjoyed his fill, he was soon bored and went off looking for more stimulation within his territory and was gone as soon as he had appeared.

The sparrows however remained, squabbling among themselves on the very outer edge of the ring of crumbs. Greedy for more, the bolder ones rushing in to then be mobbed by the others for the booty they had grabbed.

Elisabeth had one crust of stale bread left in the bag she had brought out with her, two rounds had already been distributed among the birds and word had got round it seemed, as several species of garden bird now swooped in to take up post in various stations, waiting for their opportunity to cash in. The sparrows and starlings were the most abundant, with the occasional black bird hopping in at the side, wary but confident, almost appearing regal compared to the squabbling masses of the flock birds.

Elisabeth liked the sparrows and the blackbirds best after her Rufus. On the face of it the starlings should be considered as beautiful birds with their colourfully speckled plumage that shimmered and glittered in the changing light of the sun as they moved, yet they took on an almost sinister, greedy demeanour as they prowled around waiting to hijack the smaller sparrows, their beady eyes and long sharp beaks looking almost evil compared to the cute stubby features of the sparrows.

Elisabeth would attempt to shoo away the starlings without upsetting the sparrows, gently admonishing them with "you'll get yours you greedy things". A wave of her arms would see all the birds sparrows and starlings alike flutter back to fences and bushes before steadily coming back to start the whole process again.

This particular morning, Elisabeth had spent hours sitting on the grass, her bottom numb now, but her mind focussed totally on feeding the birds and coaxing them closer and closer. She had identified with one particular little fellow that was getting bolder and bolder. She dreamed of feeding the little chap from her hand and had sat for so long with her hand outstretched that her muscles were screaming with the effort, yet she persisted, a large wad of crust about an inch in diameter pinched between her finger and thumb, held out in line with some smaller morsels on the ground about a foot away.

William and his eldest brother Simon had been watching this from Simon's open bedroom window. William didn't see too much of Simon, as he was in full time work as an engineer and was particularly gifted in this field, but he had idolised him. Simon was fastidious in everything that he did, a perfectionist with a real skill for accuracy. Simon had influenced William in many of his hobbies such as model making, buying him his first Airfix model for Christmas when William was seven, a spitfire, what else?

William wanted to shout at the birds so that they flew away and spoiled his sister's pleasure, but Simon put a finger to his lips and had a glint in his eye that William recognised as a plan worth watching, he just smiled back at his big brother and waited to see what the plan would be.

Elisabeth was totally absorbed in the moment. It was going to happen. The cheeky little sparrow was getting closer and closer. Pressing forward in a diagonal approach, one wary eye fixed on the big human, head cocked back, muscles tensed ready to burst into flight at the merest hint of any danger.

Less than a foot away, Elisabeth felt sure if she just reached out her hand she could stroke the little man, but she patiently waited for the bird to come to her, keeping absolutely still, hardly daring to breath. Ten inches away now the bird appeared to be regarding her, as if making a decision to take the final bold move, Elisabeth felt they were in rapport and she was willing him in her own mind "go on little man, I won't hurt you, take it, go on take it . . ."

"THWACK"

The bird spun and contorted on the floor, a strained little scream coming from it as its wings spread like a fan touching the floor yet unable to lift it from the ground as it gulped in vain for its last breath.

For a dream like moment Elisabeth didn't comprehend what had happened, the events played themselves again quickly in her head and her brain then put all the noises together from the hollow sounding "puck" closely followed by the sickening "thwack/smack" as the air rifle pellet found it's mark and hit the sparrow square in the chest, a mortal shot that would take only a few seconds to render the creature dead, a small entry wound barely showing a hint of blood as the feathers matted around the hole made by the .22" calibre pellet.

As the bird lay dead, beak open, lifeless eyes, once black and bright now glazing over to a dull pearlescent grey looked at nothing. Elisabeth couldn't move, couldn't breathe, she couldn't even scream. She was just transfixed on the dead bird. All the others had flown and gone. Up in the window that overlooked the back garden, William and Simon gleefully gave each other high fives. To them, it was just another pest gone with the added bonus of upsetting their pathetic sister. Simon, satisfied that the shot had been perfect, gave it no further thought. William in his inexperience was going to milk this one for all it's worth.

Then the screaming began.

Back at the breakfast table now, days later, the siblings sat glaring at each other. Elisabeth was still devastated by the killing of the sparrow, William still resentful of the beating he had received from his father after several return taunts at his sister's expense. Following the confiscation of his brother's air rifle, William had felt compelled to take any opportunity to have a little dig at Elisabeth which usually provoke her enough to lash out and give him the excuse to lash back. The whole incident had come to a head when

Elisabeth had waved a kitchen knife at William in temper and he had been unsure as to how serious she was so he stuck his tongue out and ran as she made a mocking lunge her heal caught in the kitchen floor, snapping it clean off her shoe, much to Williams delight as he howled with laughter, she howled in indignation and fury. William received a thrashing after much protestation, his father judging that he had gone too far and this would be an end to the matter.

In truth, William realised that his sister now had him on two counts. He had gone too far and while he hated to admit it, he did feel a bit ashamed, and now to add to the problem, she was a bit too close to the mark with her accusation. That gut twisting nag of instinctive guilt was eating him again, and he was angry with himself, his pride hurt once more and mixed with the emotions that Silvy was provoking he was confused and needed to do something. He needed to run.

"I'm going out!" he swiftly got up, ran out the door, pausing to snatch a jacket from the back of the chair and was away. The last thing he heard before the gate clanged was his mother's voice.

"Make sure you're back for lunch at one . . ."

Top Tips - *"No-one has the power to affect your state of mind without your personal consent" Eleanor Roosevelt.*

This now famous quote is famous because it is powerful and true. It effectively says that if something or someone upsets you, it's because you allowed it to get to you. That is quite something to buy into sometimes when some total idiot is really getting in your face and totally contradicting your own set of values, how very dare they???

We are all guilty of rising to this and it's easy to see why. What the clever first lady was suggesting however, is to take a little moral high ground and change your own psychology to the extent whereby you can take the stance of "why should I give you, you grubby little person, the power to affect my mind? It's you who are the problem, it's you who is causing the friction, so I will choose instead to smile back at you safe in the knowledge that actually, I'm fine thank you ☺"

When you have the strength to do that, it has an incredible effect in a positively empowering way for you, and in a satisfying (for you) out of control kind of way for your protagonist.

It's the same mind-set that some incredibly pro-active people have been able to achieve throughout history, Victor Frankle (Author of "Life's last ultimate freedom") and his survival of the Nazi death camps for example, Ghandi under immense political pressure before bringing the largest empire the world has ever seen to its' knees with a simple un-violent act.

These people are special in that their determination, resolve and passion in their values have set them apart from us mere mortals. Yet that passion is within us all when our own set of values is compromised.

So the next time something, or someone is in conflict with your value system, don't give it or them the satisfaction of seeing you get out of control and allowing them to win, simply say to yourself "you know what? You are not strong enough to control my mind, you can have your own opinion and you can be as unreasonable as you like, the one thing you can never have is power over my mind, that is mine alone, and I am stronger than you as a result."

Shooting then or their pet's with an air rifle is not a great option either and is, incidentally, illegal in most countries so do try the whole moral high ground thing first, it's a lot better all round really.

CHAPTER 7

FIGHT OR FLIGHT

He ran and ran hard until his lungs hurt with the effort. The thoughts whirring round in his head and the emotions tumbling round in his stomach like a washing machine were temporarily forgotten with the simple exertion. The flight or fight response to being backed into a corner, had enabled his body to disperse the chemicals that were released into his system and he felt better.

He had run across the playing fields opposite his house, cut through the old and overgrown cemetery that had spooked him so many times when he was younger, down a mud path to the river and along the bank towards the town bridge. He slowed to a walk while he sucked the precious air into his lungs quickly regaining his breath with the fitness of a young man in good condition, hardly sweating yet hot he wanted to be able to talk properly if he ran into anyone, Silvy maybe . . . "you never know" he told himself aloud almost to test the stability of his voice, his breath not quite back yet, the words came out strained.

He had thought about "that" kiss with Silvy, a lot. He craved contact with her, he couldn't wait to see her again and in his mind was planning what he would say, what he would do. Would she let him go further? His young body, pumped full of hormones would respond at the thought and he spent a lot of time with his hands in his pockets adjusting himself uncomfortably. Or sometimes a little too comfortably.

William's mother had told his father about his movement into adulthood being reflected in the laundry basket, bed sheets were in need of frequent changing and she wanted his father to speak to him about the delicate subject. His father had dismissed it as normal behaviour that would pass "let him get it out of his system love, let's not embarrass the boy". Reluctantly his mother had conformed and just got on with running the house, turning a blind eye to the frequently unsightly random patterns left half way up the sheets on a regular basis.

His mind lost in thought of what might be, William unconsciously walked toward the town centre on this Saturday morning, hoping to bump into Silvy, but knowing the chances were slim. As he rounded into the high street, the traditional meeting place of his peers came into view. The steps outside Woolworths were a favourite spot for teenagers to hang out and hook up. Today William's mates were there and beamed when he walked up to them.

"Hi Will, I heard you won't go hungry for a while after eating half a person at the disco ha ha ha" the laughter was echoed throughout the group and William took a while for the penny to drop before he let himself be sucked into the group dynamics.

Seeing an opportunity to hog the limelight he fell into the easy banter of a proud ringleader to gain control, "well you know how it is, when you're as good looking as me it's bound to happen"

"yeah right haha"

"Seriously Will, what on earth was that all about?" it was John Tansley who asked the question, one of his Cadet friends who had wanted Will to go up the fair next week. John was a small, nervous lad whos eyes were never still, his hair never seemed to lay flat, not that it ever looked like much effort had been put into combing it. He had yet to see the attraction of girls who were just a pain as far as he was concerned, but he also felt there was no way they would ever be attracted to him anyway so what was the point.

"What was what all about?" answered Will more innocently that he felt.

"Snogging the face off of what's her name, at the disco last night"

"What?" William had a smug smile on his face, but was beginning to realise that not all of his friends actually thought it was cool. In fact some looked horrified.

"That flat chested minger you were getting off with, looked like a boy uuuurgh"

William felt a surge of anger at this slight, that wasn't how he saw it at all, Silvie's figure to him was lithe and made him feel almost queasy with desire, how could they think she looked like a boy?

The flash of anger in his eyes was picked up and John had taken an unconscious step back, all too aware that he stood no chance if Will decided to whack him.

Pride and peer pressure kicked in and William heard himself say "Well, it'll do for now."

That seemed to do the trick. The group went very quiet and almost appeared to stare past him. Sensing he had his audience back he carried on, "Spit will do till I can get a better one."

Still no response came back so William went on to explain his joke unnecessarily. "You know, Silvia, saliva, like spit the dog, on my lead acting on my command. Down spit, beg spit . . ." William was swept up in his narrative once again commanding an audience or so he thought, then he sensed that they were not looking at him and he turned to see Silvia behind him.

His heart sang for a brief moment, she was here, she had come to find him . . . Then, he saw the tears in her eyes and the broken look on her face, her eyes met his for less than a second but it was enough for William to see the pain in them. There was no anger in her eyes, just bitter sorrow and hurt, as the tears finally tumbled down her cheeks she turned and fled. All the hope that had filled her heart since last night, all the elation that finally she had someone who thought her attractive, thought of her as a young woman, who wouldn't make fun of her, who could hold her and make her feel wonderful like William had last night. All broken, all smashed to pieces, her confidence shattered her world torn apart, how could she ever feel safe with a boy again? She ran, her hand clasped to her mouth, unable to breath, the sob stuck in her chest needing to explode out but she couldn't be anywhere near the source of her pain when it happened.

Like William, she had been drawn to town like a moth to the flame in the hope of seeing him. Her heart had leapt in her chest when she saw him, only to have her world torn apart by what she then heard him say about her. It had been too good to be true after all.

William, turned back to see his friends faces looking at him, "Plenty more fish in the sea!" William had heard his father use this expression to his sister so many times, it never seemed to help his sister and it felt an empty statement now, but it was all William could think of to say.

"Mate, you're a legend, haha" John Tansley was actually very impressed with the nonchalant way the William had brushed off this little incident, he could never have handled that so coolly.

The group all laughed and were now slapping William on the back, all safe again in their known world of the young male. A sense of safe normality had fallen over the group once more.

William however, felt sick. His day had gone from bad to worse. He drifted along with his pack in a surreal, disassociated kind of way. Nothing was in control any more. The more he thought about it, the worse it got. He had ruined his chances of seeing Silvy again and the thought of facing her at Cadets was intimidating, there was an option of giving up Cadets and losing that piece of his solid little life, the thought made him feel hopeless. He was unwelcome at home after the incident with his sister, and wouldn't find much comfort there. His mates were acting just like they always had but he was not sure that he felt like that anymore. Events had completely over taken him, and it felt frightening.

In reality, William was facing for the first time on his own, a few problems that he had little control over. Prior to today, problems had been easy, you either hit it or ran away from it, fight or flight. He could do neither of those things here without losing a big part of his life. William was feeling stress.

"Wassup with you Will?" it was the voice of Andy Brown, Bruno, the lad who had tackled him in the game of bulldog and introduced him to Cadets months earlier.

"Nothing" the hangdog body language gave away the opposite message.

"It's that GN 'int it"

"No!"

"Mate, it happens, you'll be all right!" slapping William's shoulder he then shoved the ends of his fingers into the pockets of his very tight jeans, managing to force them down to the second knuckle, and loped off to the front of the gang who were now moving through town toward the new arcade, William was mooching at the back caught up like a piece of driftwood on an ebbing tide.

The group had moved into the arcade and William, still lost in the numbness of his crumbling world, became slowly aware of the new environment as the distinctive noise of space invaders penetrated into his consciousness. By the sound of it, someone had got a fair way through the levels and the speed of the aliens munching down toward the frantic laser turret of the defender was reflected in the urgency to the synthetic sound effects it produced. William looked over to the machine to see a crowd of people gathered round watching a frantic lad swaying his body, fast fingers flicking at the fire button while dragging hard at the toggle joystick as if hanging on the controls with all his strength would somehow move the graphics quicker.

An explosion noise signalled the end of the game and the player punched the air with a shout of "High score, get in!" and the group dissipated away from the machine, one of three in the so called arcade which actually was a music record shop that had taken the visionary step of installing the machines at great cost. The bank manager had warned it would never catch on, yet another fad just like the skateboard, these silly on screen games would never hold teenagers attentions for long enough to make any money, not when they could be outside playing football . . .

The other two machines were being used and William moved to the now vacant machine while his friends had gone to the record counter to inspect the chart positions and latest picture discs that were out, speculating over the movements that would occur the next day when the nation would tune into the top 40 on Radio One. William looked down at the slot, the little plaque riveted next to it advertised

20p per play
50p per 3 plays

William reached in his pocket and felt the cornered edges of his 50p, pulling it out to inspect it, the proud figure of Britannia and the words FIFTY PENCE confirmed his ownership of what his Dad and elder brothers still called a ten bob bit.

He rested it in the opening of the slot, pausing, could he justify three games with his week's pocket money? At the last minute he changed his mind and pulled the coin out, he wasn't really in the mood. With a big sigh he analysed his miserable lot once more. Looking round for his mates, he saw another new machine near the counter, bright lights lit the interior, and inside were rows and rows of different chocolate bars and cans of drink, shandy bass, lager and lime, vimto. William had never seen anything like it, a machine to buy sweets from, what on earth was that all about?

"How come you're not selling sweets off the counter now? What's with this thing?" William had directed his thoughts in the form of a question to the owner of the record shop, who was leaning on his counter reading the back pages of his paper.

"Fed up with cheeky little toe rags like you stealing my profits while my backs turned"

Ignoring the general insult, William turned back to the machine as something unusual had caught his eye, a big bar of nougat. This was not a normally available purchase from his local corner shop where he had been used to spending his limited pocket money, rationing out the coins value with a mix of chews and maybe one bigger treat like a sherbet fountain or a swizzle lolly.

The combination of his mood, the new technology and the nougat led him to drop his 50p into the slot and press the buttons A & 5 that were denoted next to the nougat displayed for the princely sum of 30p. With a bang and a thump the nougat was pushed forward by the mechanism holding it in place and it hung perilously threatening not to drop for a second before landing in the bottom of a metal tray. His 50p had also dropped and gone forever it seemed.

"Oi, it's taken my bloody 50p!"

"Got your stuff out didn't you?" replied the store owner without looking up from his paper on the counter next to where the vending machine had been put.

"yeh, but that was only 30p, I wanted the change for the space invaders."

"tough"

"you're joking, where's my change?"

"it says no change given, exact money only, don't they teach you to read at school these days, makes a change for me to be robbing you, you little bastards ha ha" very pleased with his little joke he continued to guffaw into his paper, not concerned one bit about the loss of Williams money.

William wanted to protest, but he felt tears welling up inside himself, he just had to get out. His emotions were getting the better of him, he felt hopelessly the victim of everything all of a sudden and it twisted his guts. He felt a profound anxiety but couldn't understand why. So he walked out of the record store come arcade and began to trudge slowly home, his friends forgotten, he wallowed in his own self pity. Half way home he became conscious of the nougat bar in his hand, 8 inches of almost pure sugar. He peeled the wrapper off the sticky bar and tried to sink his teeth into the firm hard nougat, eventually it began to give and with a final yank he had one corner in mouth and began to chew. It was lovely, he loved nougat, he had only ever had it once before when his sister had brought some home from the fair, and now he had his own whole bar . . .

He recognised the low grumble of the Jensen engine as it rolled up beside him and as he looked inside his father's face did not suggest his day was going to suddenly take a turn for the better. As the electric window came down, still the only one William had ever seen it was a cool feature, his father's words were fierce.

"Where, the bloody hell, have you been? Your mother has had your dinner on the table for the last hour!"

"Oh Christ sorry dad" William was trying to open the door to get in the car.

"Don't you think your getting in here, you can bloody run home, and you had better bloody run too otherwise I will tan your backside when I get home."

The Jensen roared off and William stared after it for no more than a second before fear and shame motivated him to sprint for the second time that day only this time in the opposite direction. He was convinced that his father was going to get home first and would be waiting for him, his massive hands ready to smack the flesh of his backside if he were not there before his deadline. His mind played the story of what might be, the nougat now felt more like a murder weapon in his hand than a source of comfort and so William threw it into the nearest hedge as he sped along the path home. The tears now came, in floods and floods, gasping for breath with tears and snot running down his face he made it to the back gate and let it slam behind him as he raced in the house. Looking for his father who was nowhere to be seen, it dawned on him that the Jensen had not been in the drive.

His mother burst into the kitchen to find William in an exhausted state, uncharacteristic defeat written right through him. Gasping for breath, sobbing, almost wailing, her mothering instinct whipped the hanky out of her pocket and she went to William who fell into her arms for the first time in a very long time. Part of her was torn up over the state of her youngest boy. Another part of her was guilty in enjoying the cuddle and the fact that she could still give comfort to her offspring. She had no idea yet, what the matter was, she just shhhhh'd and rocked like only a mother can.

"I'm s s sorry M Mum" finally came the gasped apology between sobbing breaths. Even his sister had backed out of the room having come in to see what the fuss was about and then sensing her mother's body language realised that this one would have to keep.

"shhhhh, what's the matter?"

"Dad said you were mad"

"I am disappointed William, I said to be back by one, but it's not that bad surely, what has gotten into you?" She had never known William to be this upset over a simple punishment, she couldn't believe her husband would have done anything to cause this fuss. "Is this all over being late for dinner Will?"

Then it came flooding out, omitting the details of his part in upsetting Silvia, he opened his heart to his Mum, his guilt over losing his pocket money, wasting it, then having to throw away the treat for fear of a thrashing, everything. He sat empty and suddenly very tired on the kitchen floor where he had come in the back door. "Shall I eat my dinner, I'm hungry now Mum." In truth, William was now in need of food, his emotions had spilled out and he was genuinely hungry and slightly light headed with it after all the physical and emotional energy he had used.

His Mother suddenly felt guilt and helplessness of her own. William could see his dinner, still piled on the plate on the dining room table through the door. Sausages and mash with homemade mushy peas, almost a Saturday ritual, and one of Williams favourite meals. "Sorry Will, your Dad said you had to wait till tonight now to eat it. If you can be selfish enough to be late for dinner, you can go without till he gets home." She took on the stern tone that he had used and roughly repeated his words from around thirty minutes ago.

"Where's he gone?"

"To play golf"

"Then he won't be back for about 6 hours . . ." The new information made Williams stomach grumble an audible protest.

His mother looked on in sympathy and helplessness, she could not, dare not go against her husband's instructions, but he didn't know the full story. She made a decision

"William, you are not to tell your Father about this." She stood up and bustled around the kitchen hastily putting together a big doorstep sandwich, as if making it quicker would remove the evidence of her audacious misdeed.

"Eat that, then wash everything up except your plate, I'll cover that for later. Then I suggest you find something to do out of the way for the rest of the day, your sister's new boyfriend is coming round and she really doesn't need you to meet him today."

For once William was happy to be out of the way, and once his chores were done, he slipped up stairs to the safe world of his large bedroom where an unfinished model of a Lancaster Bomber would take up the next few hours of his attention.

Order had been restored to his life, and while the sandwich had only kept the rumbling away for a short while, discipline was being served, and control had been handed back to him. With control the stress began to subside to be replaced with the resolve to bounce back. But not today, not yet . . .

Top Tips - Coping with stress.

There is a widely accepted definition of stress that is used throughout the armed forces that goes like this:

Stress—The state which occurs when the mind overrides the bodies basic desire to punch the living crap out of some arsehole that desperately needs it.

Now, given the organisation that particular definition was born from you can hopefully forgive and understand the relevance of the language. But it's not actually too far from the mark. Stress is a malformation of the fight or flight response that we are genetically wired with. In caveman times when faced with adversity one had a simple choice, hit it or run away. In order to do either of those things the body very quickly produces chemicals such as adrenaline, neuro-adrenaline and cortisol (a steroid). Unfortunately in the modern world, when faced with adversity we still produce those chemicals but because we can't go around slapping every idiot we see without going to prison, we end up having to allow our liver and kidneys to work their magic and get rid of these toxins for us. So when we are stressed our liver is working over time to get rid of all the chemicals we produce, and what do we do? Go home and have a gin & tonic to relieve the symptoms of stress ⊠ that way we don't even get a proper night's sleep to let the body fix itself either. The "red wine" sleep may take us out of consciousness quickly enough, but it does not allow for REM (rapid eye movement). Over time, because our liver is so pre-occupied with processing stress chemicals, it has less time to keep the immune system running properly so we start to pick up lots of little bugs and viruses, we become a victim of stress related sickness.

What can you do?

Well you can decide to have a detox for a week or so and get better sleep as a result (top tip by the way), or chill out with a massage or mini break, but who has the time and money for those every five minutes. If you are stressed you need to fix it, and preferably NOT by pumping yet more drugs in. A detox works, as does good deep breathing to clear out the lungs of toxins. So a brisk walk to clear the head and lungs can work wonders. However prevention is better than cure.

There is one key word in the prevention of stress:

CONTROL

Driving a car at 200mph is not stressful. It's exciting, but it's not stressful. Losing control of a car at 200mph, now that is stressful.

If you think about it the only time you really feel stress is when something is happening that has an impact on you, that you have little or no control over.

So be responsible with control. Learn how to take control of the "controllables". If you are stressed, take control of the small things and have an influence on them, the momentum will help you to feel better about controlling the bigger things. Don't worry about the things you really can't control, they are not your problem. If you are that worried about them, find a way of gaining some control over them. You may argue that if you are stuck in a dead end job with a heartless boss giving you stress that you can't control that, but you always have a choice, you can choose to get out and do something else, it's just a question of how badly you really want it.

If you are a leader, think about control when you delegate. If you delegate responsibility without giving your subordinate any control, you have just delegated stress. If you delegate all the control you have just given yourself stress, being a good leader is about balance and empathy.

Look at the very successful people that you know, they are generally in control of their own state. They deal with things calmly because they are looking for a way to bring control to a crisis. They only focus on the things they can control now, not what "might" happen. If you only ever look at what might happen your life will become one big risk assessment. On the other side of the coin, a control freak will stress everyone out around them. They will also stress themselves when they feel they don't have control of something. Get the balance right. If you feel stressed because your letting something go, why not try this little tip. Delegate whatever it is and then at the point of delegation, politely ask for an update as to progress in a few days. You will have every right now to ask for that update if it hasn't been given to you and you will feel as though you still have one hand on the steering wheel, thus some control and less stress.

CHAPTER 8

THE TURN OF A DECADE

As the following weeks slipped by, the incident faded into distant memory. His father in typical fashion had let the matter go after establishing that the lesson had been learned and carried on putting emotional deposits into his family bank account by playing his role as the solid rock of the household. His style of strength and consistency mixed with humour and the odd overused quote from John Wayne movies, made the house seem normal and safe.

Summer turned to winter, winter brought Christmas and a New Year, 1979. 2T2 was working out well for William, and his work had improved along with his happiness in class.

There was an opportunity for boys in the top stream to sit a scholarship exam which would earn them a place in the local Grammar school. It was a good school, mixed, established and only for the brighter children. It also happened to be very close to William's house on the more affluent side of town. His cricket coach, Harry, also did some coaching at the Grammar School so there was a lot to tempt William into have a go.

There was however, a big thing putting William off. The minimum *sentence* to serve at the school was five years, this meant stopping on for lower and upper sixth years on a compulsory basis. This was an option where he was, and William had already decided that he wanted to get out of school and into the world as soon as he possibly could. He was in a dilemma.

There was a confusing and abundant plethora of advice being issued to him. Some saying that it was an incredibly simple decision and that of course anyone would take the opportunity of Grammar school. Others sharing that it wasn't the be all and end all, and pointing out something else that William hadn't thought of, which was that with the current top fifty pupils moving to Grammar it would clear the way for those that were left to thrive and grow as the academic top dogs, therefore benefiting from the attention of the best teaching available here. Having already experienced what it was like to be the bottom of the elite pile, William was erring toward enjoying the top of the masses instead.

He turned once more to his father for advice, and once again he got exactly what he needed, though it didn't feel like it at the time.

"What should I do Dad?"

"William, it's up to you!"

"That's not fair Dad, I don't know what to do"

"You have to be happy with what you decide, not with what you feel other people want you to do. If I told you to go to Grammar school and you hated it, then there would be no going back and you would resent my advice. It's time for you to make the first big decision in your life. You are lucky"

"How am I lucky Dad?"

"Because you only have two choices, things become very simple when you only have two things to choose from."

"How is it simple?"

"Well the fact that you are so torn between them for one thing tells you that either option is good, so whichever you choose won't be a bad choice."

"That's true, I hadn't thought of it like that." As William pondered that realisation, his father smiled.

"And on that basis, if you still can't decide, toss a coin."

"What? You're joking" William was genuinely shocked that his highly intelligent and business minded father could come up with such a suggestion for such an important decision.

"I've done it loads of times with important decisions that I can't decide on and I am comfortable with the outcome of each one."

He said with a smile. "Heads you stay where you are, tails you go to Grammar. When the coin comes down and you find yourself saying best out of three, then you'll know which one is the right decision in your heart Will."

And so it was that William decided to stay at King Bill's as it was nick named for obvious reasons, and 1979 was the end of a decade and the start of another phase in William's life.

He was enjoying the summer term at King Bill's. Once again his pastoral cricket team had beaten every other form in the school, even the fifth years. The sixth form didn't really engage with interschool activities and were almost a separate school in themselves.

Three of the best players in the side were destined for Grammar school and had already made it clear they were going, and so the talent in the side was far too strong for the older boys to cope with, "next year might be a struggle" William thought to himself for a fleeting moment during the final, but the game in hand snapped him back into concentration. Cricket is a wonderful game for that, you have to be there from moment to moment, totally immersed in the game as you never know when the ball will come to you, or if you are batting, what the next ball you face will do. If you don't concentrate at the time then you will either get hurt of at the very least fail. It looks boring to the observer, but the test of remaining focussed for long periods of inactivity is as mentally challenging as a game of chess.

In class he was happier too. He had found new friends, his intellectual equals, but with a much more grounded outlook on life than some of the high flying academics he had left behind in 1T1. In 2T2 his humour was appreciated, especially when it was directed at one of the weaker teachers in the school.

Mr Wells was a hard working, timid man that had spent his entire life in a class room of some sort, or surrounded by books at his home. He found comfort in books, they didn't answer back or challenge. Books added light and wisdom to an imperfect world. Books represented safety to him, he liked safety. He liked everything to be in order. His desk had a very precise layout, and he would panic slightly if this were moved when the cleaners came in at night. In fact he would leave notes for them specifically requesting that his desk be left alone, a fact that William had noticed.

At home, Mr Wells lived alone, his house, a tiny one up one down cottage, was sparsely furnished but immaculately kept. Shelves of books lined the walls, he knew exactly where to find each book he owned, as they were all catalogued and kept in such a way that would make the most organised librarian wonder at his efficiency. Each book was arranged by subject and then alphabetically. Even the fiction books, of which there were many, some classic some modern, were arranged by genre. Mr Wells liked safe, he liked logic, he lived austerely, he even wore the stereotypical tweed teachers' jacket with leather patches on the elbows. He hadn't noticed that there was a fashion with the boys this year of a similar look. Many of the boys had taken to wearing pure wool jumpers that had the elbows worn through in no time and to Mothers' delight everywhere, the look that was demanded was leather elbow patches.

His rapport with the boy's of King Bill's was tenuous to say the least. To the extent where he had been coached by the head of year to become more assertive with them, or they would walk all over him. His tactic with this was to bluster and demand five minutes absolute silence, thus achieving a temporary respite for himself. He would feel his face flush red with anger as volume levels increased with classroom babble, he would put off the moment, stealing himself to move out of his comfort zone before standing abruptly and while holding up his open hand, palm facing outward and fingers splayed would shout "Five Minutes!" The whole class rather than conform immediately would replicate the phrase, with echoes of "five minutes, five minutes" roaring round the room before settling into a quieter babble.

Had he been given one of the lower forms to teach, it could have been a whole lot worse. At least these boys had a reasonable set of values and a propensity to learn.

One day however, William saw an opportunity to take centre stage in a prank that would become a school legend to be passed down the years and exaggerated by each telling of the story.

Andy Birch had brought into school a fishing reel for reasons only known to Andy Birch, and while the class was assembling, absent Mr Wells who always left it to the last minute before coming into the room, thus minimising his exposure to the brutality of thirteen year old boys, was showing it to his desk mate behind William. William had a brown furry pencil case which he had just taken out of his bag and put on the desk ready for the lesson and an idea sprang into his mind.

"Birchy, can I borrow that?" said William turning to face the two boys at the desk behind him.

"What for?" asked Andy, William leaned over and whispered in his ear and a smile broadened across the boy's face as he gleefully handed of the reel and William set quickly to work attaching the zip of the pencil case to the line.

Once he had it attached, he paid out some line and took the pencil case over to the teacher's perfectly laid out desk. He checked the time . . . he had only a couple of minutes. A few of the boys began nudging each other as they realised something was happening, and low buzz went round the expectant room. William lifted the A4 sized pad that was perfectly lined up with the top left hand corner of the desk and carefully placed the pencil case under it. He then traced back to his desk three rows back and in doing so took the opportunity to wrap the reel and line round the leg of the teacher's desk, then the chair and then back under the desk and on toward his own. The other boys were now willingly accommodating the plan by getting out of the way while he set everything up.

A hush fell over the room as they waited for Mr Wells and William's heart was pounding with expectation. He was committed, there was no thought of backing out, and adrenaline was coursing through him.

As the hour hand reached one minute to the hour on the standard school issue clock above the roller black board, Mr Wells walked into the room and bellowed "Silence!" as usual. He hadn't even noticed that the boy's weren't actually that noisy. What he did notice was that his desk had an unkempt appearance to it "Those damn cleaners . . ." he thought to himself as he strode over to his desk, eyes fixed on the pad that was not only askew but appeared to be resting on some foreign body, "what on earth had those cleaners done? Left a cloth behind or something? How could they be so stupid?" his internal rant was consuming his thoughts as he reached for the pad to lift it.

William was like a coiled spring, the moment Mr Well's hand touched the pad, William reeled in as fast as he could.

The result was phenomenal, beyond his dreams. The pencil case shot from under the pad like a blur. All Mr Wells saw was a brown furry creature and he unconsciously screamed in shock. He screamed like a terrified girl in a teenage horror movie, high pitched and panic stricken. He had a phobia of mice and it was as if his worst nightmare had come to haunt him. He jumped on the chair at the same time the pencil case whipped from under the desk to follow him and go round the chair leg. Mr Wells screamed again, now in abject fear and jumped off and away from the chair which slid from under his feet for him to land with a slap on the tiled floor. All he could think of was to get away from the creature as he scrabbled on all fours over the polished floor to cower near the wall under the blackboard.

The chair had now tangled the line and the prank had ended, while the class erupted, having never seen such sport ever before, Birch was up and desperately trying to untangle his precious fishing line.

William was getting slapped on the back and the class was going wild.

Mr Wells was still wide eyed with fear and bewilderment as the door opened and the imposing figure of Mr Tucker boomed into the space it created. "SIT!" was all it took, instantly the room was silent.

"What on earth is going on?" Mr Tucker was looking directly at Mr Wells, he respect for Mr Wells's knowledge of all things but had never really liked the man, however he was astonished that a teacher was in the room, he was expecting to come in and find unsupervised boys.

Mr Tucker, concerned as to why his colleague was on the floor, bend down to help him up, "Are you ok? Are you hurt?"

"I can't handle them, I just can't handle them . . ." the teacher whimpered and was close to tears as the shock began to give way to emotion.

As he lifted him by the elbow he hissed into his colleague's ear "Man up for god's sake, they will eat you for breakfast"

Mr Tucker at that point saw Birch under the teacher's desk and went into mode. "You boy! Here! Now!"

"But ..."

With two gigantic strides Mr Tucker was over and reaching under the desk for the boys collar and dragged him out. "Go and inform the Headmaster that he will have a visitor Mr Wells" Mr Wells was only too pleased to get out of the room and fled to the staff toilet to compose himself, before obeying Mr Tucker.

"Out!" yelled Mr Tucker to Birch and helped him on his way with a boot up the back side which landed with a soft thump "Wait outside boy!"

"What happened here?" he looked out over the hushed room, not expecting a response, as he was conditioned to the denial of the lower form boys who were belligerently innocent of all offenses. He was astonished when a hand went up, and immediately disliked the boy, he was clearly one of those sneaky 'tell tales'. "Speak"

William confessed humbly "It was me sir!"

"What?" this had taken Mr Tucker by surprise somewhat.

"I played a trick on Beetroot, erm Mr Wells sir." Mr Tucker had heard that the nick name for his colleague was beetroot because he was always going a deep shade of purple while he wrestled with his emotional turmoil's.

"What kind of trick boy?"

As William retold the story, Mr Tucker was secretly thinking to himself "Genius", but he was never the less professional enough to know that it was unacceptable to let boys get away with terrorising teachers, where would it end?

"I want to beat you myself boy!"

"Yes sir" said William his face down and sullen, accepting that he had enjoyed the fun and that there was an inevitable price to pay. At least he would still have the respect and adoration of his classmates when it was finished, cold comfort, but none the less he had kind of budgeted for it, just not from Mr Tucker, and that was the scary bit now.

"But, it is not for me, this is far too serious. The Headmaster will probably want to expel you from the school."

This hadn't occurred to William and his face drained white.

"Go and join the other Plebeian in the corridor!"

"Yes sir" as he stood up to walk out, his legs felt like jelly.

A blubbering wreck stood in front of the headmaster in his office. A weak man that now resembled a boy making excuses rather than a professional controlling an incident. The Headmaster quietly considered this version of events and pondered the situation carefully. "Right, well let's not leave Mr Tucker to fend for himself up there, he has his own class to deal with."

"Surely you don't expect me to carry on teaching them today?"

"That is exactly what I expect you to do, and I can guarantee you that you will have no further trouble today. That is until we speak again at the end of school."

He walked out of his office purposefully with a meek Mr Wells falling in behind, and strode up the stairs to the classroom in question where he found the two boys outside. He looked at them and immediately the whispers between them ceased to be replaced by silence, fear and uncertainty. Turning to Mr Wells he asked "Are these the boys who created this disturbance Mr Wells?" Mr Wells could only dither as he stood in confounded silence, feeling the pressure of the situation more that the boys themselves. In truth, he had no idea.

Sensing that Mr Wells had lost control, the headmaster took it. "My office! Wait outside it! Do not sit! Do not talk! I will be back directly to deal with you both! GO!" The two boys scuttled off and conformed exactly to the headmaster's instructions.

The atmosphere in the room was far more comfortable than Mr Wells had expected. The boys that were left had no fear as they were not in the firing line. They had also had their fun and plenty to look forward to by revelling in the speculation of what would happen to Dole and Birch. They also knew that with all attention now focussed on this classroom, there would be no further frivolity, so they happily sat and awaited the next instructions.

"Carry on with your class Mr Wells, you will find the pupils most conformant I am sure." He made the last assumptive statement as his eyes deliberately probed the room, it was as much an instruction to the boys as it was information for Mr Wells, and it had landed.

"Thank you Mr Tucker, I am sure that your class would also benefit from your presence at this point."

"Indeed headmaster, thank you." Mr Tucker walked across the corridor and into a rowdy class which instantly silenced at his re-emergence. The headmaster smiled to himself as he heard a burst of laughter characteristically provoked by Mr Tucker as he controlled his class in his own style, so suited to the delicate and sometimes volatile nature of his special boys. At least he had someone in Mr Tucker that he could rely on.

As he got back to his office the two boys were as he expected, stood respectfully outside his office in the waiting area just outside the headmasters office which was an annex in part of the oldest section of the school tucked behind reception. They were avoiding the seats put there for people to use who were waiting for the headmaster under less formal circumstances, as he had instructed. He noticed that one boy had an air of confidence and yet acceptance about him, while the other was more fidgety and nervous. He was weighing up the task ahead, using all his years of experience and his eye for body language in order to extract the best long term outcomes from the next few minutes, both for the boys concerned and for the school's wider interests.

The boys were expecting to follow the headmaster directly into his office, but he gave no indication of that and did not offer eye contact, so they made a move to follow which faltered back into standing once the door had been closed. This was a tactic that the headmaster had used for years.

Once behind his desk, thoughts composed, he boomed "Enter" in the same voice that William had remembered from the first time he had encountered the headmaster two years ago while he had still been at primary school. That seemed such a long time ago now, a different world, so much simpler looking back . . .

"Who will explain to me, why it is that I have had to invest my precious time engaged with petulant boys, who's behaviour is beyond comprehension in civilised society?" He was quietly enjoying the opportunity to express himself with alacrity.

"I will sir" it was no surprise to him that the more confident boy had spoken up and he noticed the other one relax slightly, happily prepared to take on the role of follower.

William took a deep breath and with a quake in his voice that surprised him, one he was finding more and more difficult to suppress as his heart beat increased in frequency he began his speech, "It was nothing to do with Birch sir, it's just his reel sir . . ."

"Ah yes, the fishing reel" As the headmaster produced the reel from under his desk, a tangled mass of line in a birds nest around it, as it had been presented to him by Mr Tucker, Birch's eyes were drawn to it in horror. With a deliberate plonk, he set the reel down on the desk and clasped his fingers together as leaned forward for the rest of the story. It was as though exhibit A was on the table as evidence in a murder trial and the prime suspect was talking in the dock.

"I just borrowed it sir and . . ."

"And you let him boy?" the headmaster switched his attention to Birch, who reddened at the unexpected twist, wrenching his eyes away from his prized possession.

"S sorry sir, y yes sir, I . . ." his mouth was gaping open and shut like one of the many fish he had caught with the reel and hauled up onto the river bank.

"This is a school boy, not the multi-coloured swap shop, for you to bring a menagerie of toys and devices into."

"Yes sir, sorry sir"

"Is it expensive?"

"Yes sir, my father bought it for me, he'll go mad if I don't take it back sir."

"Will he now? Perhaps I should invite him in to collect it . . ." it was now Birch's turn to feel the blood run from his face and his knees trembled at the thought of the headmaster's suggestion.

Seeing the message land, he allowed the boy a few moments of silent torture before releasing the tension. He was above all else fair, the boy appeared decent enough. "You may go!"

"Sir?"

"GO BOY" louder "back to your class, goodness knows we cannot afford for you to miss a moments education if you waste your time on such pursuits, be gone!"

"The reel sir?"

"Not now boy, come back at the end of school, you may collect it then."

"Sir" it was a subservient sir and a little grateful, he gave William a sympathetic look as he happily scuttled free.

The headmaster turned his attention to William, who was actually feeling ok albeit a little humble, the head had just shown some fairness and consistency. "Well, to your credit, you have taken responsibility for this debacle. Tell me why on earth you found it acceptable this morning to disrupt my schools efficiency to the extent that you have. You have destroyed a lesson, imposed upon another lesson by drawing their teacher away, so far that is around sixty people who have missed out because of you, not to mention that you have stolen from me."

William looked incredulously at the headmaster, ready to refute any accusations of theft. "I have never stolen anything in my life sir!" said William with conviction and a little bit of venom.

"You have stolen my time boy, and time is something that you cannot return. It has been stolen from me, by you and I need an explanation." The words were carefully chosen in order to open William's mind to the wider ramifications of his actions and give him a lesson. It was something that the head believed strongly in. There was always a learning experience to be found in any situation, a good teacher had to look for the opportunities where ever they existed.

William, felt crestfallen once more and his shoulders sagged as he relived the moment in his brain, which now looked ridiculous while stood in the environment of the headmaster's office.

"I'm sorry sir, I can see all that now, and I am sorry. It was just supposed to be a joke sir, I didn't honestly expect him, Mr Wells sir, to freak out like that. I don't know what else to say sir." William looked down at his feet.

"Well at least you are not trying to wriggle of the hook, I'll give you that." The headmaster couldn't resist smiling at his own joke and the truth was that he was indeed uncomfortable punishing a boy for the weakness of a member of his staff. He took that responsibility on his own shoulders. However standards of discipline had to be maintained, there had to be a visible consequence that would have the wings to fly round the school when it left this office. "What would you do if you were in my position Dole?"

Williams head snapped up at the mention of his name. "The headmaster knows my name?" he thought to himself. He didn't know whether the question was sincerely put and needed an answer, or whether it was metaphorical, so he decided to play safe and stay quiet, sensing that the next phase of the incident was about to progress.

"Well, what would you have me do with you?"

Blimey, it was real, even more pressure.

"I don't know sir?" Mr Tucker's words were still ringing in his ears about expulsion, he needed to down grade the punishment from that, maybe there was an opportunity here. "I suppose the cane sir." There was a quake in his voice as he said it, but it was better than expulsion, how would he explain that to his father? It was only a few weeks ago that they were choosing which school and now he faced the prospect of no school.

"I am going to give you a choice Dole." William looked up once more, this was ominous. "You can have the cane, or I can call your parents in and discuss ways that they can deal with you."

William thought back to the conversation with his father around a choice of two and decided that sometimes when faced with two choices they were not always good ones. A coin toss would not work here, this was to be the lesser of two evils. It was a no brainer for William.

"I'll take the cane sir please." Resigned to his fate, William was preparing for six of the best, the maximum allowed at the school.

The headmaster had some respect for this boy, still young, only a second year, clearly fearful of his parents' discipline, and it had to be said resourceful in his prank from what he had heard too. "Over the desk, let's get this done." The head stood up, grabbed his cane from the bucket that stood in the corner behind his desk, and moved round to the other side where William was now bent over leaning with both palms face down on the leather surface of the headmaster old style study desk.

The blow came with a biting sting laid carefully across the buttocks. It felt like fire through the tight grey school trousers,

William's athletic buttocks were all muscle and there was no give. It was as if a hot poker had been laid across his back side and had remained there. The next blow was skilfully administered an inch away from the first, the pain even more intense than the first blow, which was already swelling and engorged with blood. The pain receptors were alive and sending fight or flight signals for the boy to get out of this situation, ramping up the sensation. William didn't think he could stand the next four and he bit into his bottom lip and tasted blood as a result.

The third blow, never came. There was no third blow. "Stand up!" William turned to see the headmaster's outstretched hand. It took a while for him to register what was required, then he took the hand and shook it firmly as his father had taught him. Once again the head was impressed by the boy. "The matter is closed, I will inform Mr Wells that the matter is closed and you are to continue your studies diligently in his class. I do not expect to see you in this office under these circumstances again, is that clear boy?"

"Yes sir, thank you sir"

"I cannot have you back in that classroom today however you don't deserve sympathy of the other boys, so you will spend the rest of this period unravelling this mess in the office, then instruct your partner in crime that he may collect it from the receptionist after the bell this afternoon." He handed William the reel, which William gratefully took, especially given that his pencil case was still attached. He hoped that his mates would bring his bag out of the lesson.

The headmaster, had another dilemma to ponder now. How would he deal with Mr Wells? Sadly the cane was not an option, he suspected that if it were, the teacher would cope less well with it than the boy just had. Two had been enough to make the point, and they were two that had been laid on hard. The boy would not forget the pain in a hurry, and had took it well. He had a spine that one.

He dismissed William to the office next door, where the two friendly ladies that manned reception, sympathetically set him up in a quiet corner. Then the head opened William's file that was on his desk and made a note.

The summer holidays brought the end of another school year. Next year William would be back into 3T1 given the gap made by the Grammar school graduates, but this time he would be with a set of like minding classmates and he would genuinely be top of the tree. He was looking forward to it.

The holidays were full of fun, cricket, cadetting and his first experience of independent travel.

He had subscribed to weeks summer camp with the Cadets at HMS Seahawk, which is otherwise known as RNAS (Royal Naval Air Station) Culdrose, in Cornwall. It was a fun packed week full of activities including a trip up in a Sea king helicopter, fire fighting with the air station training crew on the old wrecks of aircraft set aside for that purpose, trips to the coast, and a flavour for living in Naval establishments for real. William absolutely relished the whole prospect of engaging with the activities the lifestyle and the other cadets from around the country, comparing badges and stories.

He had been issued with rail warrants to get him to Redruth, and he was going with another Cadet from his unit and they were to travel down together.

His mother wasn't at all happy, but in typical style William's father was happy to allow the experience to develop his boy. The issue was getting across London and connecting at Paddington with the GWR service to Penzance. William couldn't wait, the other boy was older than William at aged 14 and was supposed to be the responsible one of the two because of this great age. The 13 year old Williams father was less convinced, having taken the opportunity to check him and his parents out when picking William up one evening.

Jack Dole's perceptiveness played out to be accurate once more, when during the trip in question the older boy was homesick for the entire week. So much so that he ended up in sickbay, ill with some mystery virus much to the relief of the other boys who had taken an immediate dislike to him.

Naturally when they had first been shown into the accommodation block with its classic layout of thirty bed spaces made up of fifteen bunk-beds each next to two lockers stacked one above the other, the two boys from the same unit were bunked together. Quickly the rest of the boys had singled out William's unit mate as a weak link in their team and cruelly cut him from the group.

William was happy that he had been shipped out of the mess because he felt that the others had tarred him with the same brush by association. His popularity soared when he was without the shackles of his unit mate.

It was day three of the trip, and the boys had been put through an action stations simulation in a mock-up of a ships compartment which was then flooded with salt water while the boys attempted to shore up the various holes and tears in the steel as they had been shown, with softwood wedges and braces pressing mattresses and other bits and pieces to stem the cold gushing flow. William had done well and had typically got right into role play. He had taken the lead without realising it, he felt the urgency of the situation as if he was really there and the consequences of failure were drowning. His eyes had been everywhere, shouting instructions and encouragement at his teammates as they struggled with the cold water that he was used to. The instructors had labelled him as one to watch. His adrenaline had been pumping all day, he was loving every minute of the activities and the popularity he was building.

The officer in charge of Cadet Training had come down to the damage control school and the room was promptly brought to attention as he walked in.

"Thank you PO" said the officer to the Petty Officer who had called the class to attention. "Could you send Ordinary Cadet Dole to me when you have finished here please, I'll be in the DCTO"

"Yes sir, we'll just be two minutes sir."

"Very good, carry on PO."

"Sir"

The DCTO was the damage control training office and was at the end of the building they had been training in all day. William was escorted down the corridor by a member of the training staff who was a serving RN rating, he couldn't help but take the opportunity to enjoy the situation. "What you been up to then?" there was a Devonian slur to the ratings accent that made the "then" sound like "tharn" as he smirked toward William with a knowing look that hid a more sinister meaning.

William didn't respond, he had no idea why he had been summoned.

"There's only two reasons as why you get called to the bosses office, and I don't recons ee'll be gettin' a medal, hehe! 'ere I 'opes you got your cap" the word cap sounded like carrp.

"What?"

"you're cap, if you's in the shit proper, you 'as to off caps afore 'ee gets wa's commin'" The thick accent was laced with Navy twang giving it an older than it's time timber.

"Of course I haven't got my cap, should I get it?" he was still in his wet overalls. The rating was thrown off his story he was building by the question, he had been told to just deliver the boy yet it did feel wrong going in front of an officer without headgear. At the same time he was enjoying the wind up, or bite as it was known in the Navy.

"Well I 'as got my cap, so I'm alright Jack, haha, not sure about 'ee though" He left the thought hanging.

As they reached the door to the office, the rating knocked firmly and waited.

"Come"

He opened the door, bustled William in and snapped to attention in front of the officer noted that he was not wearing a cap so did not salute and began his report "As requested sir," it sounded like zurr "Ordinary Cadet . . ." he paused as he tried to remember William's name "the ordinary cadet you requested sir, Able Seaman Martin reporting sir."

"Thank you Pincher, that'll be all."

Motivated by the informal use of his nickname, the rating puffed out his chest and dismissed himself "Sir!" he gave William a last smirk as he hovered at the door.

"Thank you Martin"

"Sorry Sir, I'm gone sir." Knowing exactly how much cheek he could and could not get away with, Pincher Martin slipped out and closed the door behind himself.

"How are you enjoying Culdrose Dole?" the officer used the Fleet Air Arm name for the base which was in keeping with how people felt here rather than the Royal Navy's administrative name HMS Seahawk. It was an air station first and foremost.

"Brilliant sir!" William beamed, and then his smile faded as he had the feeling that the officer was building to something else and he waited patiently, the words of Pincher Martin echoing in his mind.

"I have been getting very good reports about you."

"Really sir? Thank you sir"

"Yes I am told that you possess leadership qualities, do you consider yourself a leader Dole?"

"I've never really thought about it sir" where was this going?

"I need you to do something for me Dole." Here it was . . .

"I need you to visit the sickbay and spend some time with your friend there."

"Sir? Why sir?" the thought was not appealing to William who had got used to the idea of him not being around.

"He needs a friendly face Dole."

"He's not really my friend sir."

"But he is your unit mate Dole, and it may interest you to know that he won't go home without you."

"Sir?"

"He wants to go home, but refused to make the journey without you. It appears that you have been shown that leadership can be a burden as well as a reward Dole. Now it's time to show some more and visit your mate. It's rather full in there at the moment, there has been bad weather out at sea and we have some casualties that have been rescued from the Fastnet race, you may get to see some real heroes." August 14th of that year had been a sad day in the history of the famous race with many of the yachts wrecked in the storms and many casualties resulting. RNAS Culdrose had been instrumental in the rescue mission.

William visited his unit mate in the evenings every other day for the rest of the camp. He was thrilled when one of the recovering yacht racers spoke to him from his bed on the other side of the ward. He had introduced his unit mate and now looked forward to visiting so that he could get his share of the stories that were being told of high seas and yacht racing. Inspired by the cheerful outlook of the survivors who only days before had been close to death, and the activities of the camp mixing with serving personnel who all seemed to have an endearing ability to turn unpleasant tasks into fun, William was becoming hooked on the idea of a life on the ocean wave.

As they travelled back on the long train journey from Redruth to Paddington, he peered out of the window as they past Devonport, seeing the grey ships alongside, he yearned to be on them. His future had just been decided in his own mind.

<u>*Top Tips - Set goals that really grab you*</u>

Have you ever played on a computer game or read a book that was so addictive that you just couldn't put it down? Have you ever been stuck on a level in that game and thought to yourself "just one more go . . ." and that one more go turns into so many more goes that when you glance at the clock it's 3am and you need to be up in three hours?

Did you then get a sense of elation at having completed the level or finished the chapter that you heard your weary brain compelling you to just have a little look at the next one . . . ?

That is what it feels like to be motivated toward a truly engaging goal.

Imagine if your working life had such engaging goals that you felt the same passion to tenaciously continue until the end result you wanted was achieved and then you started looking for the next challenge . . . That is exactly what successful people feel. It's because they set themselves compelling goals that really grab them. They know what makes them tick internally and they wrap their goal motivation around these values. When you want something so badly, you will move heaven and earth to get it, sometimes at the expense of other things. So there is a cautionary message here too, make sure the goal you are looking at is really what you want, or you will burn everything around you in order to get something that leaves you unfulfilled.

William decided on his journey home that he wanted to join the Navy. What compelled him? He could visualise himself on one of those warships, he had context from the serving personnel he had met the previous week, and he had a strong desire in his belly to get there. In the following few short years, everything he engaged in would be in the single pursuit of that goal. He wanted it so badly that it showed to those around him that could have an influence on his outcome, and of course this helped to, it became infectious. The recruiting officers could see it, the teachers at his school, the officers at cadets, all of whom could have input into the outcome.

William was lucky to have found this thing to strive for, as many don't. But then William was also happy to look and brave enough to pursue it, to risk failing but to never give up the pursuit.

Ask yourself this . . . if you set out on a journey to the airport to go on holiday and you come up against a traffic jam, do you turn back and lose the holiday, or do you find an alternative route because you really do want to go on that holiday? You have you answer I suspect, so make sure you want your goals as much as you want that holiday and you will succeed.

And that is what I mean by goals that grab you, it's not just about financial targets or security, it's about what you will do with that security when you get it. It's about the journey, it's about your values, it's very emotional, so think about the emotions you want to feel.

Likewise, if you are in a position of leadership and you want to set compelling goals for your team, think about what would motivate them emotionally and make the goals "sexy". Write goals in their language so that it really means something to them. Remember that progress motivates so break them down a bit too. Take time to discuss them and translate them into meaningful outcomes. For example, a company I have worked with in the past has a value which simply says "Love what you do" this language came from employers who when asked why they work there replied "Because we love what we do!" The leadership team when talking to individuals about this value can take it to whole new individual levels of performance, but that's another conversation.

The summary of this tip it to think big about goals, but think personally. Make them realistic and engaging. Make them down to earth yet rewarding. Like William did, visualise yourself at the end goal, think what that will really mean to you when you get there, if that feels good inside, then you might just be onto something.

CHAPTER 9

WHAT'S GOOD ON THE SHIP?

William always knew that his father was in a good mood, if the answer to any kind of closed question was delivered in John Wayne style "the hell I am".

"Dad?"

"yes son?"

"Can I have a motorbike?"

"THE HELL YOU CAN! Hahaha"

Pleased with his assertive comeback and slightly nervous at the question, Will's Dad chuckled at his own joke and shook his head.

"Why not Dad? If I save up . . ."

"No way Will!" his face was suddenly more serious but still in a jovial mood, Will had timed his question well, "you're not old enough for one thing"

"Paul Clarke has got one, he's got a scrambler, he rides it in fields . . ." the hopeful tone in Will's voice needed squashing with empathy and humour, that was the judgement of his Dad.

"Get of your bike and drink you milk! Hahaha" even William was starting to laugh, caught up in some unconscious feeling of levity. "What on earth makes you want to do that Will? They are death traps, you could be the best rider in the world, and all it takes is one idiot to not see you and you're history! There is no way I will ever let you get interested in those things son."

"It's just exciting Dad, I am desperate to have a go, it would be so good . . ."

William's father recognised at that point at part of his own character in his son and he warmed to it. His boy was a risk taker. His own success had come from a combination of hard work, calculation and being brave enough to take the risk. The difference was that experience had taught him how to manage the risk and know when to change direction. He needed to inspire his son to get his kicks from another challenge.

He was in a great mood and he relished this opportunity to enter into a negotiation game with his bright boy.

"So, tell me Will how many times have you had your breath taken away this week?"

"What?" William had never heard his Dad talk like this, where was this going? He was enjoying the moment but could feel himself being manoeuvred already, but it was kind of fun. It didn't help however that he had no idea what the question actually meant.

"Will, life is not measured by the number of breaths that we take, but by the moments that take our breath away!"

This didn't help.

A confused look fell upon Williams face as he asked "Dad, is that John Wayne again?"

"Haha, no son, I don't know who said it, but he was a clever man." In those days, it always had to be a man that came up with pearls of wisdom, or at least were allowed to think that they had come up with it . . .

"It means that you know you are alive when you can feel your heart pounding it your chest." A pause while this sunk in "When was the last time a cricket ball scared you Will?" Will's eyes went up to the left as he tried to recall the last time that had happened. Seeing that he was on to something, Williams Dad pushed on, "You're cruising Will, you need something to push you, you still enjoying cricket?"

"Dad I love cricket, you know that, but they are rubbish at school and I can't get in the colts over here."

The fact was that the cricket club was strong, and the youth side was made up of 16 year old talented boys many of whom would go on to play county cricket, this meant there was no place for a 14 year old to squeeze in, so cricket was a cruise for now. He was looking for some stretch, he didn't know it, but he needed more in his life that was going to push his boundaries both physically and emotionally. His Dad could see it but his Dad had also learned from his own experience with coaching teenagers, they didn't generally take direct advice well, they had to come up with their own ideas.

"How's Cadets going Will?" he knew he was proud of his uniform the way he spent hours polishing his boots, little circles with a duster, building up layers and layers of polish, then patiently mixing polish and water from the lid in little circles on the toe caps till they gleamed. The way he displayed his certificates on the bedroom wall, best dressed cadet of the month, cadet of the month, best shot . . . there were many certificates all pinned to the old picture rail high up on the high ceilinged bedroom walls. The room was large but the rail was full. This told William's father that it was a good area to push on.

William's eyes gleamed as his thoughts drifted to Cadets, his body language slumped almost as quickly as it had surged. The last few months at Cadets had gone well since his initial fear around Silvy, they had kept a distance from each other, and every time that Will had seen her, his guts twisted, not with desire but with a sickening feeling of guilt. The longer the silence between them existed, the bigger the void became between them. To his relief, she hadn't left, but she was very careful to avoid him at all costs. So William had thrown himself into Cadetting and had been promoted as far as his age would allow, once again he was ahead of himself and had nowhere to go in the short term. He was stuck!

"It's great Dad, I love it, but I can't get any higher for ages." His shoulders were slumped in frustration at his lot.

"I was in the Army Cadets you know!"

"Were you?" William was genuinely surprised, he knew very little about his father's life, he was interested but only ever managed to get a few stories out of him. His years in the forces were not something he ever spoke about other than some standard stories that were intended to cover the whole saga neatly without getting into any detail.

William's father could see that he had his son's attention and was enjoying the comfortable rapport with his youngest offspring. They had something in common that none of the other children had, a link with the armed forces, albeit in Williams case a passion fuelled by the glamorous perception he had built in his own head, and from his father's point of view a realistic and sometimes gruesome memory of the realities of active service.

"Yes, I was in the Army Cadets till I joined up, I was a Cadet Sergeant!" he puffed his own chest out in mock pride, and put his heels together with a stamp of his right foot after raising the knee parallel to the floor, and smartly fell into the familiar position of attention.

William laughed out loud, rarely did his Dad display such open vulnerability by entering into this role play. "Dad, all that stamping around it's just not necessary, the Navy drill is far more efficient!"

"That's because you're lazy!"

The inter-forces banter and rivalry was something that both William and his father fell into as millions of others have over the years. And while they had never done this with each other, they had the same come backs on each other as the proud British Forces had used for decades. Just like the British Forces, the banter was cementing a strong bond between them without embarrassing each other with patronising or even gushing compliments, rather a mutual respect wrapped up in that unique sense of British humour, manifested by what can only really be understood in Britain, what's known as "the piss take".

"It's because we are clever Dad, the silent Navy, no need for stamping, we are in and out and gone before you know we are there" Will had a smug look on his face.

"Well, we like people to know who it is that is about to be better than them!" an equally smug look was being transmitted back as their eyes met, "besides, it's smarter!"

"It's because your too slow in the head, you even have to put an extra pace in the come to the halt!" this was a fact as the army drill does require the order for the halt to be given on two consecutive beats of the left foot rather than the right to facilitate the exaggerated stamp so recognised around the world from footage of the changing of the guard and various other moments of pomp and circumstance.

They both began to laugh and Will's father cuffed him around the ear as he spoke through his laughter "you've got me there, ha ha . . ."

The ice was broken, the rapport was close, so William's father took the opportunity to move the conversation further.

"So while you're waiting to get promoted again, why not work on some more badges?"

"I've got all the slot's filled up Dad." Unlike the scouts, there was only a limited amount space within Naval Dress Regulations to display specialisation badges, and while they were a great motivator to get, badges were not the be all and end all. William had done well to get himself qualified up in the various boating skills, seamanship and even electrical skills, he was a natural shot and loved the rifle range, but the opportunities for shooting were scarcely on offer, though he loved everything about the range. The musty smell of the sand bags and the scent of spent ammunition, added to the sense of something special, the discipline required to be safe on the range something that again William identified with and fell into role play imagining that he really was in the military. A marksman's badge was the one he really wanted. "I can't get a marksman's badge without going away Dad."

"Where would you put it if you did?"

"On the right cuff, there are not many people who have a badge on the right cuff, they are all special ones."

"Well there must be more than just marksman badges that go there, if they are special, why not ask next week about other options?"

"I s'pose . . ."

"Well you won't get to be an Admiral if you don't ask a few questions"

"Imagine that, wow an Admiral! Prince Philip got it easy, he was only a Lieutenant, all he did was marry the Queen and hey presto, he is Admiral of the Fleet."

"Haha, well there you are then Will, just go an marry a Queen"

They were both laughing comfortably and enjoying each other's company, a rare and wonderful moment to be treasured, and what's more a seed had been sown.

"So then Admiral Will, what's good on your ship?"

"What?"

"That's what Admirals do Will, when there isn't much going on, they look at all the good stuff they have at their disposal then work out what they are going to do with it! So what have you got that's good?"

"I don't know Dad?"

"Haha, well maybe you should think about that before Cadet's next week, if you were the captain of your own ship, what is that ship capable of and how are you going to captain it?"

"Sorry Dad you are talking in code!" William was trying to make light of his misunderstanding, but his father could see he had opened a window of intrigue in his own son's language.

"Right, HMS William, how is it at boatwork?"

"Good!"

"What about swimming, could it swim ashore and take a harbour?" He was dragging William into a state of role play that would help him to put a positive spin on his talents and it was working.

"Yeh!" William's eyes were glazing over as he imagined himself as the starring role in a war movie.

"Think about it Will!" and with a ruff shake of William's mop his father moved off to busy himself in the garage while William drifted away into his own little fantasy world, his mind analysing without effort, all of the good things he could add to his ships manifest.

That night, his head was full of scenarios and stories that he was role playing through in his head before he drifted off to sleep, his unconscious happy to reconcile the positive enquiry it had been given.

What William didn't know, was that his father had a working association with the Commanding Officer of the Sea Cadet Unit. The only contact that William had with his C.O. was through Cadets, he had never even considered that his Lieutenant

Commander was actually a volunteer who had a "proper job" during the day time, and certainly not that he might be one of his father's suppliers. The fact was that there were few people who his father didn't know, one of his many throw away lines being "it's not what you know, and it's not who you know, it's what you know about who you know that counts!".

William's father knew better than to interfere with the way that things were being run at the unit, he certainly didn't want to be one of those annoyingly pushy parents that aggressively turned up at clubs and organisations putting pressure on their own children as well as the willing volunteers who had the thankless task of trying to provide a balanced experience for the eager partakers.

But it couldn't hurt to make a casual enquiry as to how his son was doing. He made a point to ask at the next opportunity. Per chance that week, his secretary buzzed through a call from Bernie Thompson of BT Printing, William's father smiled and took the call much to the surprise of his secretary who was expecting to have to make up some excuse about meetings or phone calls, her levity at not having to tell a white lie shone through in her voice as she transferred the person that William new only as Lieutenant Commander B Thompson RNR.

"Hi Bernie, what can I do for you?"

"I didn't expect to catch you actually, you are such a busy man normally, it's like trying to track down the Scarlet Pimpernel!" Bernie added a theatrical chuckle on the end hoping that his little joke would be received well.

He was relieved when Jack Dole, a man who he didn't mind admitting intimidated him, laughed back. "Well you have caught me at a good time Bernie, how's business?"

"Yes, very good thanks. Not enough hours in the day, what recession that's what I say."

Jack Dole smiled at the standard purple spin that people always seemed to sugar coat their businesses with. Jack new that the truth was somewhat closer to the fact that they were so desperate for work that BT Printing were prepared to drop prices drastically to keep the presses busy at the moment. "I heard through the grapevine that you have got some serious special offers going at the moment Bernie, I hope you're not funding them through the profit you're making out of me!"

The line went quiet and Jack smiled as he could feel the man squirming on the other end of the line, he let him off the hook with a cautionary statement "haha, I know you wouldn't do that to us."

The relief was evident in Bernie's voice "haha, of course not" well he certainly wouldn't now, which had been Jack's intention all the time "in fact that was why I was calling, just to see how we can bring your prices into line with our promotional items." He was caving in already, out manoeuvred in a negotiation he didn't even realise he was going to have when he rang. His call objective was to attempt to get more volume out of Jack and if possible upgrade the profit margin, it was almost uncanny that Jack had sensed he was making a lot of profit from him.

Jack had finished playing the game and was ready to close this part of the conversation off "Bernie," an assertive upward inflection immediately got Bernie's attention and once again controlled the conversation "why don't you make an appointment with Frank, I'll let him know you are going to call, see what he has for you, no promises though Bernie, bring your pencil sharpener with you."

"Thanks Jack, don't worry I will." There was genuine gratitude in his voice as the lead into a wider part of Jack Dole's organisation was not to be sniffed at.

Now was Jack's moment, "How's Will doing Bernie? Is he doing as he's told?"

Bernie was slightly taken aback by the casual question, Jack was usually totally business focussed, never the less he was very grateful for the chance to build the relationship on a more personal note. His answer was completely sincere "Jack, he is the best Cadet on the books, and I am not just saying that!"

"Haha, Bernie that won't get you any extra margin!" Jack knew that Bernie was being genuine, he could hear that the blurted response was an honest answer to a question.

"No, no please don't think that!" there was panic in his voice.

"It's ok Bernie, I just can't switch off the haggle gland you know that." He laughed once again to ease the conversation once again "So what's so good about him?"

"Well he has a certain, I don't know, awareness I suppose that the others at his level just don't seem to have. To be honest I am a bit worried that we can't give him enough to stimulate him until he gets older, but my hands are tied on that, we would hate to lose him though."

So Bernie had sensed it too, that was encouraging but also a little worrying.

"What's your plan then Bernie? Knowing you, you will have something in the pipeline already . . ." He knew he wouldn't but he would be wracking his brain for something now. William's father had just managed to bring his son's development top dead centre on Bernie's radar.

There was a pause before Bernie responded "Well, it's pretty timely actually, I am planning to run a little session next week around what each individual cadet would like to achieve over the next year, so we can make training provision for the ambitious ones."

William's father had made his point, Bernie had bought himself some thinking time. The phone call had been fruitful but Jack Dole had already moved his brain to something else. "Well, thanks for calling Bernie, no doubt you'll sort it, I'll talk to Frank for you, bye!"

Bernie Thompson hung his phone back on the cradle and took stock of the conversation. He came to the conclusion that he had just been "Doled"!

Top Tips - When you feel like you're drifting . . .

Have you ever felt like there just isn't anything to get you motivated? That you are drifting along but nothing gets you sparked up? We have all been there! And the more life experience we get then more evidence we have to cope with these times!

As a young person we have all the energy and exuberance of a puppy, not unlike William during this chapter, but when things get frustrating and there is no source of challenge or excitement it is easy to convince ourselves that all is doom and gloom. Experience should tell us that these times don't last and that all we really need to be motivated is something to get excited about.

It is often easier to coach somebody else on this principle than it is to convince ourselves, because we risk less when we talk about other people. However the principle is the same, take stock of what you have that is good, and use that to find something to move forward with, rather than wallow in the past.

One of the greatest examples of this in practice, has been mis-quoted and used as a metaphor for disasters ever since it happened, but let's look at the real story of Apollo 13 and how a very powerful piece of thinking saved the day.

The mis quote "Houston, we have a problem!" was actually broadcast as "Houston, we have had a problem!" ok, mute point and somewhat pedantic but everyone has heard of that phrase, and many people use it when the "wheels come off" in their own little world or the project they are working on. What most people don't realise is the power of what happened next, the reply to that statement . . .

Now just for a moment, put yourself in that situation, you are mission control, you can see on your instrumentation that there is a problem, the people in your care up there in space are likely to die! What do you say to that? How are you going to find something that will motivate the crew toward positive action???

The words that came back were "OK Apollo, what do we have that's good on the ship?"

Now just think about how powerful that simple statement is. It says, we have got what we have got, so let's understand what that is and not panic just yet. It says, let's put some energy into finding a solution instead of wasting it on things that are out of our control. It says, we are here to support you, you are not on your own, but you have got to drive this thing so take actions that will get you home. It doesn't hide from reality or make out something is gold when really it's lead, it doesn't sugar coat the problem, it simply says, "we have got what we have got, now let's take the best of that and make it work."

So when you feel stuck in a rut, or even when you back is against the wall, take stock of what you have got that is good on your ship, be honest with yourself about the positive things you are capable of, if you are struggling, ask someone you trust to help you, you will be surprised at the answers you get. You could find this simple positive enquiry about your own ships manifest could change your life . . .

CHAPTER 10

NEW HORIZONS

William was in a good mood when he arrived at the Cadet Unit that week. Tuesday was the night when it was just the boys, the girls had Monday to themselves and Friday nights were mixed nights, the unit was usually heaving on Fridays. William had always loved Friday nights as there was always a real buzz about it. However, since his young male ego had destroyed any hopes of a relationship with Silvy, he had been wracked in guilt every time he saw her, so Friday nights now had a feeling of trepidation about them too. The attempts he had made to say hello on Friday's had been met with a blank look and a turn of the shoulder from Silvy. She seemed happy enough around her friends but he was simply not on her radar, he kept his distance, but it always added a nagging feeling to Friday nights for him. He brushed over it with his usual bravado, but inside his values were telling him something wasn't right about it.

What he couldn't know of course was that Silvy was still slightly besotted with him and had developed her own coping mechanism by going into complete shut-down mode around him. The messages she sent out were very clear, but inside she was more confused than ever.

Tuesday for William, was his night to own, he could be his confident boyish self, leader of the pack. And on this Tuesday he was looking forward to getting down on the river and bending his back against the tidal waters on the rough loom of an oar. He enjoyed the exercise, and the feeling of power he got as his back and arms flexed into the clumsy wooden tool that had been used through the ages to propel ships and boats alike. He was developing physically way beyond the strength of other boys in his class at school. He didn't see it himself, but other boys noticed with envy how his arms bulged in all the right places, while their own still looked like boyish sticks hanging out of their shirts. His hands were also getting toughened by rowing with a rough oar, or pulling as it was known in the Navy and therefore the Cadets. He was toughening up!

As William bounded up to the main entrance of the Unit, he stopped to put his cap on ready to snap out a perfect salute as he crossed over the threshold, a practice that was rigidly enforced. Vessels of Her Majesty's Royal Navy, during daylight designated hours fly the White Ensign from aft and the Union Jack from forward. In fact the only time the Union Flag can technically be referred to as "The Union Jack" is when it is being flown from the bow staff, or Jack Staff on one of Her Majesties Ships. The Ensign however, which is flown from the stern of the ship, has special significance and is revered in much the same way as a Regimental Colour. The Ensign is therefore saluted by all Officers and Ratings when coming aboard or leaving the ship, even when it is not within line of sight, one simply faces aft (to the blunt end) and salutes. This culture had been applied to the Sea Cadet Unit which had been designated as a stone frigate. Some Cadet's found this part of the regime a little over the top and almost embarrassing, William had totally bought into it, and took a huge sense of pride and belonging from engaging with all of the ceremonial culture of the Corps.

He paused to ensure his uniform was all in good order and his cap straight, before opening the door. It is a big no no to salute without ones cap on in the British military. As he threw open the Lower Deck (ground floor) door, and prepared to salute, he was suddenly face to face with Silvy, who stood like a rabbit caught in head lights looking directly into William's eyes.

It took what seemed like an eternity for William's brain to register what was going on. It didn't add up. Was he dreaming? What was she doing here?

Both individuals were paralysed for a moment, staring onto each other's eyes. William saw something in her eyes, almost pain or was it fear? He didn't know, but it was more intense than he was comfortable with. She looked as though she would say something any second, but then William's sense of duty kicked in as he brought his heals together, pushed his chest out and snapped out the perfect Royal Navy salute. Unlike the flamboyant army salute, the Navy salute is efficient, the right arm staying close to the body as the first finger is snapped up to a position just above the right eye brow, fingers together, thumb tucked in line with them and the palm angled down at around 30 degrees, forearm parallel to the deck (floor). A pause of two marching paces (116 to the minute) before the arm snaps back down to the position of attention, fingers clenched first and second knuckle (a part of the drill that would change in the late 90's to fall into line with a more common tri-service approach to ceremonial.)

In the four seconds that it had taken William to perform his ceremonial, Silvy had walked away. He felt a pang of disappointment in this, he was going to talk to her, realising suddenly that he really wanted to talk to her and she had looked ready to engage with him for the first time since that embarrassing day in town. Yet surely she should know that he must salute, in fact he had been very careful to make this particular salute as perfect and vigorous as he could, wanting to impress her, and now all he could see was her back as she walked away, no it was more a trudge.

"Women . . ." he uttered as he moved into the unit. He had heard many adult males use the same tone when talking about their wives or colleagues, it usually got a chuckle or acknowledgement from other males in their company, and like them he was struggling to understand what was really going on, so he decided to move on, and set about trying to find somebody to ask about why the GN's were here on a Tuesday.

Silvy's heart was pounding, and she felt desolate once again. Just for a moment of eye contact she thought that she would just fall into Will's arms and everything would be ok. She saw in his eyes something that she liked, a warmth, maybe he wasn't a pig after all but the wonderful boy that she really wanted him to be, the one she had kissed for the very first time . . . Then he broke the spell and did that thing he does, all arrogant and pompous, sticking his chest out and over exaggerating his drill, why did he need to do that? It was embarrassing, nobody else had quite the same swagger when they saluted, or did any drill for that matter. The officers seemed to all think William was special when he did all that, "watch Dole and learn!" they would say. She didn't want to watch him, she wanted to kiss him again, but once again he had broken her bubble and once again she would run and bury her feelings. "It's not fair . . ." she mumbled into her tissue as she tried to find the courage to stay for the rest of the night.

Silvy had been told, like the rest of the GN's, about the special night during their parade the evening before, so they had the advantage over the boys who thought they were in for a normal parade night. By the time that colours, the ceremony of hoisting the ensign which precedes the start of each day on ships all over the world, and therefore is done at the start of every parade in the cadets, had started word had got round as to why the GN's were on board. The C.O. (commanding officer) had planned an evening to present, to the entire unit, a range of courses and options for all the cadets to engage with over the next twelve months. His objective was to motivate the whole unit and to get as many of his cadets booked onto the coveted opportunities that the Sea Cadet Corps was able to provide such as going to sea for a week on a Square Rig sailing ship as a crew member, or going up in a helicopter, or even spending a week on a serving warship. He also had the words of Jack Dole ringing in his ears and thought that this would be a great opportunity to make a difference.

Colours was always a squeeze on a joint night, the small main deck was cramped. It was a nostalgic room, the building was old, and the first floor main deck really did take on the appearance of an old ship. The tick wooden floor boards were warped and far from level, the years having twisted the building in all directions. There was a thick, round spar around ten inches in diameter running from floor to ceiling and while this provided some functional support, it also gave the room a dynamic that suggested a mast was running through the ship in much the same way it would below the decks of an old sailing ship. There was also an overwhelming smell of hemp rope, a kind of musty yet not unpleasant scent that was almost like wet wood but not quite.

The Cadets all mustered (the Naval term for gathering together in an organised way at an appointed time) and the senior Cadet of each division took charge of falling them into squads. The layout of the main deck was such that a mast area was at one end of the room, this was significant in that it represented the stern of the ship where the ensign would be flown from, and therefore the rest of the room's allocation came from that frame of reference. To the left of the room, as viewed from the mast, were the cadets of Port Division in one squad, with GN port division fallen in behind them, both facing into the centre of the main deck. To the right was Starboard Division, again two squads one boys and one the girls. At the opposite end and facing the mast were the New Entry Division, all dressed in civilian clothing as they were yet to pass the various tests and drills to qualify for wearing what many people believe is the finest uniform the world has ever seen.

As the Cadets waited for the Officers to march onto the deck, there was a low hum of conversation which the adult senior rates (NCO's) tolerated, before a precautionary order was barked that snapped everyone into silence

"Ship's company . . ." there was a dwell as everyone braced into the ease position, merely a relaxed position of attention, feet 12 inches apart and hands clasped behind the back fingers overlapping, "Hoe!" the directive command was a sharp shout and was the signal to come to attention. In unison around forty cadets moved their left feet, without stamping, to meet their right, heels together and toes splayed, at the same time the arms were brought smartly to the sides, fingers clenched first and second knuckle, the thumbs pointing down along the seams of the trousers. You could hear a pin drop.

The senior rate then in an assertive tone gave the next order "Report your divisions", "Ship's company, stand at . . . ease!"

A frenzy of activity as each squad commander took control of their divisions, bringing them to attention and marching up to the senior rate, taking turns to make their report, William ached for the day when he could be the senior cadet in his division and make the report, he thought he could already do a better job than the lazy leading cadet in charge of Starboard Division which William was proud to belong to.

When his Leading Cadet was next in line to make his report, William craned to hear how well it was done and cringed as Bruno (Leading Cadet Brown and no relation to Andy Bruno Brown) mumbled his way through the report "Eeerm' Leading Cadet Brown reporting starboard division, eeeerm . . . ready for colours PO!" his leg always did a funny twitchy thing while he reported that drove William wild with despair, this was his Division he was reporting, why wasn't he better? William had no concept of the fact that most people were very nervous when under pressure and in view of their peers, pressure does funny things to people performing the simplest of tasks.

"How many Cadet's Brown?"

"Eeeerm, twelve I think"

"Think? Think? You should bloody well know! Come on Brown how many times have you done this?" as Brown looked behind him, the Petty Officer barked "Don't look round you muppet, go back, count, report again, properly this time" The PO was very fond of the word muppet, he claimed it was his own saying and stood for "Most Useless Person PO Ever Trained" this wasn't strictly true.

"Yes PO"

Pride hurt, face red, Leading Cadet Brown turned right, paused, marched back to his division, realised of course that he had twelve simply by the formation of four cadets in three ranks with no gaps. Unable to make eye contact with his division, who were all glaring at him with some contempt, he turned about, reported again and this time was better.

"Leading Cadet Brown, reporting Starboard Division ready for Colours PO, thirteen Cadets including myself."

"Better Brown, if you want to keep that hook stop being a muppet"

"Yes PO"

The hook to which the Petty Officer was referring was the fouled anchor badge that Brown was wearing on his left upper arm that signified his rate of Leading Seaman.

As the officers marched onto the main deck, more reports were made, this time from the duty Petty Officer to the First Lieutenant, then the First Lieutenant to the Commanding Officer as the ceremonial that had existed for centuries in the Royal Navy took on its own persona and identity in the unit, and finally the unit was ready for the actual ceremony of Colours itself, where the ensign was raised.

At the end of colours, something slightly different happened. Normally the order would be given to dismiss the hands to classes, however this time as the First Lieutenant (second in command) reported to the C.O. he was told "Thank you number one, have the cadets arrange chairs on the main deck facing forward, and a table and chair for me facing them, I will return in 5 minutes, make it so" forward was pronounced forrard.

"Aye Aye sir!"

And so it was that William was about to be offered an opportunity to further his horizons once more. As the cadets were all seated the babble of anticipation and whinging about not going boating was splitting into all sorts of sub conversations. One of the New Entries was asking why the P.O. had called Bruno a muppet, he had seen the new show on ATV but couldn't see the link between that and Bruno.

William proudly displayed his knowledge of all things trivial, he was especially keen to do so when there was a humorous connotation attached too. "Most Useless Person Pusser Ever Trained"

"Who's Pusser?"

"Ha ha, not who, what! Pusser is the Navy, well sort of. Pusser is the Royal Navy term for Purser, the purser is someone who holds and is accountable for all the stores and equipment, therefore if you are in the Navy Pusser owns you, you belong to Pusser!"

The New Entry, didn't really get it but decided not to pursue his questions any further as William's attention had already gone elsewhere. His status was much higher than a New Entry, he remembered how it felt to revere the cadets in uniform and didn't want to dilute that feeling of reverence for the new entries now either, and then of course there was pride and ego.

It had been over a year since William had first gone into the stores to be fitted with his uniform. It had been one of the proudest moments of his life, the elation of being told first of all that he had passed his new entry test and served his time, coupled with being invited into the stores, a room he had not been in before. It seemed like he was being invited into an out of bounds area, his status elevated. The smell of serge uniforms was very strong, in the stores, like the smell of mothballs mixed with polish. As each piece of uniform was issued to him the significance of each article was reverently revealed by the senior rate in charge of the stores.

The blue collar, considered lucky to touch, while on the modern uniform a significantly striking piece of decoration, was originally designed to keep the tar used to tie back the sailors hair off their uniforms. The black silk scarf, that formed a V across the chest and tied together with the white lanyard, both accessories from 18th century gunnery where the lanyard was used to fire the great cannons and hung round the neck, the silk as a crude sweat band. Both of these ramshackle items were formalised into something smart and seaman like. Even the creases had significance, in the trousers for example there were seven horizontal creases, alternately concertina exactly four inches apart. These were said to represent the seven seas, however in shorter ratings there were only room for five rather than seven and their origin was born when sailors would continually roll up their trousers to swab the decks, this left un-intentional creases which were then more formally adopted as compulsory creases that all looked the same. The strange looking uniform with such an interesting history around how it had formed through convenient adaptations of necessary tasks under difficult conditions, was instantly recognisable all over the world. Indeed, it had been copied by almost every other Navy in the world, possibly because the Royal Navy in its hay day had been larger and more powerful than the sum total of the rest of the world's Navies put together and indeed the envy of the world in terms not only of its size but also its operational efficiency. In other words, British sailors had historical significance that was something to be justly proud of.

The Royal Navy that had been sold to William, was one that had its roots in Empire, but a history that went way beyond that and a present that was proudly hanging onto the past through the stories handed down through a code of values and standards that stood the test of time.

As William had been issued with his "rig", he was told with passionate earnest "This is the finest uniform the world has ever seen! Wear it well lad because the millions that have worn it before you will turn in their graves if you don't!"

Many of the cadets took this line with a pinch of salt, William however felt the words burn into his sole and he took them on board because he wanted them to be true. He wanted to belong to something that had evidential pride. As humans we are hard wired to be motivated by a sense of belonging. William didn't find the senior rates words patronising or corny, he found them inspirational and slightly intimidating. Every time he put the uniform on he felt an overwhelming sense of pride. This pride would never leave him for the rest of his life, whenever he wore **the finest uniform the world had ever seen**, in any and all of its forms.

The chairs were in place and the cadets were all waiting in anticipation, the individual chatter causing a hum around the main deck that was steadily rising into the kind of cacophony that many frustrated teachers would empathise with, but few had the influence to deal with in the same efficient way that happened next. Why? Because the individual youngsters all had something in common, they all chose to go to the unit, they all had a sense of belonging and pride in being a member and they all had respect for the discipline and code that they were required to adhere to.

"Ship's Company ... HOE!

Immediately there was silence as every cadet assumed the position of sitting to attention, feet and knees together and arms crossed in front of them held up parallel to the deck, head and eyes to the front. How many teachers would love to have that much influence???

The C.O. walked onto the main deck and took his place at the table facing the expectant faces. "Sit easy everyone, remove head gear, those of you who are old enough may smoke, those of you who are not old enough to smoke but have cigarettes give them to me, I have run out."

A ripple of laughter went round the room and a few under aged nervous glances were shared between the guilty offenders that did enjoy a crafty smoke at stand easy (break time). The C.O. suppressed a smile as he noted the unconscious movements of guilty hands covering bulges in pockets. The baggy flares of the Navy uniform had the benefit of being able to hide a multitude of sins.

The cadets all trusted the C.O., he had a real authority about him, yet he was somehow able to show vulnerability without giving any of that authority away. Leader's who give off an impression that they are too good to be true, are most often exactly that. Showing vulnerability in appropriate leadership situations, allows those leaders to demonstrate their human side, and that gives their subordinates something to identify and believe in. It breeds trust, and trust is crucial in leadership. Here, he held absolute authority, he felt in control and he used it to good effect. He was well within his comfort zone, his mind briefly flicked to the phone call with Jack Dole, how different the feeling of control was now . . .

Lieutenant Commander Thompson RNR, brought his mind back to his eager audience, "Well I suppose you are all wondering what tonight is about?" expectant faces met the question without answer, knowing that soon the plot would come out.

"As you know, the Corps offers many opportunities to those who are brave enough to deserve them." They didn't know, but they accepted it now, the statement sounded so evidential, how could their minds think anything different.

"Every year her Majesties Royal Navy, the finest Navy the world has ever seen.,." he was milking the dramatic affect and sucking his audience into his spell ". . . invest vast amounts of money into the training of the finest young people in the country. For some reason, they have allocated some of that money for me to spend on you instead." His mouth curled in an ironic grin and there was a ripple of chuckles from those who got his little joke.

"So tonight I will present to you the courses on offer from Her Majesty on board her shore establishments and for the boys only on board her warships. Girls you will also get your chance to go to sea on T.S. Royalist, I'll tell you all about her in good time."

There was a hubbub in the room, some Cadets actively disengaged at that point, knowing that they would never be selected to go or have the support at home to allow them to. Bernie knew that so he played another quick card.

"For those of you who do not wish to travel or spend time away from your precious *school work* for a week at a time . . ." more irony was met with enthusiasm and pulled the room back together again, ". . . we can also map out a plan for you to advance, or not in your case Greene" another chuckle as Greene was patted on the head from behind by a teasing mate "and, I also have something special lined up for all of those of 14 years and over. I will be introducing some civilians to you later, I expect they will leave here with a lasting impression of our fine standards. In fact I shall go further than that and insist that they do."

The plot was becoming thicker and thicker, civvies? What were they doing here? What could they possibly add to the mix? Williams mind was fully engaged and open to the next couple of hours.

As the C.O. took the Cadets through each course and opportunity, telling vivid stories about the exploits that they might get up to, from flying in helicopters to running assault courses, sailing in the square rig Training Ship Royalist and much more besides. The Cadets put their names in the mix to be considered for each opportunity. William had wanted to be considered for a week in the summer holidays on HMS Flintham, a ham class inshore minesweeper, one of 93 in her class all of which were named after English villages ending in ham. HMS Flintham was affiliated to the unit and one or two others and gratefully enjoyed training a few of the cadets from time to time, it broke the ships routine and gave a few of the tight crew some leave while the youngsters took over their bunks and their jobs. He had also applied to go to the HMS Seahawk summer camp. HMS Seahawk was the name of the Royal Naval Air Station at Culdrose in Cornwall, and the week's camp there was a real treat.

His mind was drifting toward what might be if his application was successful and his parents said yes. They always did say yes to things like this, he had no fears there, but he also knew there would be hundreds of other Cadets around the country that would be applying for the precious places too. As the sound of 8 bells rang in four groups of two, signifying 2000 hours and the end of the dog watches, there followed a call from below "Stand easy, stand easy!" This was the break time, and as the C.O. stood up, the senior rate once again called the deck to attention. As the C.O. walked away he returned the salute of the senior rate, uttered a curt "carry on P.O." and was gone. The senior rate dismissed the class, and that was when William caught the first fleeting glimpse of her . . .

Stand easy, was a frantic affair that night, chatter around the previous session and what might happen next. The usual banter between the boys and the girls took place, some flirting and some discreet contact between some of the older Cadets who had formed relationships as boyfriend and girlfriend. But William's mind could only think of the vision he saw walk into the Wardroom (officers mess) with an older lady both in civvies. Who was she? Why was she here? She was lovely.

The second session had begun much the same as the first, the normal ceremonial out of the way a more relaxed tone took hold of the evening. There was a hint of formality for the benefit of the two guests however, the younger of which William was completely fixated upon.

The C.O.'s voice broke the mystery "I'd like to introduce you to Sarah Miles who is going to talk to you all about The Duke of Edinburgh's Award Scheme. Sarah . . ."

The what??? William had never heard of it, however he was interested, after all the Duke of Edinburgh had made Admiral of the Fleet simply by marrying the Queen, maybe he had some tips . . .

As Sarah Miles, a middle aged lady who looked like she would suit a Girl Guide uniform in her demeanour and by the way she was talking, took the group through a fascinating journey of how the D of E Award Scheme worked, William only had eyes for the demure, elegant, pretty, blue eyed girl sat next to her. Her hands placed in her lap with her knees together in her school pencil skirt, the hem just above the knee. Her shiny dark hair was loosely tied yet down, in stark contrast to the tight buns that the GN's had to wear. Her white blouse was open at the neck for the first two buttons and William could feel his heart beating in his chest as he looked at her. Her eyes were so blue, so very blue that he felt he could dive in like he would a swimming pool. Her features were almost noble as she sat un-phased by all the attention her presence was bringing.

Sarah, was giving a great presentation around all the elements of the award, of which there were four at bronze, silver and gold level and had made the point that to achieve gold was quite a thing and that recipients would be awarded their gold at Buckingham Palace by the Duke himself. The four sections at each level were; community service, sport, skill and expedition. None of these things phased William, but then he wasn't really taking it on board until something happened . . .

"At this point I would like to introduce Samantha, who will tell you all about her recent expedition training and how she would like you help to go on to her next project, Samantha"

Samantha, her name was Samantha. Wow how pretty did that sound, Samantha.

Samantha stood up and smoothed her black pencil skirt, her hands rubbing in one motion down her thighs. An innocent move, but as William watched it he was totally besotted with her. She confidently began to speak and her voice had a soft timber that sounded to William like the voice of an angel. It reminded him of the sound of Debbie Harry's voice, soft yet strong, sensual and knowing, like melted chocolate silky smooth. The Juke box in his head began playing a Blondie song "Pretty baby, you look so Heavenly . . ."

As Samantha talked through some of the activities she had begun on her Bronze journey, her eyes darted around the room, and William was hoping beyond hope that she would look at him. He had not heard a single word that she had said, she was explaining how tonight was helping her to gain confidence in her presentation skills and her eyes met with William's as she closed her address

with ". . . and that's why I hope you will come and join D of E."
Her eyes were so blue, and William suddenly felt embarrassed as
she awkwardly dropped her head and blushed. Had it been their
eye contact that had forced that?

His heart was audible in his head and his face felt flushed.
He would from that day forward be committed to the Duke of
Edinburgh's Award Scheme, and another pivotal moment in
his young life was about to begin. He was on the brink of a new
horizon.

Silvy looked at him as his tongue was hanging out at the posh
looking scruffy civvie bitch, and she thought at that moment that
she hated them both. But she knew that if William came over now
and asked her out she would say yes immediately . . . Fat Chance!

Top Tips - Start looking for good things, they will come!

It's easy when things are at a low ebb to start thinking "what can go wrong next?" We use language like "these things always come in three's". We actually start actively looking for the next thing that will have a negative impact on us, thinking that this will get all the bad stuff out of the way. The problem with that is that we get into the habit of looking for bad things and grab them with both hands when they come. We become our own self-fulfilling prophecy.

The brain begins to play tricks and does it's thing on us. Have you ever noticed that when you start looking for a new car for example you suddenly notice lots of the ones that you are interested in on the road? Your awareness of that particular make and model has become heightened and because you have sent this message to the brain that you want to see them, it obliges and picks up on them for you. The unconscious mind loves to serve. Sadly it works for negatives too, if you program it to look for them it will.

However as we collect evidence over the years we know that good times come again after the low moments, and in those moments of laughter some of us reflect that maybe life is not so bad after all. The longer we live the more good times we have, that is statistical fact, therefore we become more robust about the fact that good times will return during the doldrums.

A lovely quote from an author called Robert H. Schuller "tough times don't last, but tough people do!"

This quote has held our own author together on many an occasion, when a stiff upper lip was required. Because of course, there are bad times, they call it life. We cannot constantly pretend that everything in the garden is rosey and that everything will be ok. But what we can get into the habit of looking for the positive things too, and take the time to notice them more when they come. Suddenly you will find that, just like the metaphorical car in this top tip, you start to see more of them. This is an extension of the generative enquiry, what's good on your ship?

But it goes further than that. I was inspired when chatting randomly to a stranger at a conference and building rapport by asking open questions about life in general. It transpired that the very confident looking lady I was talking to had a terminally ill small child aged six, a little girl. It struck a chord with me as my daughter at the time was the same age and it almost brought tears to my eyes as I imagined the pain in my heart I would feel if that were me. Yet this lady was bravely facing life and all it's challenges, it put things into context on it's own however when I suggested that she was incredibly strong, she told me she had to be strong for her daughter and that it never occurred to her not to be. I was genuinely moved by this and asked how she managed to do it, she simply replied "There are bad days and good days, and on the bad days, we talk about the next good day we are going to have."

I was inspired beyond belief and my trivial problems melted away.

Looking for good things sounds such a simple thing to do, and that's because it is. There are wonderful moments happening all around us, enjoy them, recognise them and look for them again. The bad stuff will come and go, sometimes it will stay with us for longer than is welcome, but remember we have an evidence file that we are capable of enjoying the good stuff. Refuse to let the bad get the better of you, fight it, because tough times don't last, but tough bastards do. (I modified that, not just to give it a bit of bite, but because that's the one I use for me, I promise you it works!)

CHAPTER 11

BAGGY TROUSERS, DIRTY SHIRT

William had gone home that night beaming inside. He had missed his opportunity to talk to Samantha, as she had slipped away with her leader immediately as the evening colours ceremony was concluding. William of course was trying to stand out as the smartest Cadet on parade and in doing so completely missed the moment that she slipped away. His heart was fluttering when he realised he had missed her, but he knew exactly where to find her, he was definitely going to enrol on the D of E program.

As he skipped through the door, his father enquired "good parade Will?"

"Blinding Dad!"

"What? Somebody stabbed you in the eyes with a bayonet did they?"

"Hah hah, very funny Dad"

"So what made tonight so good then Buster?" William liked it when his father called him by the affectionate name that he occasionally used and had done since he was a toddler. However, he was becoming less keen on it when it was used in front of his mates.

"I'm joining D of E!"

"What's DV?" his father was shouting from his comfortable chair in the living room through the open door to the dining room where William was taking of his boots, the process of undoing the laces and loosening them enough to slip each foot out was a lengthy one.

"Deeee of Eeeee, not DV"

"OK what's Deeeee of Eeeeee?" Jack was pleased that something had happened, clearly his chat with Bernie had worked, his son had a real fire in his bearing tonight.

"It's Duke of Edinburgh's Award Dad, when you get it you go to Buckingham Palace and everything, I am going to do the lot Dad, it will be really good, you get to go camping and do sports and loads of skills stuff and . . ."

"Woah, slow down son, when exactly are you going to do all this?"

"Wednesday Nights Dad, It's perfect, I don't miss Cadets"

"What about homework?"

"Daaaaaaaaad" the inflection went from high to low and then high again in the way that only teenagers really can, it's as if they all go on a course.

"Okay, okay, just don't let it slip, I'll get my best suit ready then shall I?"

"what?"

"For Buckingham Palace! You can shine my shoes, you need the practice" He pointed down at William's boots which were now slightly scuffed but the evidence of a brilliant shine on the toecaps was there. William spent hours on his boots, perfecting the technique of little circles, getting the mix of shoe polish and moisture just right. Some people preferred spit, but William found that water was better.

William was in the living room now and sat down next to his Dad and playfully took up the routine they silently fell into of finger wrestling. Jack had fingers like thick steel rods, and William thought him to be invincible. Jack however was beginning to find it more and more difficult to get the balance right as his son's strength improved, from time to time he was in genuine pain when William trapped and twisted one of his digits. They would spar for hours trying to get purchase over one another, William's stronger right hand against his father's weaker left. This silent battle was a comfortable and credible contact between a proud father and an equally proud teenager. As the battle commenced, Jack smiled to himself at his son's mood, then regretted his lack of concentration as his thumb let out an audible crack, with a supreme effort of will he suppressed the squeal of pain that was desperate to escape him and set about freeing himself.

William had to wait a whole week before he could attend D of E. The very next night was not possible as he needed to get the details at the next parade that Friday. It was one of the longest weeks of his life. His thoughts were totally consumed by Samantha. That first night, after the finger wrestling, he went to bed and tried to recall the image of Samantha, he panicked when he couldn't see her face in his mind's eye. He tried and tried and couldn't for the life him remember. Then he thought of her blue eyes and he saw them. Like topaz gems, her eyes had seemed to look into his soul, and as he remembered them the features of her face came slowly out of the haze and he smiled. His guts turned over and he felt like he did as a small boy waiting for Christmas, but this was different, there was something else going on too. It was exciting, yet stomach churning. He began to question, what if she didn't like him? What if she had a boyfriend already? What if he didn't see her again? What if . . .

He decided instead to imagine scenarios that would have them together, with him as her hero. Fantasies, which found him looking after her out in the woods, after they had been chased out of the camp site by armed thugs while on a D of E expedition. He would protect her and use his skills of survival learned on proper Sea cadet camps to keep her safe. Her blue eyes would be looking gratefully into his as he made her feel safe. With such thoughts, he drifted off to sleep.

As he biked to school each day over the next week, he sang to himself over and over again the Elton John song, "Blue Eyes, babies got blue eyes. Like a deap blue sea, on a blue blue day . . ."

He was smitten and helpless. He had no way to communicate with his new fixation. All he could do was hope that she would be there next week, and that she would like him. Maybe she had a boyfriend already . . . his guts tightened up at that thought. As the week drew to an end he found it increasingly more difficult to pull up the picture of Samantha in his head and the whole thing was getting to him so he decided to change the song in his head. His favourite Madness record, the one that had taken him aback with the sound when they had their debut on Top of the Pops and a very boyish looking lead singer in a pork pie hat was interviewed briefly before opening a career that would last for decades with the first words "Buster, he sold the heat . . . with a rock steady beat . . ." and with their tribute to a legend "The Prince", they had their first of many hits and William was hooked.

His father had often remarked, with some frustration, that if William could learn his schoolwork as well as he could retain the lyrics in his head from his favourite songs the he wouldn't have to worry so much about his homework. William treated the remarks with the same distain that most teenagers have and will forever.

As he pulled into the bike shed with the usual two minutes to spare before pastoral registration class was due, he carefully took his A3 folder of the back rack that he had protected all the way to school. One subject that William really enjoyed was technical drawing, and he was very proud of the work in progress that was held within the buff coloured folder that made the cleverer boys stand out as the subject was reserved for the top stream.

The pastoral set up was designed to allow boys of all abilities to mix at the start of the day and was a throwback to the old days of houses and competition. William had embraced this in the early years and had taken an active role in representing his class in sport.

As the years went on however, the void between intelligence and the application levels of the boys began to tell and gulfs between values began to grow. Most of the boys in the lower performance streams were actively disengaged with academic achievement and despised the boys that were. William was in the middle, he liked the humour of some of the lower streamed boys, but also knew he had to do well and actually enjoyed a lot of the work, especially with certain teachers who really brought subjects to life for him.

As he rushed in to class this particular morning, he put his Adidas bag down next to him and consciously laid the Technical Drawing folder next to it.

A stand in teacher arrived a moment later and sat quietly behind the desk at the front of the class and allowed the babble of the form to continue as he familiarised himself with the register in front of him. His presence hadn't gone unnoticed and almost unconsciously the whole class took a slightly more rowdy demeanour. Maybe it was the way that the unfamiliar teacher slunk into the form room without asserting himself, but there was a sense in the room that something was going to happen.

William just wanted to get through registration and onto the Tech Block where he could safely deliver his drawing and engage in one of his favourite lessons of the week. As this thought went through his mind, he glanced down at the folder, to see it being dragged back to the seat behind, where to his horror one of the known trouble makers was gleefully provoking William by threatening to spill the contents of the folder on the floor. "What's the matter dolly boy Doley? You want your little pickies?"

"Give them back!"

"Nah, let's have a little look shall we?"

William began the panic slightly, the boy had no idea, no concept of how proud William was of his work, the effort and time he had put in, and how such a stupid joke could ruin it in a heart-beat.

"Back! Now!" the panic was beginning to galvanise into anger at this ignorant act. There was menace in his voice and it flashed in his eyes.

"Why, what you gunna do posh boy? You gunna make me are you?" The boy was trying to provoke William, his reason to push the temporary teacher and ultimately show off to his other classmates from the dregs of the academic gene pool.

William was thinking fast, he wanted to get out of that class, work intact but also his own pride intact with the added bonus of not being in trouble with the teachers either. "I'll arm wrestle you for it" he said with a confident smile. His thought process was sound enough, the boy wanted a show down, this would do it and William knew he would win hands down.

What he hadn't thought through was that it was also clear to the bully boy that an arm wrestle would be one sided, and not what he wanted. "Nah, not my style . . ." the boy threw the folder on the floor, and as William followed the fall with his eyes, the boy threw a punch that landed squarely on William's nose.

The pain registered immediately and the metallic taste of blood in the back of his throat, was exacerbated by the fact that the blood had come from a different sense organ, giving it that unique sparkly numb feeling that comes from a bloodied nose. He literally saw red and flashed with rage.

However, he was snapped back to his senses by the teacher who was up on his feet and moving purposefully with a confidence they had not seen as he entered the room in the beginning. He grabbed both boys by the scruff and dragged them to the front of the class with a strength that had remained hidden to that point. He placed a boy in each corner of the room and calmly took the register in double quick time. Then ended the registration with a curt "all you boys out now, you two . . ." indicating the two boys he had grabbed "stay right where you are!"

Once the hubbub had died down, William was astonished to suddenly be bearing the brunt of the teachers onslaught. In his own mind, not only was he the innocent party, but he had also shown considerable restraint in not striking back. He had rationalised all of this while waiting in the corner, feeling sure that he was going to be allowed to go straight to his lesson while the other boy would be punished.

"Name boy!"

"Dole sir"

"Why did you provoke this boy to punch you?"

"What?" William looked incredulously at the teacher while his attacker looked innocently smug.

The teachers hand lashed out and slapped William round the head, "Don't what me boy"

"But sir . . ."

Whack, another slap to the head, in exactly the same place.

"Sir?"

"you must have said something, look at him, he is much smaller than you boy, I cannot tolerate a bully do you hear me?"

It occurred to William in that moment that just maybe this teacher had been bullied all his life and was enjoying his own moment right now. He had to think fast.

"Sir, I'm not a bully, it's just a personal thing sir, he doesn't like me sir."

"So, you want to get him into trouble do you?"

"No sir, I just don't want to get any blood on my work sir" William decided to milk his bloody nose and draw attention to the fact that he was the studious one.

"That's your work boy?"

"yes sir!"

"Not your work?" he said turning to the other boy who now began to squirm as the tables turned slightly.

William seized the initiative as the other boy stood with his mouth open, "I think he just wanted to see what work looked like sir, in case he ever has to do any when he grows up sir."

"Insolent boy!" William was rewarded with yet another smack to the side of the head, and to his utter surprise the teacher went on, "you boy get out of my sight" the confused, yet thrilled other boy bounded out of the room, "as for you . . ." turning to William, ". . . detention tonight!"

"But sir, he hit me"

"Then let that be a lesson to you." And with that the teacher turned on his heal and left the room. William was glaring after him, feeling angry yes, frustrated for sure, but moreover profound disappointment that somebody in such a position, a figure to be respected, to trust, had got it so wrong. How could that happen? How could it be allowed to happen? Why was that teacher so weak, why hadn't he at least tried to understand. William looked around him in that room alone, took in the sights he could see, the desks with graffiti scrawled upon them. The brown floor tiles all dull and scuffed, worn down by years of teenage traffic, only shiny at the very edges of the room. The roller black board, dusty with chalk. And at that moment he made a deal with himself that he would remember this room at this time and the feelings that he had right now, and if he ever should be in a position of power, he would take a lesson from this and handle it a million times better.

With that, he left the room, went to the toilets and cleaned up his nose. Then ran as fast as he could to his lesson, the school had already taken on a different aspect as the lessons had started, and rather than the usual bustle of boys fighting their way to class, there was a strange feeling of emptiness to the corridors, muffled sounds of lessons in progress, and sense that he was missing something and the anxiety built once more.

As he entered the room, "Your late Dole, that's a detention for you tonight."

"But sir . . ."

"Want another one?"

"I've already got another one sir" the class burst into laughter which abruptly ceased as the master turned and used his eyes to calm the class. This teacher had respect, he was helpful, knowledgeable, funny at times, but strict and fair.

"And, how pray tell, did you manage that Dole?"

"It's a long story sir."

"Then you may tell me during your break instead." The truth was that the technical drawing master liked William. He also needed to show he had flexibility while not losing credibility, it seemed like a good compromise and was genuinely interested in William's story, might be a good one to share in the staff room at lunch time.

William groaned inwardly as he accepted his fate for the day. But he was, never the less, angry that his own set of values had been turned upside down by that scum bag from the dreg pool. "How simple life must be for the thickoes" William thought to himself, as he sat down at the spare desk and pulled the drawing board that sat upon it toward him and began to unload the contents of his folder. He had a helix to finish within this double period. As he mounted it onto the board and clipped it into place, the master observed a beautiful piece of work, the fine work of the 2H pencil barely visible yet precisely drawn enabling the much bolder 2B make up the outline of the helix by joining up the sector points. The mathematical stretch along with the creativity gave William a little buzz and as a result he put a lot of effort into Technical Drawing.

His mind focussed once more he went to work. As he worked, his mind began to play a tune that had embedded itself from the day's activities so far. ". . . baggy trousers, dirty shirt, pullin' hair and eatin' dirt, teacher comes to break it up, bang on the 'ed with a plastic cup. Baggy trousers . . ." an image of the saxophone player flying through the air, winding his way up in a perfect helix . . .

The rest of the morning went ok, the break spend with the TD master had actually been quite good fun, and William had enjoyed receiving some well placed and well delivered recognition. As he felt in his pocket for the 60p that would buy him a dinner token, he pulled the two coins out and looked at them for a moment, then made a decision. He said out loud "Yeh, sod it, it's been one of those days". With that William headed over to the hole in the wall that was the tuck shop serving hatch and joined the free for all scrum that was far from a queue.

Around 30 boys were pushing and squeezing to get to the small hatch in the wall. As one boy wriggled free with his purchases, so another would fall into place and the whole sausage machine would move slightly. From a distance it looked like a bait ball of fish swarming and wriggling as one entity, up close is was brutal, but accepted as the norm. William picked his spot and squeezed his shoulder into the moving mass of teenage male body odour. In fact one boy in the middle of the four or five deep mess (it was difficult to tell) farted loudly and began laughing at the comedy of the situation, knowing that he alone was about to enjoy the smell that they would all be trapped in. The groans and curses said it all, to the observers on the periphery it was equally as funny as it had been to the boy who had been responsible for the social relapse. "Well if you'd all stop squeezing me I would have to." said the laughing voice of the slightly chubby boy. Another strained voice replied "You need to go and shit some out, not put more in you smelly bastard."

William recognised the voice, and his earlier rage returned, taking him slightly by surprise. It was the bully boy from pastoral, this time William held the cards.

It was fairly easy to work his way across the bait ball, through the middle. All of the force was pushing forward and squashing in from the sides, as some boys were using the wall as leverage to squash in behind the throng. As he got closer to his target, he fixed his eyes onto the other boys face and they were full of menace and meaning. Eventually the boy sensed he was being eyeballed then turned and saw who it was. There was something about William's eyes that struck fear into the boys heart.

As William brought his head near to the boy's ear, he spoke with a slight quake in the voice that the other boy wrongly perceived as fear. In fact it was passionate rage, pent up rage, a week of frustration about not being able to know or contact Samantha, pressure from school generally and now this day's miss-justice. "You dropped me in it you cowardly little shit!"

"haha yeh whatever . . . argggh!"

William had grabbed the boy by the bicep, his strong fingers pushing between muscle, bone and tendon easily. The more the boy cursed and wriggled the more William squeezed, the hours of finger wrestling with his father having strengthened his grip and his own tolerance to pain.

"I could have dobbed you in, but I didn't, and you let me take the rap, well you wanted a fight, you've bloody well got one, and this time you'll bleed you shit."

"Let go, let go, please I'll give you my dinner money, please let me go."

"You cowardly little weasel, I don't want your money, you make me sick. I don't think I will let go, I think I'll squeeze harder."

At that point William recognised sheer terror and helplessness on the other boys face, and it touched him slightly. He was not a bully, but he recognised that this bully could be scared when the table was turned, and it felt like justice for all the weak kids that had fallen prey to this lump of turd. He thought for a moment about the likelihood that the money he had been offered was probably some that had already been prised from a younger boy.

"Nah, you're not worth the effort you spineless monkey." William twisted hard for a second and let go, to a shriek of pain.

"I'll kill you, you posh twat!"

"No you won't, but if you want to try you can find me near the tree after this, and if you bring your mates, I'll find you again, and again on your own, and every time I do I'll hurt you, so it's up to you dick head. You're either brave enough to face me, or let's just say you'll never bother me again shall we?"

William spent his 60p on a frozen mars bar, which lasted ages for obvious reasons, some fizz bombs, a packet of space dust and a panda pop. He took it to the tree that had served as wickets on many occasions and waited for the boy for the remainder of the lunch hour. Now the adrenaline had left his body, his stomach began to twist in fear and anxiety. Had he been a bit too rash with his threat? He was convinced that any minute now there would be a gang of boys purposefully walking over to give him the kicking of his life. Every fibre of his being was telling him to get out of there, and remove himself from danger. But a stronger motivation was keeping him sat at the base of "his tree". Pride. The electric sound of a siren invaded the buzz of the long school lunch break to signify its ending. The boy, or his gang of thugs never came, and he would never hold eye contact with William again.

William got up, grabbed his bag, and with a spring in his step, sang in his head as he went off to his next lesson, double maths. "All the teachers in the pub, passing round the ready rub, trying not to think of when that lunch time bell will ring again, oh what fun we had . . ."

Top Tips – Making tough decisions

We all face tough decisions throughout life, some tougher than others. What makes them tough? Have you ever thought about that? It's usually because the decision will have a high impact outcome, whether it be positive or negative. Sometimes you have a choice between two or more things that all have a fantastic potential outcome and the dilemma is to choose the best one. In reality when this happens there can be no bad decision because the final result has to be a good one, and more than likely a close call or there would be no dilemma. In these circumstances the toss of a coin can have a great impact. Seriously, if you toss a coin, and hear your inner voice say "best out of three" you have your answer. As to the risk, there is none as both outcomes will be good.

But what of the really tough decisions, the ones that have consequences? Sometimes the outcome of any decision will have negative impact on your life, then the process becomes one of damage limitation. Sometimes we avoid making the decision by burying our head in the sand, this course of action may well get us out of immediate peril, but it will not be future proof. If you have time, you need to consider the cost of inaction as well as the consequence of decision. Often a bad decision is much better than no decision at all.

It's as simple as "what happens if?" play the scenarios through and make an informed decision.

Panic is not an option, panic kills. Snakes know this, they inject venom and rely on their victim panicking, running around, raising the heartbeat, pumping the venom round the system faster, while they patiently wait. The smart thing to do, is to remain calm, apply pressure between the bite and the heart to stop the flow of blood, and get help. Easier said than done, but this is how survivors survive. Recommended reading is the true story "touching the void" by Joe Simpson. This is a heart wrenching story of survival where the ultimate decision of life or death are made, to cut the rope and kill my friend, or hang on and kill us both . . . (you should read the book).

The ability to make decisions under pressure separates great leaders from weak ones, and of course it becomes easier with experience because experience comes from evidenced outcomes. Some people seem naturally gifted even at an early age, often they become rising stars of any organisation they are in. They weigh risk versus benefit and take action. If they make a mistake, that's fine, learn move on. A mistake is an accident, the same mistake twice is a bad decision.

It becomes easier with practice but to start with you need tools, of which there are many, you can go onto the internet and search for decision making tools and find lots of very good models such as SWOT and PESTLE, all proven to work and assist with analysis. But to simplify the whole process look at three things:

- The cost (emotional, physical and financial)
- Impact (what difference will it make, what will be the outcome?)
- Ease of implementation

If you have a range of decisions you could even score them all over the three criteria and see how they come out. If you do this, remember that impact is the most important as this is what you will end up with so why not factor that score a bit, you decide.

In summary, tough decisions are tough because they need to be made, so make them don't hide. If you hide from decisions you will become a victim of circumstances, and therefore lose control. When you lose control you feel stress and the cycle begins, your snake has won . . .

In the last chapter, William decided not to react to the bully in class because his values kicked in and he didn't want to be seen as reactive, or disruptive to the teacher. However he also decided that the issue was not finished. The tough decision was to bury his pride and play a longer game, but he saw it through and the outcome, on this occasion, was good for him, and most likely a few others that probably didn't suffer due to a change in attitude from the bully.

CHAPTER 12

HEARTBEAT HEAVEN

It was Wednesday. William liked Wednesdays. He had double maths in the morning, followed by games. Then in the afternoon, metalwork, a good timetable in William's view. He liked maths, there was a logical conclusion to make, the answer was either right or wrong, none of this subjective interpretation that was involved in English based subjects. In truth, he had an issue with his English teacher, which was probably shared, he was convinced that his work was judged too harshly, so he focussed on subjects he knew he could prove an answer to.

This Wednesday was different though. This Wednesday was the Wednesday that he would go to D of E in the evening. So this Wednesday, despite the engaging lessons would drag. As he cycled to school, he hardly noticed the driving rain as it beat into his bare hands on the handle bars. He considered that gloves were for weaklings, and wanted to toughen his hands up, it was working. The rain stung his face as he squinted his eyes to see the way ahead, yet all these sensations were subliminal to him compared to the butterflies of anticipation welling up in his gut.

His mind was racing ahead to the night he had been looking forward to, for what seemed like weeks. His mind was flip flopping between excitement and fear, and it was almost making him feel physically sick. He thought about the feeling in his stomach, trying to analyse it and likened it to watching clothes flop round in the new tumble dryer they had, which still amazed people that saw it when they came round. One minute he was exalted at the thought of seeing Sam again, planning what he would say, how he would engage her in conversation, how good it would be ... the next his heart was gripped in fear, what if she wasn't there? What if she didn't like him? What if she already had a boyfriend ... ?

He constantly pushed the negative thoughts aside and focussed on what he could control, how would he play it this evening? But the nagging doubts kept creeping back. What if she wasn't there? How would he find her again? The reality of the time was that there were no mobile phones, no internet, no social networks, communication had to be face to face, or at best a phone call on landlines conducted either within earshot of your parents at home, or from the smelly confines of a phone box cut short by beeps at the end of your 10p or 2p call. That's if you had the number ... William decided there and then that he had to get her number tonight come what may.

He didn't hear the noise, the wind and rain driving into the hood of his blue parker coat with the grey polyester fur lined trim thickly lining the hood that he had deployed over his ears. Green was the fashion, but Navy blue was his colour, he was never bound by fashion. His sight could not play a part in his protection either as the car was skidding toward him on the wet road from behind ...

The sensation of being hit by the car was almost dreamlike. The Raleigh Wayfarer, blue in colour of course, bicycle was pushed rather than knocked from under him as the bonnet of the Ford Cortina slid into the back wheel and went on to mount the pavement that William was tracking to his left.

It was like slow motion, as if it were happening to someone else, there was no pain as William was bounced onto the bonnet, hitting the screen of the car and for a frozen moment looking into the wide, panic stricken eyes of the girl in the passenger seat of the car, before sliding off the side and hitting the pavement with a crack.

Immediately, William made to spring up onto his feet and as he put his hand down to push up with, a searing pain shot up his wrist and seamed to grip his very being. He slumped back down to the ground as fresh sources of pain began to take hold of him. The sharp pain in his wrist began to throb, but there was an uncomfortable ache in his side too and he didn't quite know where to put himself, he tried to roll over and felt the soreness of open skin on his knee and looked down to see blood oozing through his trousers, already darkened by the rain in was difficult to tell how much blood was seeping through. He decided to lay back down on his back, and wished the screaming would stop.

The girlfriend of the man driving the car was sat in the passenger seat, hands tugging at her hair, in a completely hysterical state, the man next to her was blindly looking forward as if in denial of what had happened. Then a voice in his ear, calming, controlled "you ok son?"

"yeh, yeh . . ." William made a move to get up, he felt embarrassed to be laying on the floor like this.

"Stay still lad, don't move, help is coming, what's your name?"

"William"

"Good lad, don't move, let me check the others."

William began to worry at that thought. Was it that bad? What had happened, oh no!!! what about tonight . . . ?

"Calm down love, breath!" his assertive voice broke through the hysteria enough for the wide eyed girl to snap her attention toward the man that had opened the driver's door, her boyfriend had put his face in his hands and was leaning forward onto the steering wheel. "Is, is he dead?" she tentatively enquired, panic beginning to rise in her once more.

"No he's not, no thanks to you!" the man had directed his attention to the driver now "What the hell were you doing?" the engine was still running and the driver who hardly looked old enough to be behind the wheel was still slumped over the wheel. "Are either of you hurt?" he looked at the girl who shook her head in sobbing jerky denial "Hey" he had put a hand on the drivers shoulder "are you ok?"

"How's my car?"

"sod your bloody car!" with that, the man went back to William just as his wife came running back from the phone box "they are on their way Bill" she said "We've got another little Bill here love, brave little sod too." He said smiling down at William

"It's Will not Bill"

"Ha ha you'll be ok, by the way I saw it all, he just ran right into you, he can't have been looking."

"Police and ambulance are coming, we'll stay with you." Bill's wife had kind eyes, a mothers eyes, William saw a sadness in them that he could not have known was down to her own longing for a child of her own, but at 40 it was unlikely to happen now after all these years of trying. All her built up maternal instinct was channelled toward this teenage boy laying injured on the wet pavement, and she began to cry.

"Not now, for goodness sake Shirley . . ." her husband frowned at her, and gestured with his head toward William as if to suggest her tears would send him into shock.

She pulled a hankie from her sleeve and stifled her sobs uttering an apology.

The driver had heard the exchange and was beginning to panic. In truth his attention had been elsewhere at the time of the collision. How things can turn in a heartbeat. A few moments ago, his left hand had been caressing under his girlfriend's skirt. He had just picked her up to take her to college in his new pride and joy. He had passed his test a few weeks ago, and was the envy of his friends. The ability to pick up his girlfriend had given him not only kudos, but the opportunity to snatch some privacy with her in his own little world. It hadn't taken him long to execute the plan he had been forming for days and his hand had slipped from the gear stick to her leg. She didn't seem to complain as she wriggled in the seat to give him easier access. His clumsy attempts to reach under the three tiers of her new RaRa skirt had been less than subtle, as he reached the material of her cotton underwear she had felt a gut twisting yet pleasant feeling from within and the action of squirming in her seat not only gave him better access but helped her feeling along. She was ready to be touched, she had kept him at bay long enough, she craved to know what it felt like to have a boy touch her there and her heart was pounding in her head. After all she had just turned eighteen last week, surely it was ok now, decent, it had been legal for two years in fact, but she hadn't felt ready. The feeling of his hand hot on her bare thigh had dispelled any thoughts of denying him again. There was something about being in the car that made her feel all grown up and ready for what was about to come. She felt the tight sensation of her body taking over and producing that dampness down there that she found embarrassing yet exciting all at the same time. She closed her eyes and bit down on her bottom lip.

He couldn't believe his luck as he felt her legs part slightly, and he felt his own blood surge to cause an uncomfortable restriction in his skin-tight jeans. As he made his clumsy progress he thought he was going to explode, he was working his fingers in such a way as to move the material to one side, trying to make it appear as an accidental fringe benefit, yet they both knew what he was doing. As his tenacious efforts progressed, they both gasped. Though she craved for him to slowly tease her and build the sensation that was growing hot inside her, the only thing he could focus on was his end goal. She was beginning to doubt herself, this wasn't how it was supposed to be, it was hurting now . . .

All of his expectations had been built through listening to his gang of friends, and they were now being redefined. He was also eighteen and felt way behind the game in comparison to all his friends who seemed to have had so much experience with the opposite sex. Everything was far more complicated than he had imagined, the anatomy and the reaction to his advances were taking him by surprise in many ways. His failing attempts were making him angry and impatient. As he moved his hand more roughly, pulling aggressively at her clothing once more to give himself easier access, he was making her very uncomfortable. He knew she was in pain by her movements and noises but he was so close now he had to reach his goal, he didn't care about her feelings at that time (surely she would like it eventually?). His frustration was making things much worse, and when she suddenly screamed aloud like a wounded animal, he jumped in fear, his hand falling away. For a moment he thought he had damaged her in some way and didn't register what was happening as the dull "thwump" of his bonnet hitting the bike was followed by the crunch of William landing on the windscreen.

His girlfriend was in emotional meltdown, her heightened state of feeling turning to confusion, revulsion and panic.

Her screams were driving him mad with anger, at her, at the boy on the bike, at his own frustration that his plan had been smashed along with his car.

Then the man, the smart arse do gooder, drilling him with his eyes full of accusation.

His mind was churning everything over and none of it was good. He felt trapped and out of control, stress was beginning to take hold of him. He put his head in his hands and could smell the musty scent and it now made him feel sick. Through the confusion of overloaded senses he slowly picked up the drone of his engine, still ticking over and tapping as one cylinder was slightly misfiring. He made a snap decision that would add a nasty twist to events.

Suddenly and violently he engaged first gear and slammed his foot on the accelerator pedal, hauling on the steering wheel to bounce the car back down off the path and onto the road, snaking away as the wheels spun on the wet tarmac.

"What the . . . ?" Bill looked up astonished as his wife's hands went up to her face "Oh my . . ."

They watched in horror as the car sped off, Bill swore under his breath "stupid little shit"

Shirley was left with the image of the girls face as she peered back through the window, she was trying to work out the look, was it fear? Yes but there was something else, panic? No it was simply saying, begging almost "help me!"

"That poor girl . . ."

"What?"

"Bill we have to do something!"

"Never mind that, the police will get them, little buggers! Little Bill here needs us right now"

"It's WILL!" said William "And I'm fine, I want to get up"

"You stay right there son" and then to his wife "Did you get the number?"

"What?"

"The number plate Shirley, did you get the number plate?"

"No I didn't, did you?"

"Dam, no I didn't, bloody stupid of me."

"Well we didn't know he was going to do that did we."

"Little sods the pair of them."

"She was frightened Bill, I didn't like the look of that boy, he had mad eyes. God I hope she's alright." And Shirley began to cry.

"Oh Christ, here we go, come on love . . ." as the first wail of sirens cut through the noise of the rain on their coats ". . . saved by the bell".

As the police car came toward them, the girl in the passenger seat of the car banged on the windscreen and screamed at it, much to the annoyance of the maniac driver next to her, who cuffed her with the back of his hand making her whimper and press herself into the passenger window.

The police lady sat in the panda car's passenger seat picked the handset of the in car radio up and called in a suspicious incident and stated the number plate of the Ford.

"You're unbelievable you!" said the time served PC driving, "It's not enough to attend an accident with casualties you have to wrack up more paperwork on the way! You newbies are way too keen!"

"There was something wrong about that car"

As they turned the corner at the top of the road where William had been knocked down, they saw a woman enthusiastically gesturing them toward the scene, and they knew they were in the right place.

Shirley was blurting out the chain of events as she had witnessed them. The ambulance had arrived within a minute of the panda car and was attending to William.

"He was mad I tell you, he crazy eyes and . . ."

"OK madam, what kind of car were they in?"

As Shirley struggled to answer Bill chirped in "Mark 1 Cortina, white.!

It was the WPC's turn "I told you there was something about that car." She shot an accusing look at her colleague who avoided the look by getting onto the radio and upgrading the recent message his WPC had put into the control centre about the Cortina. Taking control and asserting his seniority he turned from the radio and announced "right, it appears we now have a hit and run, very serious. Let's go and see our patient and see how he is. We'll need statements from you both of course." He said looking at Bill and Shirley who were nodding enthusiastically. "What did you say the lads name is again?"

"Bi . . . , William, William is his name, Will" said Bill.

William had sustained a hairline fracture in his wrist and some nasty bruising. He was stiff but comfortable. His young fit body had bounced well and preserved him from serious injury. They had strapped his wrist after the x-ray, much to his surprise he was not to have a plaster cast. He thought all breaks had a plaster cast fitted as standard, part of him was disappointed having seen other people get theirs signed. He would have a real story to tell tonight when he got to D of E, he could turn this to his advantage yet.

His Mother had arrived at the hospital and was much calmer than Shirley who had stayed on throughout. William's mother had been in and of hospitals with her children for the last thirty years. Once she had established that William was essentially ok, she went into supporting calm mother mode. Shirley looked on with awe and a little envy, but didn't quite understand how she was being so calm.

They all sat in silence, William on the hospital bed, patched up with various bandages and dressings. His mother and Shirley were sat on uncomfortable plastic chairs at the bedside. They were waiting for the ward rounds and the doctor's analysis of the situation to find out what was to happen next.

The nurses had taken a shine to him, his boyish cheek and stubborn resistance to pain was endearing. They were more used to the whimpering kind of patient that expected way too much sympathy, it was refreshing to care for someone like William so they all unconsciously spent more time looking in on him that the other patients in their care.

There was a sudden bustle as the nurses became overtly efficient at the approach of the consultant's ward rounds. The senior doctor reached the end of William's bed surrounded by his entourage of student doctors, the ward sister and two staff nurses. He picked up the notes from the bottom of William's bed and asked without looking at William "so what have you been up to young man?"

As William opened his mouth to answer, the ward sister interjected and shot him a cautionary glance "Road traffic accident sir, he was knocked off his bike" William gestured to speak and the ward sister shook her head at him.

"Ahhh the hit and run, yes I heard about that, nasty business. Well we shall look in on you again tomorrow and see if we can't send you home then." He glanced at William over his half rimmed spectacles, gave a forced professional smile, he placed the notes back on the hook at the end of the bed and breezed onto the next patient.

"Tomorrow?" William was flabbergasted, "but I'm ok, how come I'm staying in?" the doctors words had crushed his dreams for the evening, he had an overwhelming feeling of despair. Then, determined to make it to the evening he had been longing for, dreaming about for days, he leapt off the bed and began to follow the entourage. The friendliest of all the nurses stopped him with a panicked hand on his arm "What are you doing? That's Sir Richard, he is like God around here, he will go ballistic. What on earth is the matter?"

"He just said I had to stop in. Why? I have to get out, I have to go somewhere tonight . . ."

The nurse smiled and knowing smile "She's a lucky girl"

"What?" William was blushing

She just winked and led him back to his bed, his mother and Shirley sitting back down again having been slower to react than the pretty young nurse who now seemed to have everything back under control.

"Looks like I had better nip home and get you some Pyjamas Will, is there anything else you want?" said his mother, in an attempt to calm the situation further with something practical and caring.

"But I don't understand, he never even looked at me. It's just my arm and some bruises, it doesn't even hurt that much now."

The nurse was fussing him onto the bed now, "I'm afraid that's the painkillers we gave you kicking in, you will be sore later."

"So what, I might as well be sore doing something than stuck in here. Why can't I just leave and take some more pain killers later if it gets bad?"

She had to admire him, once again that attitude was appealing rather than the types that just came in and gave up expecting the nurses to become like hotel waiting staff, there to provide for their every need.

"I'm afraid because you had a bang on the head, and because it was part of an accident, we have to keep you in overnight for observation Will, Just in case" she said it with genuine compassion and empathy, using the informal form of his name as she had heard his mother do. She could see that her guess about the girl was not far from the mark and found it very romantic, "ahhh young love" she thought to herself, "shame they all grow up into bastards" her good looks and her uniform had attracted a lot of attention over the years and sadly she had fallen for more than one or two men that had used her and dumped her. The trouble was the other type just didn't seem to have any spark about them, she was addicted to bastards.

William's shoulders sagged as he accepted his lot, and for the first time that day he felt tears welling up inside and he felt a bit shaky too. The delayed shock was beginning to kick in, triggered by a profound sense of helplessness. He was confused by the feeling and cross with himself as he squeezed his eyes tight shut to stop the tears.

"Are you ok?" asked the nurse, and immediately regretted asking, seeing his embarrassment.

"Head hurt a bit?" she gave him a life line with the question.

He nodded, not trusting his voice and keeping his eyes tight shut.

"Never mind, you just lay back for a bit and I'll come by later. Get some rest, I'm afraid the police are going to need to talk to you later too."

The nurse left them all and William rolled on his side to face away from his mother and Shirley who was now beginning to feel a little out of place and made to get up and go. William's mother thanked her for all she had done and with a sympathetic look over her shoulder she bid them both goodbye and left awkwardly.

"Do you want me to stay for a bit Will?" asked his mother. She was feeling his pain with her mothering instinct, and while all she wanted to do was sweep her baby up into her arms and hold him close, she knew from bitter experience of bringing up three teenage boys that she had to stifle that desire and let them come to her.

"If you want Mum" "Actually, Mum no, I just want to be on my own for a bit." The words stung her, but she heeded them never the less.

"OK if you're sure love. I'll nip home and get some things for you and come back with Dad later."

She kissed his head and left. At that moment, William suddenly felt tired and lonely. The events of the day had shaken his world upside down, all he wanted to do was see Samantha, now he wondered whether he would ever get to see her at all. For a moment he began to feel sorry for himself and slipped into a depressed state of mind that threatened to poison him with toxic negativity. Then he looked up and looked around and thought of all the other people who were suffering in this place and he quickly pulled himself round.

"Get a grip" he said it out loud, then looked round again, this time in embarrassment, hoping nobody had heard him. It appeared they hadn't. He set his mind racing toward how he would turn the whole experience into a positive, rolled over and went to sleep, dressed in the hospital gown they had given him when they cut his school clothes off him earlier. "What would Bodie do now?" he thought to himself as he drifted off, running scenarios through his head in a morphed fantasy of becoming his favourite TV hero and sweeping Samantha off her feet bravely despite his injuries . . .

He woke up to strange voices and as he opened his eyes he looked straight into another pair that he recognised yet somehow couldn't place. His head genuinely throbbed now and as he cleared the fog of a day time sleep from his thoughts, he tried to assimilate the worried looking face before him. Where had he seen that face before?

Then it struck him as he flashed back to that frozen moment in time when they had held eye contact before, earlier that same day, through the windscreen of the Cortina. It was her, it was the girl in the car. He noticed that she had a bruise on her right cheek, she must have hit it in the car during the accident, but how? The bruise emphasised how pretty she was, and once again the eye contact was intense, like it had been in those few fleeting micro-seconds of the collision. What was happening today?

She opened her mouth to speak when he awoke, but no words would come and she looked like a fish out of water gaping and closing her nervousness all encompassing.

The policeman suddenly picked up the change in mood and looked over to see William awake, breaking the conversation with William's father whos attention now was also with his son.

What time was it? William thought to himself. The ward seemed to be different, was it darker? No but certainly artificial light gave it the feeling of evening.

"We can do this very quickly now, and tie up all the loose ends sir." The policeman was saying to William's father.

"Hello William" he said smiling "how are you feeling?"

"Fine thanks" but he felt a stab of pain as he attempted to push up onto his elbows and sank back down into the pillows to re-plan the manoeuvre.

"This is Catrina Hemmings" he gestured toward the young lady who now blushed and looked down at her feet. "Do you recognise her William?"

"Yes, yes I do"

"Could you tell me where from?"

"From the car, she was in the car!"

"Where in the car? Sorry William, but this is very important"

"In the passenger seat." He was looking directly at her now and as she raised her eyes to meet his she attempted a thin smile and was evidently relieved when she saw that there was not a hint of malice in William.

"Thank you William." The PC was writing in his notebook "This young lady has been very helpful William and sadly is as much a victim in all this as you, we'll find him"

William looked confused, as Catrina meekly said to him "I'm so sorry."

"You have nothing to be sorry for" the impatient voice of a man who must have been her father cut in from behind her "can we go now?" his question was directed to the policeman.

"Yes, thank you for all your co-operation. Look after her."

"I've been doing that quite well for years young man!" the man turned on his heel and hailed Catrina "Come along then, let's get you home." She glanced one more time and William, an apologetic look, one that almost said that she didn't want to go, but then she was gone.

The policeman explained the events that unfolded while William had slept. How the girl had come to the police station and reported the whole thing. How her now very much ex boyfriend had tried to take her away with him, to "go on the run" as he had put it, but she had screamed and screamed until he stopped the car and she opened the door and fled, not looking back but hearing the squeal of his tires for one last time as he sped away. This had made the investigation so much simpler, and William's unprompted corroboration along with the couple who stopped to help tied it all together nicely. Now they just had to catch the little bugger and they had a juicy case to take to court. Even better, the lad was well known to the police as a bad egg. A bully boy who was rotten, but they had never had anything to charge him with before. They suspected he was into petty crime, but now they had a list of serious charges to levy against him and hopefully it would be one less baddy at large very soon.

As the policeman left, William's father said his formal goodbyes, something in his natural manner causing the policeman to act subservient, he almost saluting as he withdrew. "you ok buster?" the affectionate name his dad used when they were alone.

"Dad I'm fine, I want to go to D of E."

Jack Dole looked down at his son and smiled at the fighting spirit he saw laying in the hospital bed. Of course he had felt the knot twist in his gut earlier when he had heard the news, but he was satisfied now that his boy was just fine.

"Why would you want to do that when there are all these pretty nurses fawning over you?" he said with a chuckle. "I wouldn't mind a day or two of it . . ."

"Daaaaad . . ."

His father was right, he was the centre of attention, and had made headline news in the otherwise routine little district hospital, but all William could think of was the missed opportunity of meeting Samantha again. He closed his eyes to dream of her as he had done so many times in the last few days, but the image of her face would not form. Had he lost her? The pain he felt in his heart unlike the rest of his body could not be cured with drugs, it was his to bare alone, it would be a long and lonely night.

Heartbeat heaven had almost turned into heartbreak hell.

Top Tips - Managing pain.

It may seem a little pretentious to suggest that one can manage their own pain, but from personal experience and evidence gathered from other people I can absolutely attest that you can. Physical pain is easier to manage than emotional pain, as most of us can testify to, but the process is almost the same. That said, we are all of us different, however if anyone takes anything from this and it helps them in future then I will feel a sense of achievement having helped someone.

For Millions of years humans have survived without pain relieving drugs, animals of course still do. That said, our quality and longevity of life has been vastly improved with the introduction of drugs and medicines. Because of that I am certainly not going to pretend that there is some mystical inner strength that means we can all do without modern medicine. That would be a hugely regressive step for us. However, unless we are very very lucky, most of us at some time have to cope with pain (yes ladies, I agree we men don't know the half of it).

We know that when faced with adversity or trauma, the body releases chemicals such as adrenaline, neuro-drenaline and chortisol (a steroid), which act as a pain relieving drug. This is the bodies way of getting us out of immediate danger so that we can slip into the cave and "lick our wounds". But how is it that people are able to cope with unbelievable sustained pain? Do we just get used to it and become desensitised? To an extent I would say yes, but that's not the answer.

My personal story around pain management :

I learned the technique on the parade ground in Winter during my basic training. Wearing a sailor suit in early February when the wind and snow and rain are lashing at you from the coast, is not a pleasant experience. The upper chest and neck are completely exposed, the square necked, white fronted shirt is just a thin layer of cotton. You cannot wear a vest underneath, as it would show, and the heavy serge jacket forms a V down to the middle of the torso. The cold hurts, but actually it's not the pain itself that I wanted to talk about. With bodies standing to attention all shivering

James H. Leet

uncontrollably you feel a sense of absurd pride in not giving up and letting down the rest of the squad. Not that you could without suffering the consequences, and there is the first point, often the alternative is worse than the immediate suffering . . . worth thinking about. My lesson came from a firm but friendly voice at the back of the squad one morning "Relax into it lads . . ." what on earth did that mean? When I first heard that I thought it was ridiculous, how could that help? Then I tried it! I stopped holding myself against the cold, muscles clenched in shiver mode, and just let myself relax. I trusted the fact that we were all there together and that the parade staff would not let us slip into hyperthermia. Then something interesting happened. My mind was wandering, working hard to keep active. One of the key things about standing still and not feinting on parade is to keep your brain working, running stories, singing songs, it doesn't matter, just as long as you are always ready for the next command and always thinking. I began to analyse the sensation of being cold. It was as if I was a research scientist analysing a subject. My brain became impartial to my bodies suffering. I thought deeply about pain, and the itched that I could not scratch, I analysed the sensation. Then I told myself that, while they are all very unpleasant at best, I was dealing with it right now, so I could deal with it in the next second, and the next and however many seconds it took before we could move again and relieve the pain.

That technique stayed with me. Years later I needed it in a far more traumatic scenario. I jumped off something too high and landed badly on the back of both heals. The ankle joints were badly fractured and both tubular and fibular bones were split, the fragments from the ankles ramming between them. I said Ouch I think. Then I realised that I needed to walk on them. I stood and analysed the searing pain . . . My body was doing its job, releasing chemicals. I was young, fit and mentally strong. I tried a step, it hurt, but I had stepped! So I tried another, it was worse because I had now rolled through a full sequence of movement and weight transfer, I analysed the pain and was angry with it. I had beaten it with two steps, I had evidence that both legs worked so I did it again and again. In hindsight I probably caused a lot more damage but it got me to where I needed to be. During the next week I had to keep the ankles moving so that they didn't set where they were. They needed an operation but the swelling was too bad. Three times a day a doctor would come in and "manipulate" them . . . not pleasant. The interesting thing is that during that week, I coped, and I coped well, with pride and anger keeping me going, analysing the whole time. Weeks later when I was "comfortable" I would go nuts if anyone went anywhere near them, a stark reminder of how the brain forgets pain and reframes things in line with how you feel now. You don't know what you can tolerate until you need to, case in point the everyday phenomenon of childbirth.

Mental pain is obviously more complicated but the same principal applies (to me anyway) but this subject is for another book . . .

CHAPTER 13

FOCUS AND FUN

William was a showman, he was a brilliant dancer and had a musical ear that could pick up a rhythm and just let his body unconsciously roll with the beat. William would tolerate a discussion around records for a while, but he wanted to be where the action was. He was waiting for Madness to come on, so that he could launch into his kind of dancing. Tonight he was dressed for the occasion in his burgundy stay press and pure white Fred Perry shirt. Close cropped hair being a requirement of Cadet regulations gave him the excuse he needed to complete the look without losing favour with his parents (they had absolutely refused his request for a crew cut, but they had reached a nice compromise). As the first, unmistakable bars of "Baggy Trousers" blared out of the speakers, William launched into the dance. His timing was perfect, as the energetic ska dance took him to the centre of the main-deck where his delighted friends were cheering him on gleefully. He imagined being Suggs on Top of the Pops and mimicked the movements, knees lifting high with corresponding elbows, a little skip of the other foot as the head moved in time with the almost reggae style two step beat, an imaginary saxophone using an improvised arm as the instrument, thumb in mouth as if blowing it. William loved the audience and the adoration from the other boys, but what he hadn't really considered was that the girls were also watching.

It was now 1981 and the months that had followed the accident had been a rollercoaster. He had made his entrance to D of E and had been crushed to see what he thought was going to be the new love of his life sitting on the knee of a long haired older boy he recognised from the Grammar school. It had seemed that William just wasn't her type and the more he had tried to impress her with his extrovert ways, the more he seemed to shove her away.

Despite finding his first attraction to the club frustratingly unavailable, William had taken to the Duke of Edinburgh's award scheme with alacrity. It enhanced everything he wanted to do. He was able to use his Cadet activities to earn achievements and it also introduced him to another club which was to renew his passion for swimming. He had joined the Royal Life Saving Society and become a qualified life guard in order to fulfil a section of the D of E book. He easily worked up through the Bronze Medallion award required to become a pool lifeguard, but also chose to take the Bronze and Silver Cross which qualified him in open water also. This was much more challenging and William relished the cold water and the strenuous exercise. He also relished the attention his status got while patrolling in his bright red RLSS speedo's and yellow and red skull cap. Many of the summer weekends were taken up patrolling a gravel pit that had been turned into an unofficial place of leisure by hundreds of locals. Sadly there had been a tragic accident whereby someone had drown having got tangled in weeds out of their depth and panicked in the cold waters. Unable to keep the locals from the pit which had many beach like qualities, the local council decided to invest in making it safe instead, hence the club were asked to combine their training with active patrols at the site. William had been in his element.

All of his extra, out of school activities were taking William nearer and nearer toward his goal of joining the Royal Navy. He now had a club to attend every night of the week except for Thursdays which he dedicated to as much homework as he could stand, his one driver being the qualifications he needed to get in the RN. His teachers had in the main supported him, with one or two exceptions who were actively against out of school activities that had the potential to impact on study. William chose to ignore them and committed to do the best he could with the time he had.

He was going through the selection process with the RN Careers office, who along with his father were pushing him down the route of joining as an Officer. They had suggested that if he were to achieve five good O levels he could scrape into training as a helicopter pilot, and take a degree while he was in the RN as top up to his education. When the results of his mock exams came through, they were forced to re-evaluate that position. With some regret, having identified clear leadership potential, the Officer in charge of recruitment, handed the case over to his Fleet Chief Petty Officer (the equivalent of a Warrant Officer) and recommended that William be processed as an Artificer Apprentice. This presented William with a dilemma, he really wanted to wear the uniform of a British Sailor, the blue collar the white front, the cap … He had been pushing back against the officer route because of this but now he had more reason to. Artificer apprentices were put through four years of technical training, much of that at sea, and past out as a senior rate or Petty Officer at the end of it. They wore a Petty Officers uniform from the moment they joined, but without the rate insignia and with a different cap badge. They were therefore a limbo rate that were much maligned outside their own circles. William's dilemma was between the prospect of fast track promotion weighed against a loss of identity as the proud sailor he had tattooed to his subconscious goal. It was a battle his subconscious was to win, and in the end he convinced his father and the careers officer that he wanted to be a Weapons Engineer and wear the finest uniform the world had ever seen. There were four hundred applicants for three places, and William was determined to be one of the three.

This night was a Saturday night. It was a D of E, fund raising disco. They were charging £1 for people to get in and hoping to raise £100 for the club funds. An easy win, organised by the club members, DIY discos had been an idea borrowed from Cadets and made better by one club members set of multi-coloured flashing lights, and the big hall of the youth club that was used as a base for D of E.

The paying guests hadn't yet arrived, and as the club members were testing out the equipment William took his place at centre stage with relish. While the boys whooped encouragement, the girls couldn't help but be swept up with the art.

Samantha had never really felt all that comfortable around William, in that she found him attractive physically but he was way too keen, so she had just put her shutters up. The other girls had spoken to her about him and were jealous that he seemed to like her and not them. One in particular had a real crush on him and at any opportunity would brush against him suggestively bit he would simply brush her off with a witty remark, cutting her to the bone and making her want him more. Samantha or Sammy as she was known at D of E, was strikingly beautiful and had boys falling at her feet, it was actually frustrating for her, how she longed for a boy that would make her heart race, that she could pursue, she was fed up being the fox, she wanted to do the chasing, but no one ever gave her that challenge and it made her feel like an object so she withdrew.

She was however a young woman, with chemistry flowing through her body and a quick mind that needed stimulation outside of school. She was a year older than William, she had just turned 16 and as she watched William's athletic grace on the dance floor, she thought "what the hell, I might play a game with that one . . ."

The group had decided to divide up the various duties on the night and Samantha was in charge of the rota. She had managed to work it out so that the half hour slots of free time had worked in a way that she and William were off together. The duties included running the snack bar, which was a serving hatch from the kitchen area through to the main hall, sweeping around with eyes open looking for trouble makers or alcohol that might have been smuggled in, then reporting it to one of the few parents who had volunteered to be adult supervision, taking ticket money on the door and running the disco.

As the evening came the hall quickly filled. They had sold over a hundred tickets on the door and sales were going well at the snack bar so the target had been surpassed already, the evening was shaping up to be a great model of success. Samantha and William had been working on the snack bar together and it was nearing the end of their shift. William had become conscious that Sammy didn't want him and had backed off with his attentions and was carefully trying to avoid physical contact with her in the tight space behind the counter, as he didn't wish to push her away any further. Unbeknown to him, Sammy was finding his aloofness exciting, especially given her plan from earlier, she was getting the hots for him right here right now.

The relief column arrived bang on time "Ok you guys, have fun" It was Paul, one of the other club members who was heavily into heavy metal, William had no time for that head banging crowd. He made to disappear into the crowd, when Sammy caught his hand and said "we don't have to go anywhere do we, I need a sit down but there is only that stool." She gestured to a swivel topped stool that was fixed to the floor on the hall side of one end of the serving hatch. People were pushing against it to get to the hatch but it was nothing like the queue at the tuck shop in school, just a few people at a time were patiently waiting to be served. "Get that for me will you?"

"I can't its stuck there"

"Then I guess you will have to protect me from the crowd then." She gave him such a cheeky smile, he had never seen such mischief in her eyes, he was under her spell once again and eager to please.

He joined the queue politely, his sense of duty as "an official" preventing him from steaming in like a bull at break time, then positioned himself in such a way that he was able to turn his back on the crowd and side on to the hatch counter had made just enough space for her to slide onto the stool, her back pushing into his front as he leant on the counter with one elbow facing the stool. He felt an immediate surge of blood to his system and hoped that he would not become embarrassed by it, but to his amazement it didn't seem to register with Sammy.

As Sammy slipped up onto the stool, she saw her father through the crowd catch her eye from the periphery of the hall where he was keeping an eye out for trouble makers. At the same time as she had this visual communication from her father, she felt the hard body of William against her back, and was aware of the proximity between them. Like some voyeuristic guilty pleasure, she felt a surge of excitement at this naughty act that her father couldn't see and yet was happening before him. She felt a fresh flush of excitement, and her cheeks reddened. Her senses were alive and tingling at the combination of physical and psychological stimulation.

William had naively thought for a moment that she had not noticed his closeness. Then something terrible yet incredible happened. She had slowly begun to swivel the stood back and forward, rubbing against him. How could she be so cruel? This was driving him wild with excitement, the straining feeling as the blood pounded in his ears was exquisitely intense, almost painful. His forearm was wedged on the counter, the palm of his hand turned inward, he was stuck there by the pushing mass of people which was hiding the whole private scene from the rest of the world. He groaned what he thought was an internal groan, at which she turned further to say "What was that?" her face went from devilish grin to lip biting and eyes closed.

As she had swivelled the stool a half turn toward him, the cup of his hand experienced a seemingly accidental encounter. She wore only a vest top under a silky white blouse, and in close confines of their predicament the consequences were inevitable. She had never felt such an intense feeling like this, she was aware of herself as a young woman but she had no idea she could be made so instantly charged with electricity by someone else's touch other than her own. Her pleasure receptors were sending messages through her body and mind, making her tense her muscles involuntarily as she felt heart pound in her chest.

William felt the same surge of pleasure, as the contact traced a path over his palm, he felt a sudden empathy with her and instantly this new sensation was like a thunderbolt to the brain. His mind was filling in the gaps in the picture that his brain was building from the information it was receiving, made all the more exciting because the rest of the world was oblivious to the contact between them.

"My Dad is watching" she said huskily

"Oh my god is he?" William tried to pull his self away with some reluctance, but found that he was pinned by the proximity of the crowd and was effectively stuck fast.

She swung back to the front, thereby breaking moment and said "It's OK he couldn't see"

He was however looking over at the barely hidden guilt on William's face and his protective instinct told him to keep watching this young man who was standing way too close to his precious daughter.

The touch that had come as an accident developed into a game designed to extend the pleasure.

"Do you want a drink?" asked William

"Ooh let me see what there is . . ." Samantha replied, already knowing the answer but using the excuse to swivel.

"How are the takings?" she asked swivelling once more to heavy metal Ken, who was none the wiser as to the real reason for her enquiry.

William had cottoned on quickly to her willingness to participate in the game "Do you think Ken's hair has got any longer?"

"ooh let me check . . ." swivel.

The strain was becoming too much for William, when as if on cue the slow dances came on.

As the first bars of John Lennon's hit Just like starting over beat out, the dynamic of the dance floor changed, couples made their way to smooch, and William felt the press behind him move which was his opportunity to take Sammy to the dance floor, she did not resist and relished the contact between them to the extent where she wished she was just a fraction taller . . .

As they swayed to the rhythm of the beautiful ballad, William was conscious of her father eyes boring into the back of his head. Giddy with the euphoria of having got away with not being seen at the bar, William's hands stroked Samantha's back while it was turned in the direction of her Dad, then slipped to her just above her bottom while his own back was to him. Despite the fact that he had five minutes before had her literally in the palm of his hand, he now found it daunting to cross the threshold once more and each time they revolved through 360 slow degrees he edged further and further down on his journey from back to bottom.

There was a pause while the record was changed to the next slow track, Smokey Robinson—Being with you, and they settled into the rhythm once more.

She longed to feel his hands on her bottom and buried her head into his neck so as not to face her father at any time, she was disorientated and swept up with passion and desire, she had no idea which way she was facing, but had intelligently worked out William's tactics and smiled at the thought. Each time they revolved round and his hands fell to the base of her spine, she craved more and pushed into him, he responded by teasing further each time.

Finally as the third and final slow dance of this particular "erection section" (that was living up to its name for sure) came on, Williams hands slid down to hold her perfect pert bottom in his hands. Each cheek fell into his palms to the sound of REO Speedwaggon—I'm gonna keep on lovin' you . . .

He wanted with all his heart to kiss her fully on the mouth, but he could still feel the intense eyes of her father bearing down on him and decided instead to nibble her neck, naively thinking that this would be ok with her father.

The pace changed slightly with ABC's When Smokey sings, a few tried to keep pace with the new beat but the spell was broken and the floor began to fill once more with the dance moves of singular protagonists.

Samantha had been called by her Dad and squeezed his hand in reassurance as she left him with a lingering glance. William could still feel the raging urgency of his heightened state and disappeared to the toilets to relieve the pressure on his bladder at least at the urinal, hoping this would give him some small comfort.

Her father wasn't the only male in the room to have viewed the spectacle with distaste. "Look at that posh twat." Sneered the boy that had recently been let in with six of his mates, all bigger than him and all in the same class at school. It was the boy that had almost had William labelled as a bully a couple of years ago. He had stayed out of William's way at school, fearing the humiliation of another run in and fearing the physical confrontation it might bring. But here he had his mates around him, at least three of which hadn't even bothered going to school for the last year. "Let's get the twat" Fuelled on the drink that they had drunk from the off-licence, they were spoiling for a fight, and they had found their excuse in William. As they made to follow him into the toilet, they were too late, William was making his way out, and intuitively knew that something was going to happen.

He instantly picked out the gang coming toward him and knew from the body language that a physical confrontation was inevitable. Strangely however, his first thought was not for himself but for his responsibility to the club, this had to somehow go outside. The toilets however were situated half way down the hall, so William made his move toward the main entrance as the first blow struck him on the side of the head. He felt no pain, as the gang pushed through the throng of dancers to get to their quarry. They mistakenly thought that William was simply running to get away from them and had the smell of blood in their nostrils like a dog chasing a hare.

William could hear the unmistakable voice of the ringleader, happily hiding behind his henchmen, goading them on "Look at the posh little twat run"

Another blow hit him on the back of the head, and as he turned to look he caught another on the corner of his eyebrow, a warm, numb sensation told him it would begin to swell almost immediately, but still he felt no real pain, he was totally focussed on getting them to chase him outside. They couldn't ruin the disco . . .

He was almost to the front entrance before the adults cottoned on to what was happening, and he had taken several blows by now and blood was seeping from his cut eye brow. He heard an authoritative shout from the other side of the room and there was a bustle in the room as it slowly dawned on people that trouble had kicked off.

They tumbled out onto the street and the gang expected to chase William down it, but when he turned something in his eyes made them all stop. He was no match for them all at once, but the same fear that creeps into a mob of rioters when faced with an organised minority began to eat at the gang. No one individual wanted to commit and they began to circle him instead.

William knew that any second adults would be there to sort things, but he also now had his own pride to salvage. It was payback time. He fixed his eyes on his old adversary for a second and watched him sneer as he moved back behind his bigger friends. As William then scanned the group his choice was made for him, the biggest of the bunch ran at him. William let him come, and at the last second rocked to his left and swung his right fist in an arc as hard as he could. It landed with a sickening thwack square on the nose of the charging brute and instantly, in a spray of blood, the nose broke and was seemingly spread across the boy's face like a burst blood orange. His feet went from under him as they carried on under the momentum of his run and he landed flat on his back, the back of his head hitting the pavement. Seconds later he was lying in the gutter snorting blood from his nose and holding the back of his head, the fight gone from him.

William had timed the blow elegantly, all his sporting prowess combined with the strength from the physical hardship of lifesaving, rowing and living the way he did. He was balanced like a cat, and he threw out the challenge "Who else . . . ?"

"I might have known . . . it's the bloody groper!" It was Samantha's father.

The appearance of the adult was all the excuse the gang needed as they bolted into the night, lost in the streets with a minute, leaving William to face the music. "Some bloody helper you are, starting a fight on a night like this, I knew you were no good, you should be kicked out. In fact I'll bloody well make sure you are."

William couldn't respond, he stood with his mouth open and suddenly his legs felt like jelly as the adrenaline that had been fuelling his system dissipated and he began to shake.

Other's began to pour out onto the street, among them Samantha "Oh my god are you ok?" she began to run to him but was caught with a hand round her wrist by her father, who's opinion of William had been heavily influenced by the scene he had witnessed some thirty minutes before. "Oh no you don't young lady, come on, we are going home."

She looked back over her shoulder, an almost apologetic look of concern on her helpless but beautiful face. He wanted to kiss her more than anything at that moment but it was the last time he would ever see that lovely face again.

William was hardly conscious of being bundled back inside by the other adults. There was already a buzz in the room as the stories were quickly being circulated around William's haymaker that had brought down one of the biggest bullies in town. All William could think about was that look on Sammy's face. The first pain he felt was the sting of the wet cotton wool as it touched his eye and smeared away the first clot of blood. At the second application the tear in his skin protested with more pain, and systematically the throbbing began to spread. In the space of a minute he had gone from no pain, to not knowing which bit to hold or where to put himself, and he was slipping into a mild state of shock. What would Dad say? What would the careers office think? "I was just trying to get them out of the disco." There was a tearful quiver in his voice that surprised and angered William to feel.

"You should have come to us William, it's what we are here for."

But he knew he had made the right decision, there was no point in arguing about it now. "I want to go home."

"we'll call your Dad."

Top Tips - focus and fun

If you really want something, really want it, then you can have it. The decisions you make will help you get it. Those decisions usually involve the amount you are prepared to give up to get what it is you want. In other words you become obsessive about your goal and the feeling you have inside is a little like the one when you are playing an addictive game and a little voice says "just one more go". You know it's bed time, you promise yourself to turn the game off at 11pm but you find yourself heavy eyed three hours later still saying "just one more go". That is obsessive goal hunting and the gaming industry thrive on our human instinct to pursue it.

The trick in life is to get the balance right. But it is more than just work life balance. Constantly look for a stimulus that enhances both sides, fun hobbies that enhance your working life or contribute to family life. Not many of us have the perfect job, but that shouldn't stop us from obsessively striving toward it by improving ourselves along the way.

The perfect job is one that you love doing so much that you would be prepared to do it for free, then you become so good at it that people are prepared to pay you.

Unless you are a gifted football player or child singing sensation it is unlikely that you will fall into this job before you hit a decent age, but that shouldn't stop us from adding value to our lives and collecting little gems along the way that can add to the ultimate lifestyle. I am being deliberately vague because only you know what good looks like (or maybe you don't just yet). It's not about money though! That may sound like an old cliché, but the moment it just becomes about money the passion wears thin. Money will be a natural consequence of success and it will feel all the better for being generated with passion rather than necessity. It is also a great metric for measuring just how successful you are, but then so are the smiles on your children's faces or the look of unconditional love you get from that special someone, or even a pet.

So the balance is about being obsessive about what you want for sure, but then making the right decisions about what you are prepared to give up to get there, and also giving yourself the time to stop and smell the flowers from time to time.

It's your goal, you decide!

CHAPTER 14

GHOST IN THE WATER

While William's father had been concerned over the incident and the possible repercussions, he was also quietly proud of his son, not just for the way that he had dealt with yet another bully in his life but the moral values that had emerged during the interrogation that had been conducted the following day. His mother couldn't see it, she wanted him to give up all these extra activities and any thought of joining up. She had never wanted William to join up, she had too many painful memories of sitting at home pining for her sweetheart all those years ago, and now here was that same sweetheart seemingly happy to allow that whole cycle to repeat itself with flesh from her own body.

As usual, she calmly and quietly conformed and pushed the painfully nagging thoughts to the back of her mind, but the residual feeling remained in the pit of her stomach. She busied herself, resigned to whatever course of action transpired.

Gradually the scars healed and the bruises disappeared, once those evidential signs had gone, the incident became less talked about as more topical happenings came and went. The incident was one that would be talked about and embellished many times in the future depending on which side of the story was told, thereby consigning it to the status of mini legend.

William had been more concerned with losing contact with Sammy. She had never returned to D of E, every week he looked around expectantly whenever the door of the hall opened, only to feel his heart sink when it was someone else who came through it. He had looked for her number in the phone book, not knowing her father's name he had systematically gone through every number with Sammy's surname, spending his bag of 2p's at the local phone box. None of his calls were successful. She must have been listed as ex-directory. He had then begged for her number every week at D of E and was told that it was absolutely out of the question to share that information. He wrestled with the idea of going through the filing cupboard while nobody was looking and dismissed it as the wrong thing to do, tempting tough it was.

Dick Binns was a lad that rarely turned up to D of E but when he did was always vocal as if he had the answer to everything. He had been there forever and achieved nothing. In the beginning William had respected him for his seniority, but as time had gone on and William had moved up through the system with his sights set on achieving the Gold award, Dick had been left in the Bronze group. William had asked him about this, dick had merely replied that he had loads of time and if he didn't get it till he was 24 so what? In a strange way William envied his lazy approach, he seemed happy, but William felt a sense of urgency burn in him for everything he did and knew he could never be like Dick.

Dick came over to William during the break on one of his rare visits and said "What's up with you, you are normally the life and soul, why so quiet?"

"I'm not!" said William defensively.

"Yes you are" a defiant smile was plastered on Dick's clean complexion. In that moment William envied his good looks and clear skin, his own face had recently suffered an eruption of teenage acne which he was suddenly very conscious of. Dick's hair was long to the shoulder and had a shine to it unlike some of the dirty looking dishevelled rock fans, the type that were associated with the greasy biker club. He was taller than William and a little unconventional in his appearance, certainly not fashionable in the way he dressed, yet there was something enigmatic about him that made him likable.

"Doesn't matter"

"ahh so there is something" the smile broadened as if he had found the first clue to a great mystery and was now on the scent.

"Yes, but like I said, it doesn't matter" William felt a momentary surge of anger which must have flashed in his eyes.

"OK, OK, I don't want to upset you . . ." his hands were up as if William were pointing a gun in his face, but the smile remained "I heard what you did at the disco." There was a pause ". . . and the fight hehe"

William was turned now "What do you mean *and* the fight?"

"Well that was impressive, but your real coup that night was pulling Sammy, she is a tough nut to crack that one. I had a go myself ages ago, went round her house once too, very possessive father, no boy will ever be good enough for that one!"

"What? You know where she lives?" Williams eyes were full of hope, they pleaded with Dick in the question they asked.

Dick beamed triumphantly at the revelation he had uncovered, "So that's it!" "Ha, you bugger you, don't tell me her Dad won't let you talk to her . . ."

"Chance would be a fine thing" William slumped back into his resigned state.

"What do you mean? Surely you have rung her"

"Can't, haven't got the number, can't find it anywhere."

"Well why didn't you say so old mate, I've got it!"

The words didn't seem real, they took a moment to sink in, "You, you've got her number?" it was a tentative question, seeking confirmation that he was hearing this right.

"Yep" Dick was smiling back, and not with any malice or teasing intent to get a power trip out of the situation. That kind of thing didn't really motivate Dick. "You want it?"

William was almost trembling at the thought. His mouth opened but no words would form.

"Well, do you?" a concerned brow furrowed on Dick's forehead.

"Yes please"

Dick recited the number from his head.

"You are having me on right? That's not really her number is it?"

"Why wouldn't it be?"

"You just made that up in your head!"

"Try it!"

"You sure?"

"Try it! I am not going to give the slugger a bad number am I, I might just be next in the firing line for a whack"

"Blimey, what was it again?"

And so it was that William had in his hand a potential ticket to heaven. For the rest of the evening his mind could only think of one thing, phoning Sammy.

He was due to walk home and so he had formed his plan, he would call her from a phone box on the way.

During the break he bought himself a carton of Calypso orange drink for 10p not because he was thirsty or because he particularly liked them, in fact they were pretty awful. He bought one because he needed to change the pound note he had in his pocket for the phone later. He now had a 50p and four 10p's. The 10p's would work and should give him plenty of time at this hour in the day, if not he had one or two 2p's in his pocket too for the last few seconds of snatched conversation. He thought of nothing else for the rest of the evening, she was bound to be excited to hear from him after the last time they met. There was no way he had mis-read any signals . . .

He had the number written down on a scrap of paper in the pocket of his burgundy stay pressed trousers, and his hand kept reaching inside every few seconds to make sure that he hadn't lost it.

By the time he got to the phone box, his heart was pounding with anticipation. He lifted the receiver and the smell of the composite handset mixed with stale urine that was unique to phone boxes reached his sensory system adding to the feeling of slight sickness in his stomach. Why did he always feel like this when it came to girls he really liked?

He pulled the number from his pocket and began to sequentially push his fingers into each number and move the dial round to the stop and wait for it to return, before dialling the next. The phone rang four times at the other end, the tinny tone reaching Williams ear as he begged her silently to answer the phone. It hadn't dawned on him that perhaps it would be her that picked up. "Hello?" It was a man's voice.

William felt a surge of panic and opened his mouth like a goldfish a couple of times before speaking, he almost forgot to push the 10p into the slot, the action snapping out of his mute state "Hello, is Sammy . . . Samantha there please?"

"Who is this?" the voice was aggressively defensive.

"It's Will from D of E"

"Ah, the groper!" it was a direct and hostile accusation, and for a moment William thought of slamming the phone down, but his own pride wouldn't let him. He remained silent, waiting to see what would happen next.

As if he had passed some kind of test, he heard the voice now slightly distant from the phone "Samantha! It's the groper! Make it quick!"

A pause . . .

"Hello?" the voice hardly sounded like the Sammy he knew, the confidence had turned into a timid whisper. "Will? Is that you?"

"Yes, hi Sammy" William's beaming smile could be heard by Sammy as he spoke over the phone line.

"Will, I can't see you again, sorry. I won't be coming back to D of E! It's exams and everything, Daddy sais I have to let things go and concentrate on school. I'm sorry Will" Her voice betrayed the white lie.

William's heart sank and he felt the pit of his stomach ball up into his chest, "But that's just crazy Sam, you can't let him do this . . ."

"I'm sorry Will"

He was sure he heard her cry just as she put the phone down on him.

From elation to despair in the space of a couple of hours, now William stood in the phone box suddenly aware that the stink was unpleasant. The mind now tuned in to negative emotion was telling him that the whole world stank especially the little space he occupied at the moment. He suddenly felt sick and couldn't get out of the box quick enough.

He walked home in a state of shock, his hopes and dreams crushed, he could still smell the stale pungent aroma of the phone box and his unconscious mind was busy associating it with the feeling of bitter disappointment and nausea was presenting itself as a result.

William sucked in a big lung full of night air and looked up at the stars as he did so. The distinctive figure of Orion was low on the late summer horizon in front of him as walked home toward the South East. With its distinctive three stars in a line representing the belt of the great hunter it dominated the sky as one of the few constellations that were easy to see at a glance. William often looked at the stars, wishing he knew them all, always promising himself he would learn them but never getting round to it. He looked above Orion's belt to see the bright and sparkly star to the left, it was Beatleguesse, the brightest thing in that part of the sky that night, and he wondered if Sammy was looking at the same star . . . Then, he snapped out of his melancholy as he realised that the stars never changed, they would still be here looking down on everyone's little woes every night and not caring. With a huge sigh he said aloud "Ah well, on on!" He felt the need to run, and run he did, filling his lungs once more and purging his respiratory system.

By the time he was home he felt better. His mind had moved onto tomorrow, where he might even bump into another beauty (you never know). He was due to be lifeguarding at the gravel pits. The skill required to lifeguard outdoors was far in advance of simply supervising a pool. There was so much more to consider such as the elements, the cold, water quality, visibility, weeds, current not to mention the attitude of the public that were there toward compliance and safety. William had breezed through his pool qualifications, but the bronze and silver cross that were awarded for outdoor lifeguarding were far more difficult to achieve than the award of Merit for the pool and William relished the challenge. They also scored very highly toward the D of E gold award he was pursuing.

And so it was that the next day William found himself proudly walking around in his RLSS bright red Speedo's and the red and yellow skull cap that signified him as an on duty life guard. He was oblivious to the taunts of the boys that jeered him and his colleagues, he knew that they envied his status and would never start any real trouble anyway. The lifeguards were generally regarded as a massive benefit and the self-appointed picnic spot had been adopted by local families and sun bathers for the past couple of years. The Council had taken the approach that if they couldn't police it, they may as well make it safe and embrace it, which had gone down well in the community. The life saving club offered the council a cheap way of covering their backsides.

William was guilty of parading himself a bit on this day, his mind drifting back to last night and his pride glossing over the knock back, he puffed his chest and flexed his muscles to the crowd in the hope of impressing a girl or two.

The gravel pit was a sun trap. The gravel itself almost orange in colour was almost fine enough to feel like sand, albeit hardly the Caribbean. The old works had left a substantial bowl in the landscape that was now permanently filled with fresh water and a haven for fish and wildlife, nature finding a way to invade man's industrial legacy given half the chance. The spot was really quite pleasant on a sunny day, what had become the small lake was shaped like a kidney dish and trees surrounded the entire shore line with the exception of one section on the bottom shore of one end that had become, what you could term as a beach area. This was what made it so popular, there was a beach and plenty of privacy in trees to get changed or to have a private moment if you needed one.

William was fantasising over one such private moment, imagining a damsel in distress swooning over the handsome lifeguard and begging him to take her in the trees. When out of the trees that separated the two halves of the kidney shaped lake came bursting a bikini clad girl. He thought his prayers had been answered, then he registered the wide eyed panic and fear on the girls face. He was sure he had seen that look before . . . de ja vue maybe . . . she looked around frantically and when her eyes fell upon William she sprinted toward him arms gesticulating wildly.

She was gasping for breath when she reached him and almost slumped to the floor, but instead pulled at his arm and pointed "help . . ." was all she could manage through her panting distress.

William felt a burst of adrenaline and an instant almost professional distance from the situation itself and the training kicked in. "Show me!" he said firmly and dragged the girl in the direction from where she had come. As he jogged easily beside the now exhausted and terrified girl he activated his radio "Lifeguard one to base over . . ."

"Base, go ahead over . . ."

"Incident in progress, North side, scramble!"

"Roger that" it was the calm voice of the Club chairman and head lifeguard, himself an ex Royal Navy Officer who William idolised. He had introduced a military style communication system which was no nonsense and designed to deploy quickly when necessary.

Seeing someone else at the shoreline through the trees, William sprinted to them, leaving the exhausted girl behind him, to find another panic stricken face, eyes pleading with him to help almost with relief as if he would fix everything just by being there. He felt the burden of responsibility but relished it never the less.

"She she's out there, down there, oh my god help us please, she hasn't come up we can't swim."

William was quickly taking in facts and assessing the situation around him, "OK where did you last see her?"

"Just there . . ." the girl was pointing to about fifteen yards off shore to an area that William knew was thick with weed on the lake bed and about 10 feet deep. Warning signs were up telling people not to swim here.

He had no choice, he was going to have to go in and search "How long?"

"W, what?" the question didn't appear to register with the second girl.

"How long since you saw her?"

"I, I don't know, too long, oh my god, she's drowned!!"

"Don't panic, stay here!" William thrust the radio into the girls hand and waded out into the chilly water, waiting for the sharp drop he knew was coming. As he did so, he imaged that this is what must have happened, a false sense of security building in a weak swimmer in the shallows that suddenly fell away from under you into a murky, dark and cold depth that would take your breath away if you were not either ready for it, or used to it.

William was about ten yards out and up to his waist in water when he felt the sudden drop and the gravel shift from under his feet as if to suck him down. He was now happy to plunge in, knowing that there was deep water below him and little risk of landing on a discarded shopping trolley or other such hazard, so he swam the next few yards and turned to look back, treading water to get his bearings from where the girl had pointed from the shore. He saw the two girls hugging each other and heard them sobbing and whimpering.

He was happy he was in roughly the right place, took another reference from the tree-line so that he could start a systematic search pattern and duck dived down.

Visibility was very poor, at best eighteen inches. His eyes wide open he could make out the darkness of thick weed as he dived deep, his ears objecting to the pressure he pinched his nose and blew to equalise and felt his ears pop. Nothing, he could see nothing other than the fuzzy darkness of the weed refracted through the murky water to his unmasked eyes. He started a slow search, careful not to turn himself in circles so that he could reference where he had been for a second or third dive if he needed it. His lungs were beginning to burn in his chest as they protested at the lack of air, and he decided to surface. Going straight up, the last foot seemed like a mile as he burst to the surface and sucked in a great lungful of air. Immediately he referenced again with the shoreline, and was careful to stay still as he treaded water. He could see the back-up team running through the trees toward them now and knew there would be a canoe on its way from round the corner of the lake at any moment. He turned himself through 180 degrees, took another deep breath and dived again.

He went straight down so as to start exactly where he had left off and tracked back in the opposite direction. Something caught his eye, a fleeting wave of whiteness that disappeared the moment it had emerged. Was he seeing things? Was his mind making him see something he wanted to and playing tricks? He swam toward where he had seen the flash and the moving water allowed him another glimpse as the weed was swaying around to reveal what looked like a plastic bag. It was just a plastic bag! William knew that searching for a person down here was like trying to find a pin in a swimming pool. The black brick in a warm pool that was used for this purpose in training hardly seemed adequate now. Was it a bag?

He reached out his hand to move the weeds, their slimy texture taking on a sinister feel and for the first time William felt a hint of fear. There it was again, just two feet away, a swirling bag, but bags don't swirl like that . . . His heart thumped as he realised that what he was seeing was a shock of blond hair, and as he got close he could see beneath it the ghostly features in the shape of a pale face. His lungs were screaming again, he cupped his hand under the chin, it felt cold. He kicked up as hard as he could, his survival instinct begging him to let go and swim to the surface. Pulling on the chin was not getting him anywhere, the pain now almost unbearable and his kicks were beginning to become panicked ones. His hand slipped and he managed to grab the hair as he felt his momentum finally go up, but it was like kicking out at treacle, he was going nowhere. It seemed an eternity, he was going to have to let go and breathe soon or there would be two people down here in the murk to find. Something inside him drove him on. He had been under the water for almost a minute, on the edge of his lung capacity, the exertion making matters worse. He felt some progress and kicked hard once more but it was no good, he was going to have to let go. Then he felt arms under his own armpits and a sudden upward surge, he held tight to the hair as his brain fizzed with stars and pain on the edge of consciousness.

As his head broke the surface, the noise of the air filled environment invaded his ears snapping him back out of the surreal watery world that had muffled his senses. He let go of the hair, and submitted to the help of his colleague, the team having taken over the rescue.

Without realising how, his feet were now on the gravel, his wobbly legs taking him to shore, where he collapsed down onto his bottom, drew his knees up and let his head drop between them. He was cold and exhausted and more than a little grateful for the towel that had been thrown over his shoulders.

The girls were screaming and a crowd had begun to gather, as two lifeguards attempted to keep everyone away from the resuscitation effort that was going on. William looked over to see a very girl laying on her back receiving mouth to mouth, her skin was blue grey. It was as if he were watching a movie and none of this was real.

Within a few minutes the police arrived and took control of the crowd, a female officer with a very caring yet assertive voice was leading the two screaming girls away as two Paramedics swept in and took over the resuscitation.

William was sat in the lifeguard hut, his hands hugging his second hot chocolate, the two girls were being comforted by the police lady. The pit had been closed and the public dispersed shortly after the ambulance had sped away sirens wailing. A police inspector was talking to the lifesaving club chairman, debriefing the event, when a call came over his radio. He excused himself and went outside. Minutes later he came back in, spoke to the chairman once more whos body language immediately indicated something had developed. He walked into the middle of the hut and as expectant faces looked toward him he announced "Sorry everyone, I am sad to say the young lady has died on the way to hospital!"

William looked over at the two girls who were now in shocked silence, and his eyes met once more with the girl who had come to find him. He knew that look, he knew those eyes, he had seen that panic before . . . it was the girl in the passenger seat when he had been run over. "I'm sorry Catrina!" The silence was broken and Catrina burst into tears at the sound of her name, burying her head into the police ladie's tunic.

The inspector walked over to William, and with genuine admiration in his voice said "You are a very brave young man!"

Top Tips - Keep it real

We can all be forgiven sometimes for wallowing in self pity. Bad stuff happens to us all, and sometimes it just keeps coming and coming. It's an old cliché, but there really is always someone that is worse off than us, and we have to keep a reality check on the bigger picture. I am not pretending for a moment to presume that we can all think our way out of depression or make light of very real issues that individuals have to deal with on a daily basis. That said truly inspirational people do tend to get on with it and have a much more holistic approach to life.

William naturally did this when he looked up at the stars. Something else happened at that point though, something physical that he was unaware of. It is actually very difficult to feel depressed when we look up. The blue sky thinking lobes of the brain are at the back, the analytical ones at the front. So when we have our heads down analysing we become "down in the dumps" but things start "looking up" when we do just that. Keep your head held high, look the world in the eye, chin up, all these sayings have their origins based in evidence. The action of looking up helps the blood flow to the optimistic part of the brain, but in this case it also helped William think of the stars and put into context all they had metaphorically seen. The past has gone, we can't influence that, however we always have choices about the future. Choose head up and see the opportunities that are there or choose head down and analyse all the woe, each action can spiral.

Reality also means not getting over optimistic either. A lesson that was drummed into me as a boy came from one of my father's many wise sayings "Some people have their head so high in the clouds, they can't see the slub around their feet". Sometimes we just need to take a long hard look in the mirror and accept our strengths and weaknesses, and work on them both. You may be amazed at the strength you can find from within when you need it. You will also be amazed at how your body and mind will intuitively know when and how to defend itself.

It's worth asking the question every now and then "what does good look like?" then you can check reality and decide what you need to action to get somewhere near to good. One way you can get a reality check on that is to write down your goal set in the future but actually written in present tense. For example:

"It is 12 months from now and I am sitting in my living room planning a family holiday to the Maldives. There is a new car in the drive and I am running my own business. We have just signed up three hundred new customers and the business is going well."

If as you write that down you think there is no way this can be true, then it more than likely won't happen, so keep it real and tone it down to something that you can really see happening. Then make it engaging too, by ignoring traditional SMART thinking and using plain language. If you have ever used the SMART model for goal setting, you will probably have the same opinion as me, it's a great tool for being able to set metrics around success, but rarely does a SMARTly written goal ever really suck you in. We engage with goals because they are emotionally meaningful to us, not because we can measure them.

If you are unfamiliar with the acronym SMART there are a couple of versions, my favourite being this one:

Specific
Measurable
Agreed
Realistic
Time-framed
Ethical
Recorded

I know, that's SMARTER, but there's nothing wrong with being smarter.

In summary, keep it real, keep perspective, remember that ultimately you are in control of your own destiny by making the right choices at the right times. If the choices turn out to be the wrong ones, then recognising it early is crucial. If it's going to fail, then make sure it fails fast and then you can move on. Experienced business people often talk about intuitive failure. They accept that in order to innovate and evolve that it is inevitable that some ideas and projects will not be successful. When this happens it is sometimes difficult to give up on something that you have invested in both financially and emotionally, but it is absolutely critical that you do give up on it before you invest any more. Fail fast and move on.

CHAPTER 15

READY AYE
READY JACK

The weeks that followed had been no more than strange for William. He had been applauded, revered by some, sneered at by others, questioned by police but never by anyone else. He wondered why no-one else ever asked him about the day, he saw the questions in people's faces but somehow the questions never came. It hadn't occurred to him that people simply wouldn't know how to start such a conversation.

William himself had simply moved on past the day, it was as if it had happened to someone else, as if he had seen himself in the picture of a dream.

His mother had worried herself deeply over the incident when she had heard the details. She had lost far more sleep over it than had her son. She worried that William had taken it in his stride a little too easily, and she also worried in case the day came when he would break down over it. She didn't know what was worse.

William's father had left it a few weeks before he sat down with his son on a different level. He went into William's room while he was busy making a model of HMS Victory from and Airfix kit. His strategy was simple, just ask.

"Looking good Will!" he gestured toward the model, which immediately aroused suspicion in William. His father had never really shown an active interest in his modelling hobby, and only ever really gave praise for workmanship that was perfect and meaningful.

"I've noticed that you never talk about the drowning Will, do you think about it much?"

It was the first time William had ever heard anybody refer directly to the incident like that, and the question immediately cleared any uncomfortable clutter out of the way. "Sometimes Dad, but not much if I am honest."

"You ok with it?"

"What do you mean?"

"Does it feel ok with you? . . . Inside?" Jack Dole was choosing his words carefully, trying to get to emotions but sticking to the blunt reality.

"Yes Dad, it feels ok. It happened, I did what I could. I'd do it again"

"That's good enough for me son." For the first time in a few years Jack ruffled his son's hair, but this time there seemed to be a new understanding between them. An empathy that others' outside of their unique relationship didn't share, couldn't share, wouldn't understand. William was glad of the chat, and so was his father. It was done.

The end of the summer brought a welcome distraction for William, and as if he needed it, a cementation of the desire to join the RN. William had been on all sorts of Cadet activities with the Navy, but the week in October of that year spent at HMS Excellent on Whale Island, the Royal Navy's school of leadership and gunnery, was to give him a real taste of what training would be like. He was enrolled on a qualification course for the rate of Cadet Petty Officer. The course was notoriously tough, and run by the Navy. The boys were all over 15 and a half years of age and as such were treated just as hard as enrolled boy sailors, if not harder because these ones were clever or pretentious enough to want a leadership role. If William passed this course he would be automatically rated up on his sixteenth birthday early next year.

From the moment he walked over the bridge to the main gate at Whale Island and saw the gravel parade ground, William felt the hairs stand up on the back of his neck (a reaction that would never change years from that day). His ears picked up the distinctive voice of a drill instructor, commanding conformance from a squad of Royal Navy leadership students. He was to learn later that the man was famous and feared all over the world, it was Fleet Chief Petty Officer (Freddy) Fuchs, who was revered as "God, only harder".

After being booked in at the main gate, he was ushered past the parade ground, past the black cinder practice ground of the Portsmouth Field Gun crew, onto a floating pontoon, to what would be his accommodation for the next week. On the side of the old grey Fleet Tender built during the second world war, were the distinctive black markings A134 that designated HMS Rame Head, the white ensign flew from her stern which signified she was a commissioned Royal Navy ship, despite looking like a cargo freighter. As he stepped onto the gangplank and crossed the ships side, his snapped his heels together, turned aft and saluted as he knew he should.

"Get that creature off my deck!" the words were bellowed from an annex not far from the gangplank, followed by a fierce looking man in a Chief Petty Officers uniform.

The naval rating escorting William, sniggered quietly, "You dumb fucker, you're in the shit before you've even started, good luck Jack!" in the bomb proof way that only a jolly jack tar could pull off, he slunk away as if invisible with the sole objective of not being caught up in any form of disciplining.

For a moment William was confused, what had he done? Then he realised that he had saluted while out of uniform. His keenness to do the right thing had actually led him straight into the place he didn't want to be, on somebody's RADAR as a duffer.

"Why haven't you jumped over the side you maggot?" the Chief was now striding to within a few inches of William, "You love my ship boy? Is that it?"

"Chief?"

"You don't love my ship? That means you hate my ship" he was almost incandescent with forced rage, and red in the face as a result.

"Chief, I . . ."

"Prove you love her you unworthy worm, get on your belly and kiss her!"

William looked uncomprehendingly at the Chief.

"DROP!"

William dropped his kit and fell the deck, the cold steel was covered in rough deck paint, a mixture of paint and sand designed to be non slip in heavy seas. The sensation was harsh on his hands and face which was now pressed to the deck, the Chief's shiny toe caps an inch from his head served as a visual reminder of his predicament.

"How much do you love my ship boy?" the emphasis on the "my" was unmistakable, this was not an answer to get wrong.

William was thinking hard. He was damned either way, that much was clear, so what he didn't want to do was simply conform and show a lack of leadership qualities. On the basis that there was not going to be a right answer William decided on his response.

"We have only just met Chief, but there is a certain attraction already!"

That was a new one! The Chief thought he had heard it all but had to admit he might have misjudged this one, this might be a good week after all. "Well it's time you got to know her better then, she's not shy, give her fifty kisses, each time you kiss the deck push yourself up and raise your face to the ensign then drop again. Give her fifty, and arms straight, no slacking"

Fifty press ups were really not a problem for William, he regularly raced people to a hundred and had managed a hundred in 90 seconds, but the pain of the deck paint on the palms of his hands did not make it a pleasant experience.

Though he didn't feel as though he had, William had managed to earn some early respect from the Chief Petty Officer who would act as the class's leader, mentor, punisher, motivator, maker, breaker, nurse maid and general provider of wisdom. He was a seasoned campaigner, you might even call him a salty sea dog. He was feared and respected by most, hated by some and the odd few who had won his respect had learned the true value of his sage council. As William disappeared down the hatch to his mess-deck that would be home for the next week, he was glad to be out of the chiefs gaze, and he turned his attention to searching for an available bunk. Below decks the ship had an audible and physical hum caused by machinery and air conditioning. It was invasive to begin with, but soon became part of the unconscious and for William it was part of the nostalgic experience unique to being on a warship and he loved it.

There were plenty of bunks and he soon found one to his liking. The bunks were classically three layered, with around 18 inches between each, just about enough room to roll over without touching the bunk or deck head above. They each had a metal roll bar which was a really uncomfortable accessory when getting in and out of bed or when banging a knee in the night, however in rough seas they were apparently a god send as you could wedge yourself against the pitch and roll of the ships motion and get some kind of sleep. Maybe the habit of being able to snatch sleep in all conditions added a little something to the character of the British Sailor. William loved the thought of being part of that elite number and began to day dream. "'Ow do?" a happy voice thickly laced with a welsh accent broke through his day dream.

"Hello"

"Where you from then?" the you sounded more like oo and the inflection of the last word fell off as if almost sung.

"East Anglia, you?"

"The Valleys boyo, God's own country!" Valleys was split into two very distinctive syllables Va . . . lleys.

"Haha, that's what all you remote types say about where you live. I'm Will"

The Welshman grinned with infectious enthusiasm, "I'm Taff"

"No shit!" they both laughed and in that moment became friends.

"That Chief is a proper bastard, he had me doin' press ups before I had even got on board, proper fierce he is!" the Pro . . . . per fi . . . erce protraction once again exaggerating the description.

"How many did you get?"

"Bloody 50, can you imagine man? 50 bloody press ups, all in one go?" his voice seamed to get higher and higher with each inflection, it made William laugh.

"Haha, me too!" William liked Taff, but it was clear he was no athlete.

As the mess deck filled up with boys from all over the country, they began to form relationships and common ground. There were other courses running, but the Cadet Petty Officer qualifying course was the tough one, and as such had a different tempo about it. As soon as the last boy enrolled on the course was on board, the Chief had them all muster on the fo'c'sle for a briefing.

They fell in as a squad of twelve, three neat ranks of four, and listened to the sermon like briefing.

"This will be the toughest week of your life! The rate of Petty Officer is something to be earned and will not be simply given to you on a plate. Our job therefore, is to find reasons for you to fail, the fact that you are here suggests that you should already be good enough to pass so don't look for help or sympathy, if you want sympathy you will find it in the dictionary between shit and syphilis!" His glare challenged the squad to laugh, eagle eyes searching for quarry, no-one moved a muscle so he continued, "You will be expected to be everywhere you need to be five minutes before you are due there. You will not be chased, you have to be responsible, you are senior Cadets we don't expect to be running around after you. But woe betide anyone who is adrift, lateness will not be tolerated. You will be worked hard, call the hands is at oh six thirty, lights out at twenty two hundred, and there will not be a moment to waste between those hours if you are to pass. Now, as the senior Cadets in that mess down there, you are expected to keep order. Those little turds will be having fun while you work and no doubt they will want to talk all night and throw bedding around at each other, if that happens I will hold you lot responsible, is that clear?"

"YES CHEIF!" the reply was shouted in unison, already they felt a special bond that often emerges quickly in a team of people facing a tough challenge together. Pride was emerging, all of them convinced that they would not be the one to let the side down.

"Good, now, this will be the only time I expect to see you in civvies for the rest of your stay, and the only time you will dine in civilian clothing. As the senior class, you will have the privilege of eating first, the only privilege you have. We will march to the galley now where you will eat, then come back on board here, and make sure that your kit is ready for a full inspection in the morning."

"When you are dismissed fall in again on the jetty and we will march to dinner."

They did exactly that.

"This is where you will muster every morning, and I expect you to be the stand out squad, you will be immaculate every day, you will not move or talk in the squad. You will march everywhere, if for some reason you are alone you will double everywhere, is that clear?" the verb to double was referring to double time or running.

"YES CHIEF!"

Without another pause the Chief barked out the next order.

"MOVE TO THE RIGHT IN THREES, RIIIIGHT TURN!"

The squad moved in unison, and it felt good.

"BY THE LEFT, QUICK MARCH!"

Everyone knew what they were doing, each cadet's left foot hit the tarmac at the same time and a steady cadence was immediately established. William was grinning, he felt great, the rapport felt by the simple act of marching perfectly in a squad of people who had known each other for less than an hour filled his heart with a sense of pride.

The week lived up to the Chief's billing, not a moment was wasted, the pressure was relentless. There literally didn't seem to be time to go to the toilet. In fact toward the end of one lunch time, William found himself in the heads, which is a Naval term for toilet, on his own and felt a surge of panic that he should be somewhere else. The lack of anyone else being there suggested that they were all marching off to a class without him. He rushed out to find his class with some relief mustering casually, his heart rate slowed again. Such was the sense of urgency that had been quickly instilled into the group, and it would change the way William approached work in future. He was achieving more than he ever thought possible, certainly more than he had ever applied himself to at school.

The week was packed with learning and culture, it was physically and mentally challenging and William loved it. It was a Navy that was clinging onto the ideals of Empire, there hadn't been a war to fight for years, and the ceremonial element of the base was steeped in history that dragged back the values and customs through its salt encrusted instructors who had served as man and boy and now clung onto the old ways that had seen the Royal Navy become the most powerful thing the world had ever seen.

Most of it was theatre, but it felt so real to those swept up by it. And for William it was spell binding. Friday morning was divisions where he would see his hero Fleet Chief (Freddy) Fuchs in action, The feared parade marshal who claimed to "own" the parade square and therefore everyone on it regardless of rank. In truth, there were more than a few officers who feared him, the enlisted men were terrified.

The gravel parade square at HMS Excellent was huge. Its perimeter was peppered with exact replica steps for the entrances to the like of Westminster Abbey and St Pauls Cathedral, so that ceremonial state occasions could be practiced. In the corner there was a World War 1 tank, otherwise known as "Freddy's perch". He would stand on the tank and observe a parade looking for the slightest movement or mistake before marching off the tank to impale any wrong doer on his parade stick. This was a time when the term political correctness had not yet been coined and the concept was unthinkable. Freddy had phrases that would see him in a 21st Century prison, yet somehow they made him a legend and despite being terrified of him, people loved him for it. He was an icon.

The fear that he could induce was irrational in many ways, because he could never physically hurt anyone, yet the image of Freddy marching off his tank toward an individual could and did provoke flight. William was privy to the evidence of this on Friday's divisions where the whole ships company were fell in for the colours ceremony at 0800 hours. Because it was a Friday, there was a full 48 man guard of serving sailors, made up from the classes of gunners that were training there. A guard drilled with rifles, and this always drew more scrutiny from Freddy, it was a privilege to be in the guard, especially on Freddy's square. Not everyone saw it in the same way. As the guard marched on, no-one moved, all you could hear was the synchronised crunch of 48 sets of highly polished boots on gravel plus the two officers of the guard and two flank guide Petty Officers (who were also fair game for Freddy). As the order was given to turn into line and then order arms, a noise was heard that was clearly not meant to be there, the unmistakable sound of a rifle falling onto the gravel. In the seconds that followed, over 500 people held their breath. Freddy's voiced boomed across the 50 yards or so that separated his perch from the guilty sailor

"YOU FUCKING LESBIAN!!!"

And with that Freddy was on the march, closing the distance with every stride, face manic, one arm pumping almost crab like as the other clasped his parade stick, eyes like a demon possessed with hate focussed on his prey. With ten yards to go it was all too much, the rating had served for over five years, been to sea, suffered from sleep depravation, hardship, hunger, cold and the unrelenting sarcasm of his fellow sailors, but Freddy bearing down like a battleship from a bygone age tipped him over the edge and he ran. He ran off the square, out of the main gate, over the bridge and was gone. Apparently the Naval Provost found him sleeping rough in the New Forest three weeks later.

The experience underpinned for William how great it would be to be part of this. He was up for it. He had worked so hard, passed the course with flying colours, and learned a lot about his capability in the mean time. He was focussed, this was it, he was ready aye ready.

Summer turned to winter and Christmas of that year saw The Human League at number one with don't you want me baby. William liked the new sound of New Romantic, it wasn't Madness, but it was edgy and different yet kind on the ear. Though the look was something he was less comfortable with, makeup for men was not going to find its way onto Williams shelf where he still had a bottle of Brut that he was making last as long as he could.

It was a white Christmas, the December of 1981 had some of the heaviest snowfalls for years, and with the melting of the snow an old life melted with it, ushering in a new year that had the potential to dictate the rest of William's life. 1982.

It was to be his last year at school, exam year. It would also see his sixteenth birthday. These things he knew would happen and he was ready for them. Other things that would unfold in that year he could not foresee and it would have a profound influence on the rest of his life.

William had done OK in his mock exams for GCE and CSE qualifications. He hadn't really put a lot of effort into revising for them and didn't really get motivated by them. He regarded them as practice for the real thing, and as such he had decided to reserve his investment of time into the real deal. His teachers were frustrated by his approach but there was little they could do at this stage to influence him, he was too strong a character, the academics sighed at another wasted talent, while the more intuitive teachers hoped that he would fulfil his potential and quietly admired his calm and confident outlook.

William knew he would do what he had to do to get into the Navy. That was his focus, his passion. He was completely obsessed and driven by the goal of getting in. He was willing to sacrifice just about anything to get there. Suddenly the stakes were real and he was applied to making the grade. Teachers that had written him off were shocked when project work began to hit their desk. His Geography teacher was amazed at the work he had done. "Dole, why on earth didn't you produce some of this last year? I would have put you through for GCE instead of CSE, but I couldn't do that on the strength of nothing?" He was aghast with frustration.

William simply beamed back at the teacher, "It's ok sir, I entered myself for the O Level after I saw you had only put me down for the CSE. And don't worry, I'll get it too." His work ethic had changed since his experience at HMS Excellent.

The teacher simply shook his head in resignation and leafed through the project once again.

William had done the same with Mathematics. He had a huge personality clash with the teacher, who William was convinced had taken him out of the GCE stream out of spite. "I'll bloody show him!" he thought to himself as he filled in the entry form for the

O Level. He knew he had the support of his parents to pay for the extra exams, they had said as much.

He was also down to take the first ever GCSE, a new pilot scheme that was designed to combine the two qualifications into one. The subject was one of his favourites, Technical Engineering Drawing. He would end up with the honour of being the first ever person (well among the others of that year) to get an "A" GCSE.

At one stage William considered giving up all his out of school activities to concentrate purely on his exams. In fact he even tried it for two weeks. Every night for those two weeks he sat in his bedroom and applied himself to his books. After an hour or less, his mind would begin to drift, he always found it hard to get motivated to read and digest information, he much preferred to learn by living and experiencing than by filling up on theory. The reality was inescapable however, he had to demonstrate his ability to learn and earn the necessary O-levels that would get him into the Royal Navy, but not just in as a "deck ape" seaman, he wanted a technical job, to work with weapons and have the ability to develop. For that he needed to get at least five O-Levels and he was determined to get them.

As his mind drifted, his eyes would float around the room, as they did so they would fall upon all of the memorabilia he had collected from the Sea Cadets, including all of his certificates which were pinned on the high wooden picture rail in the large old room. Beneath those, he had a collection of cap tallies pinned to the wall. Cap tallies were the black ribbon tied in a bow on a Royal Navy ratings cap They had his ships name woven in gold lettering. William allowed his dream to develop as he went from name to name, caught up in the nostalgia of some of these names: HMS Ark Royal, HMS Bulwark, HMS Sheffield, HMS Ajax, HMS Phoebe, HMS Arrow, HMS Scylla, HMS Zulu . . . and of course in pride of place HMS Excellent. There were over fifty and he knew them all, he knew each ship by class from the old Tribal class frigates like Zulu to the modern type 42 destroyers like Sheffield and the sleek Type 21 Frigates like Arrow and Ajax. He liked the idea of serving on a frigate, the busy and nimble work horses of the fleet capable of defending and attacking, speedy and manoeuvrable yet still big enough to pack a real punch. The centre piece of his collection was his own painting of the Sea Cadet Corps crest, with its motto scrolled at the bottom *READY AYE READY.* He said out loud "Yes I will be!" and with a sigh went back to his studies.

It became a ritual for two weeks, but it wore him down. One Sunday evening, he looked at those three words and declared "How can I be ready if I can't be me?" As he heard the words form, he knew that the next night would see him at the pool with the life saving club after he had pressed his uniform and polished his boots for Cadets the following night. Strangely, or maybe not, he found it easier to study that night.

The two weeks of abstinence from extra-curricular activity had given William another view of life, he was focussed on success, but he had also realised that he needed to be actively doing what he needed to do in order for this new focus to maintain momentum. His teachers all had different advice, most of them selfishly condoning him to spend most of his revision time on their subjects at the expense of everything else in life. William however, was making his own decisions based on his own instincts. As he cut through the water doing swimming drills his mind would drift to his books. As he stood on the parade deck his dream of wearing a cap tally that started with HMS was almost an ache. Being at the unit for the first time in almost three weeks was the fuel he needed to keep going, this was what it was all about, this was why he was working, of course he had to be here.

It seemed to be coming together. Revising was going ok, Cadets was buzzing, D of E was progressing well, William was well on top of his D of E modules to get the Gold award which meant he would be able to visit Buckingham palace and receive his award from the Duke of Edinburgh himself. He only needed to complete the expedition which was planned for the summer, and that left the residential section where an individual had to go away and work in a team with people they had never met before for two weeks. He had hoped that some of his Cadet courses would have qualified for that, but the longest one was only one week so fell short of the mark. It had occurred to him that if he got into the Navy then basic training should be more than adequate, if they allowed it to count.

If there was an evening William could afford to let go of in favour of revision it was his Wednesday night at D of E. He had therefore been popping in only once a month just to keep the ball rolling. In his various meetings with the Fleet Chief Petty Officer at the careers office (such a different character from Freddy Fuchs), he had been told that his achievements at D of E were certainly seen in a positive way so he felt it was important to keep up a presence.

He was greeted with enthusiasm by the other club members whenever he turned up, and it felt strange to William when he did, almost like he was out of touch with the gossip by not being on the inside track. "Come and meet the new girl Will" came a beaming greeting from one of the regulars upon one such visit.

It was enough to get William's attention.

As they turned into the common room of the hall William once again found himself having eye contact with a very familiar face "Will this is Catrina!"

"I know!"

The last thing he needed right now was another distraction. He was so totally focussed on achieving one aim and one aim only that was to join the RN. But something was happening to his insides again when he looked into those eyes that were full of something he couldn't quite make out. There was something almost chemical coming from her as they held eye contact. Her eyes were a little more knowing than some of the younger girls he knew, as if she had experience they hadn't, yet there was also a hint of desperate fear and innocence. Was it innocence? No it was more like submission. Whatever it was, she was certainly sending out some signals.

Catrina had become a little obsessed with Will, every time they had met had been nothing short of dramatic and full of emotional turmoil, yet each time he had appeared to her like a rock, so much older than his years. To Catrina, Will was the hero that she wanted all the older boys her age to be, yet they could never make the mark. Despite being younger, Will had stolen her heart, she wanted him. She wanted him emotionally, intellectually and sexually, and she would do anything to get him, but he wasn't yet sixteen and that was a problem.

She had thought about joining the life saving club to meet him there, but ever since the tragic events of the previous summer, she couldn't be near water, yet thinking of the way William, her hero, had looked in his speedos, she almost caved in. Then she had heard through a friend that the reason he did Life Saving was to supplement his Duke of Edinburgh's Award. She had never heard of it, but once she researched it and found that you could join up to the age of 24, it sounded perfectly credible for her and she seized the day.

William looked into her eyes and something drew him like a moth to a flame. The back of his mind was shouting "here we go again, back off Will, back off!" but it was too late, his teenage hormones, pride and growing sexual appetite was cancelling out all the sensible messaging. He found himself smiling back, and knew something would develop that night.

The kiss that they shared at the end of that night was different to anything William had experienced before. She had pressed herself onto him in a way that he had not expected. This was new, exciting and a little intimidating, he wasn't the one setting the pace this time. She was far more experienced than he had ever known . . . the older woman.

Catrina wanted him, but she was also conscious that he was not yet sixteen, albeit only a week or so away. "On your birthday Will, can we do it?"

"What?" his heart thumped in his chest, he hadn't expected that. "You know Will! I want you to"

"yeh" he was euphoric, like it was another world, as if he were viewing a movie and he was in it.

"I am going to make you a very happy boy!" She licked her lips suggestively and winked.

"What?" he wasn't sure he was hearing her correctly, wasn't sure what she even had in mind. His mind was doing as many somersaults as his tummy.

Without saying another word, she turned and walked away from him in the most suggestive way he had ever seen, and it was clearly exaggerated just for him.

Going home that night, William didn't know quite how to feel. He was going to lose his virginity, yet he wasn't driving the pace, it was exciting yet he wasn't in control so it was slightly stressful too and that was confusing him. Something didn't feel right about it, yet somehow he knew he would go through with it.

Top Tips - Tough Conversations

All too often in life, both at home and work, situations suffer because of the inability for people to have those "tough conversations".

We tend to avoid confrontation on certain sensitive subjects, or simply tolerate unacceptable behaviour because it seems easier than tackling the issue for fear of breaking the relationship. In reality, all we achieve when we do this is an outcome where we have effectively given that person permission to behave badly by not bringing up the subject.

Candid conversations are healthy and they bring clarity to expectations. A good session of clearing the air can breathe new life into any kind of relationship and remove any potential for long term resentment.

Conversely, the cost of inaction can be a build up to what becomes a terminal argument because things have been allowed to fester for so long that all trust disappears and the relationship is broken to the point whereby the resulting discussion is so confrontational that a good outcome is beyond reach.

So why is it that we allow ourselves to get into these situations? Usually fear of what might happen, of course, but also we often simply don't know how to start the conversation, so we justify to ourselves that things aren't so bad, we'll "wait and see what happens". Hey presto, we have just given permission for unacceptable behaviour.

So how can we avoid this trap? Given that once any subject is on the table it is easier to talk about, the key thing is to get it on the table early and in such a way that it's real and specific. Our friend evidence comes to the rescue here once again.

Having tough conversations is so much easier when you can open one with evidence. Once you are into it, you can quickly decide what good looks like and get to win-win thinking (as discussed in a previous top tip). So find ways that you are comfortable with to open evidential tough conversations, such as "I noticed that . . ." If you open a conversation with "I noticed that . . ." it is very difficult to avoid or disagree with because what you say next provides all the evidence you need. If what you noticed was something that you got out of context or misunderstood, the other party will quickly challenge it or put it into context for you, or they might agree with you and immediately apologise, horrified in some cases that is has affected you in such a way and how could they have been so short sighted or thoughtless. There are any number of outcomes, but the point is you are now talking about the meat of the subject two sentences into the "tough conversation", that has to be a good thing. It also avoids the usual skirting around the real issue that we often engage in when avoiding a tough conversation we know we must have. Evidence is key, underpinned by how we feel about that and what good looks like going forward.

For example in the workplace, an opening statement from a supervisor to a lazy operative my go something like this "I have noticed that you have been a few minutes late every day this week, I feel a little let down by that because everybody else can make it in on time and while it's only a few minutes it's not acceptable or fair. I am concerned that people will start to think of you as a lazy team member and I am not prepared to have that going on. Is there anything your struggling with that is preventing you from getting in on time? Maybe we can help"

Again there are several outcomes, however this is a common niggle and more often that not, because they have got away with it once they tend to be less bothered by being late more regularly. By raising the issue in this way, the usual outcome is that the individual changes their behaviour because they now know it's been noticed. Ironically they can also be motivated by the conversation in a positive way because, guess what, they have been noticed!

"I've noticed that . . ." really works, and there are others you can use too:

"As you know . . ."

"When we first . . ."

"It's obvious that . . ."

You get the picture, and you will find some of your own that are relevant to your character and the situation. The point is they are all powerful and underpinned with evidential information within the next breath. Hopefully you can see how this will get you to where you need to be far quicker than "we need to talk!"

Once you get a reputation for having the ability to have "tough conversations" your leadership or relationship role becomes so much easier, you will find you are actually more approachable, people will know that you are happy to listen to their concerns and you will actually feel a lot more in control of relationships which as we know leads to less stress.

Look around you at people in great marriages, they have tough conversations very easily and trust is at the centre of their relationship as a direct result of that. Look back also at tough conversations you yourself might have been involved in, how much better did you feel for having it? Even if the outcome wasn't pleasant, at least you could now plan a way forward because the elephant was out of the room.

Get your mindset into the fact that tough conversations lead to great outcomes, it's not about being aggressive it's about caring for fairness and trust. Just like being a parent, you confront because you care!

Good luck ☺

CHAPTER 16

BOY TO MAN

William's head was spinning! Everything was happening at once and it felt like he was being swept up in the current of an unstoppable river of emotions and duty. He was to be sixteen in a few weeks, old enough to fight for your country, old enough to have sex, old enough to leave school and become a man. Because of his successful passing of his Cadet Petty Officer course, he would be rated up on his birthday. His exams were looming which also meant the end of school the reality of which meant that the Navy was not just a dream anymore but a fast approaching necessity for a job if nothing else.

He had a week booked in the Easter holidays on HMS Flintham, the Ham class inshore minesweeper. He was looking forward to going onboard as a Cadet Petty Officer and getting out to sea as if he really were in the Navy.

He had also been offered a job in the engineering factory where his brother worked, with the promise of an apprenticeship if his exams results worked out ok. This had thrown him a bit because he hadn't really thought about what might happen if he didn't get in, but then the reality was that he might well not as there were so many applicants for so few places. He had unconsciously began to accept that he may well be spending his life getting his hands dirty working machines and making parts. Part of him was happy about that as his technical drawing skills, metal work, maths and science subjects were his strongest and he loved making models. He also knew however that it would always be a compromise on what he really wanted.

All of this sensible thinking was constantly being pushed aside by Catrina. There was a doubt in his mind about Catrina, he didn't know what it was, it didn't make sense, but he knew inside that being with her was wrong for him. Then he would think of what she did and what she was promising and he would feel himself getting uncontrollably excited and all thinking went out of the window.

He had successfully avoided the issue for a few weeks, making sure he was never alone with her, never having any time to just hang around with her . . . to be fair, he didn't have to manufacture too much, the fact was he was very busy cramming everything into his life. But one night at D of E, she managed to get some time alone with him, her methods were brave.

As William went to the toilet during a non official break time, Catrina followed him in. As she walked in behind him she immediately wrinkled her nose at the musty smell of the men's lavatories and feeling suddenly out of her comfort zone she almost had second thoughts and for a moment considered turning round and running. Her heart was pounding in her chest at the audacity of her actions, yet she had now committed, she was here and for the first time in ages she could talk to William alone. She had almost given up hope, as he had seemed completely aloof lately, she fretted in case her forward actions which at the time seemed to have pleased William so much may have actually put him off her. Was she bad at it? Did he find her unattractive? She had to know . . . she decided to push it.

William was standing in front of the mirror over the sink, he was leaning forward his face contorted as he stretched his top lip down while examining his skin which always seemed to threaten an outburst of acne. His hands were supporting his weight on the built in counter surrounding the sink as he leaned forward pulling various faces. He heard someone come in behind him and quickly stopped the faces in time to see in the mirror just who it was. "Bloody hell . . ."

He watched her walk up beside him then to his astonishment felt her press herself onto his hand before she simply said, as if it were the most natural place to be "hello Will".

They were both suddenly stuck for words, stuck for actions. Catrina didn't move and William didn't even breathe. He could hardly believe that the back of his hand was in direct contact with her intimate organs and yet she hardly appeared to notice. Had she not realised? He had no way of telling, but it was one logical explanation.

She broke the silence without moving "can I see you tonight Will?"

"You are now . . ."

"You know what I mean Will, don't tease me!"

"I suppose . . . I don't know . . ."

"What's the matter? Don't you want me?" she was beginning to feel genuinely rejected and uncertain, but stayed still, hardly daring to move, the contact between them now seemed almost unreal, like a third person in the conversation that neither of them dare mention.

"It's not that Catrina, I just . . . I don't know!" and the truth was he didn't know, his mind was a confused mess of hormones, basic desires, intrigue and conflicting emotions, and yes there was fear too, but fear of what he had no idea.

Catrina was beginning to run out of confidence too, she stepped back, leaving his hand feeling suddenly cold and yet she herself could still feel it's presence on her. As she hurried out, suddenly aware that she really shouldn't be where she was he heard her parting words, confidently spoken almost as an assertive instruction "Buy some johnnies."

The words echoed in his brain for days. Where the hell could he get those from? This was just adding to the pressure, yet he plotted and schemed none the less. Presented with the problem that was in front of him, he simply had to find a solution, it was his way after all. The chemist was no good, far too embarrassing and too many people knew him, word would get back to his parents for sure. No, that was not the way!

Then one night at Cadets the solution presented itself, albeit not without some awkward confusion along the way. One of the cadets, a lower rank, and slightly younger than Will was skylarking (the Navy term for messing about) one parade night and Will went over to break up the noisy throng of young lads that he had around him. "Pipe Down!" William instructed, "What's going on?" he naturally assumed the role of instructor and authority and was generally respected as the senior cadet, the hierarchy worked. There was a lot of giggling and suppressed behaviour, one of the younger boys looked visibly scared of what William might say.

With a smirk on his face the ring leader made a statement that would haunt and taunt William for days, "we are just laughing about the instructions on here" the lad said defiantly. What William heard next was "put on a wrecked penis" then a splutter of laughter as the boys dispersed, the ringleader waving the packet of Durex at Will before stowing it away in his bell bottomed uniform trousers.

"Where did you get those from?"

"The same place everyone gets them from!"

"The chemist?"

The boy laughed out loud, "no you have got to be joking, the off-licence"

"Piss off! They don't sell those at the offy!"

"No, but the toilets in there has a machine"

The shrill sound of the bosun's call warbled the distinctive general call that captured everyone's attention for the next instruction as the duty bosuns mate called "out pipes, hands to muster". This was the signal that stand easy (break time) was over and thus broke off William's interrogation.

As he climbed the companion way (stairs) to the upper deck, he felt a surge of excitement at the thought of shame free buying of condoms, but at the same time total confusion about why on earth they could only be put on a wrecked penis . . . and why on earth use that term? What did it mean? It couldn't possibly be literal could it? He would have to get some and read the instructions for himself.

The opportunity presented itself a week or so later. There was only one off-licence that was well known by teenagers as fairly forgiving on the legal drinking age. It was an old fashioned style, walk in room attached to the back of a busy pub. The interior was typically dark, with wooden floors and smoke stained ceiling. A small room with a counter no more than four feet across, it smelled of stale smoke and old beer. There was a door that connected to the main bar and another that led to the toilets, that was where Will was heading, and hoped to make it before the barmaid came through. As he entered, he could see that the barmaid was busy pulling a pint, she looked up at the moment the door had activated the bell hanging just above it and rolled her eyes at seeing another teenager walk through, her attention once again directed at her paying customer. This was perfect for William's plan as he scuttled straight into the toilet.

The machine on the wall was right in front of him, the advertising promising a featherlite experience 3 for 50P. He fumbled in his pocket then felt his adrenalin rush as a man at the urine trough coughed and spat onto the wall in front of him, giving himself a target to aim at. William was like a rabbit in headlights, he hadn't thought about the possibility that there might be anyone in the toilet before he rushed in. William tried to compose himself and pretend that he was waiting for his turn at the trough, but his body language gave everything away, "You getting lucky son?" the man winked as he turned, zipping his fly as he adjusted himself.

William flushed as the blood rushed to his face, he could not hold eye contact with the man but felt compelled to defend himself, his pathetic reply was less than convincing "I'm just getting them for a mate . . ."

"Good luck son" the man winked again and was gone, much to William's relief.

With trembling hands, desperate to get what he came for and get out before anyone else came in, he found the slot with his 50 pence piece. There was an empty hollow noise as the coin fell into a void within the machine, to Williams horror, nothing happened as he turned the wheel. He pressed his thumb on the coin return button . . . nothing happened. Again he pressed, several times with more urgency and yet nothing came out of the slot beneath. Now what? He couldn't face the concept of complaining to the barmaid, he had one more 50p but could he risk that happening again? It was a vast sum of money to just waste. In the back of his mind however, he knew he would take the risk, he was here after all, he had come this far.

He held the coin in the slot for a few seconds before he allowed himself to let go. The noise this time was far more promising, it sounded as if it had engaged with machinery rather than just falling to a tinny resting place at the bottom of the machine. He screwed the wheel on the side of the machine and it crunched through gears in the mechanism and as the pressure suddenly released on the wheel, a cellophane wrapped packet slid into the tray beneath. The words on the back of the packet that William was now reading made him laugh out loud in both relief and stupidity "... erect penis" That makes more sense.

The days that followed dragged. He had taken one condom out of the packet and hidden the rest with its contents up the chimney of the disused fireplace in his bedroom. The one he had taken out was already beginning to make a tell tale ring impression in his wallet. He was looking forward to tell Catrina about the fact that he was ready for her that night at D of E.

"No William!" her face was twisted in what looked like disgust to William and his brain was thrown once more into confusion. What was this girl doing to him? "I told you William, when you are sixteen and not before."

"But what about when you ..."

"That's different"

"How?"

"It just is, that's all. How could you think that I would want to now, with a fifteen year old, ewww Will that's wrong ..."

He was shattered. His pride had been bashed again. It wasn't the rejection so much, it was the obvious disgust she had shown to the whole idea. He thought she had wanted to, hell she was driving it for god's sake. "Bloody women" he was becoming more and more familiar with the feeling associated with that phrase. He trudged home that night, and knew why men using that saying always sounded so exasperated.

The blow had led to him once again avoiding Catrina. Helped by the week aboard HMS Flintham, which served to take his mind completely away from all things female and focus on the career he now so passionately wanted. He had been really looking forward to this one, having now ironically turned sixteen and been rated Cadet PO.

He had been on before, but as a junior cadet, now he was top dog and in charge of all the cadets on board. A few Naval ratings had stayed on board for the week, having given up their bunks for the visiting cadets, their shipmates also having gone on leave. There was a level of resentment, no matelot liked to give up his pit, or have the extra work involved of moving all his kit for one week. But as always, "Jack" simply cracked on with it and faced the challenge of the day.

William was in his element, he was a capable seaman and was able to perform many of the tasks the professional deckhands did and indeed was able enough to teach them to the younger cadets. In fact the very responsibility of teaching the others added to his own learning, he unconsciously put pressure on himself to perform well and learn. The best way to learn anything after all is to teach it.

While the cadets idolised William and wanted to be like him when they became older, marvelling at his badges of proficiency and the way he handled himself. The sailors who called HMS Flintham their home found him a little too cocky and arrogant. One of them in particular felt he needed to be brought down a peg or two. Able Seaman John (imbe) Tween was what the Navy called a three badge loafer. The three badges referred to the good conduct stripes earned for every four years of good conduct served in the RN, the maximum being three which suggested a minimum of twelve years service but twelve years spend loafing around going no-where. He was a typical waster. The term waster actually came from the Navy and was allocated to a rating than was only fit to perform low skilled work in the ships waists rather than up in the rigging with the "topmen" their pay even reflected this and certainly their status with their shipmates. Imbe was the modern day equivalent. He had never been popular in any of the ships he had served in, and as such he had worked out his on method of survival and chuntered on continuously about getting out as soon as his time was up. He would use the term ROMFT all the time

"I'm ROMFED, leave me alone" (Roll On My First Twelve) and do the minimum necessary to get by. He had got away with this attitude serving on bigger ships, but drafty (the Royal Navy drafting department, who allocated human resources to ships) had stitched him up with this one and he was six months into a three year stint on a tiny little cork with nowhere to hide. His life was a misery, no "jollies" to sunny shores, this was a UK waters only draft, no decent oppos (mates) no decent runs ashore and they had even stopped the tot a few years ago, so no rum ration either.

Imbe had volunteered for duty on the Cadet week, thinking it would be his opportunity to for once have some status on board. And now he was being shown up by this spotty oike who he had to admit could splice better and quicker than him. Well, he would pull down a peg or two . . .

He grabbed his opportunity when he saw William teaching the younger cadets bends and hitches with some off-cuts of rope on the fo'c'sle. Striding over, he tried to take on a posture of authority, it didn't come naturally to him, "what's occurring here then?" the younger cadets looked up nervously as if they had done something wrong.

William simply replied without looking up from his west country whipping "Bends and Hitches Imbe, it's what sailors do when they grow up!"

Imbe felt his anger surge, but he couldn't find the words for a witty comeback. How was it that so many other sailors had such an ease with banter and would never bite at being teased, how he longed for that skill now. He had to repress his anger, he would be trooped (sent for Naval disciplining) big time if he struck a cadet.

"And is that what you want to be then? A sailor when you grow up?" it was delayed, but Imbe was pleased with his question.

"Yes, I will be" William said with certainty "and I won't be stuck in the bilges like you for long either." William had picked up on something one of the other sailors had said, a killick (leading rate, junior NCO) who William respected deeply.

"You'll never get in you little shit, you're too gobby!" Imbe was incessant with inner rage now.

"Well they let you in and you're both gobby and shit!"

That was the last straw, Imbe grabbed William by the scruff of his neck and hauled him to his feet. William reacted instinctively the years of finger sparring with his father paying dividends. He grabbed Imbe's wrist, digging his fingers into the artery commonly used to take a pulse and twisted back hard and sharp, using the mechanical advantage of angles to his favour. As he did so he allowed his other hand to fall over Imbe's fingers and he squeezed one up inside itself as if making Imbe's hand into a fist. But as he did so he pulled it hard from the very tip toward the knuckle while keeping it tight into the hand. The pain was excruciating for the surprised sailor, as William knew it would be and Imbe let out an almost girlish screech of shock and pain.

William pushed him away, looking at the pitiful sight of this grown man in uniform cowering and holding his wrist "The difference between you and me is that gobby is all you've got!"

As Imbe skulked away to lick his wounds, his real problems were as yet unknown to him. His killick had seen the whole episode from his concealed position on the bridge and was now smiling to himself, he could envisage the countless months ahead where he could extract mileage out of this one. For now he would store it away. He liked that young Cadet Petty Officer, and quietly under his breath uttered "I recon I might be saluting that little bugger in a few years ..."

On the 2nd April 1982, shortly after William had been on HMS Flintham, Argentina started what was to be a bloody conflict by invaded the Falkland Islands and South Georgia in the South Atlantic. A small force of Royal Marines bravely held the Argentinean forces at bay on South Georgia before being overwhelmed and sensibly doing something that the Royal Marines simply don't do, they surrendered. William had only ever heard of the Royal Marines performing a "tactical withdrawal", but on such an Island below the Antarctic circle that option did not exist. Britain duly declared war on Argentina, and the first live televised war the world had ever seen was to be broadcast in all its stark reality.

There was a period of four weeks while the task force sailed the 8,000 miles in record time where nothing really happened other than debates about why on earth would anyone want to go to war for islands that no-one had ever really heard of? And, actually where the hell were they anyway? Some even thought that the Falkland Islands were somewhere off the north coast of Scotland.

But soon enough, images of air battles where British Harrier pilots vastly out classed their Argentinean foes were bringing a sense of invincibility in British military mite to the living rooms of Great Britain. Shocking though it was to see enemy aircraft exploding in mid air, people were somehow detached from it. Then new images came in from the sea battles where first it became clear that a ship was no match for a submarine when the Argentine battleship General Belgrano was sunk with a massive loss of life, then shortly after it became even more clear that a ship was no match for an aircraft when British ship after British ship was hit by modern missiles from modern aircraft. The images now were of British seamen, exhausted, burned, dying, surviving . . . the reality of war at sea and on land in a remote, cold and distant place, there live and for all to sea. Some of the Cap Tallies on William's wall would have a different feeling about them now, Sheffield, Ardent, Antelope, Coventry then Atlantic Conveyor and Sir Galahad would all be condemned to the bottom of the South Atlantic Ocean.

William's father was always quiet during the news as was the rest of the family as they knew he insisted upon it so that he could hear every detail, but during these scenes you could almost hear his silence, as if he knew more than everyone else about what those men on screen were feeling. As William watched his father, his Mother watched William. She knew his passion for joining the Navy, and now this was tearing her apart. She was bursting to plead with him not to go, but feared it would push him and his stubborn streak further, she also knew Jack, her husband, would not be pleased with her if she did, they had spoken of it.

William however watched the images and listened to all the reports, propaganda or not, he was convinced that the British would win. He himself felt bombproof, if he were to enter a similar theatre of war, he knew the odds were in his favour to come out victorious. He now wanted more than ever to get in and stand alongside the brave boys he saw. He had two friends who were down there, one an older cadet who had joined two years ago and was serving on HMS Arrow a type 21 frigate that sustained some minor damage when hit by cannon fire, and someone he had met at HMS Seahawk, the Royal Naval Air Station at Culdrose, who was now serving on the carrier HMS Hermes. William wanted to be there, he was completely detached from the danger and the horror, he just knew it was what he wanted to do, his mother wept at the thought every night.

When the task force arrived back in England, battered, tired but victorious a surge of pride rushed through William as he pressed and polished his Sea Cadet uniform. That same sense of pride in that uniform again.

Life was a blur, his exams came and went, he found them easy enough, certainly not as stressful as some of his classmates seemed to find them. He was very much of the attitude that they were finished and he couldn't change what he had done in them so why worry about the results? He had left school, his birthday had also come and gone without event, he had started his job in the engineering factory and Catrina had disappeared completely from the scene.

Work was exciting to begin with, he enjoyed getting his hands dirty and picking out the steel splinters gave him a feeling of machismo. He also enjoyed the status of walking around in overalls rather than school uniform, he was beginning to feel like a man. His first wage packet made him feel like a millionaire. He had worked 163 hours in his first month and on his hourly rate after tax and national insurance he had taken home £211.08. He paid £50 to his mother and the rest went into his wallet. He felt like a god.

"We need to get you a bank account set up son." His father had said once his mother had informed him of the £50 transaction. "I'll make you an appointment at The Midland, ask for the manager tell him I sent you." William hated it when he had to declare that he was the son of Jack Dole, it always made him feel embarrassed and somehow under scrutiny as the boy who had to rely on his father's name, this was far from the truth.

"It's ok Dad I'll do it"

"William, you need a current account, I'll tell them what you need it for and they will set it up with you, don't be arrogant on this one it's important"

"O K" the reply was protracted as Williams eyes rolled at the same time, he had to concede he hadn't thought about a bank account other than his savings account he had building up. It did make sense, though the cash in his wallet did feel nice. He looked down at his wallet where the tell tale ring of his purchase some months ago was now permanently forged into the soft leather.

The next week, he went into the Midland bank one lunchtime. He was dressed in his overalls, smelling of soluble oil and suddenly feeling a little out of place. He was usually proud to walk round looking dirty, to him it showed he was not afraid to get in amongst it and work hard. Lifted the heavy cast iron blocks that were to be machined onto the tables of milling and drilling machines was a dirty and arduous task. He suddenly felt very uncomfortable standing in the queue of people waiting for the next available teller. He scanned the faces behind the counter and his heart skipped as he saw a beautiful face with a fashionable perm flowing either side of it. He hoped he would get her . . . and he began to work out how many people were in the queue and what the odds were on him being next in line when she became free.

At that moment the manager came over and singled him out in the queue, "Mr Dole?" he asked it as a question, but it was clearly a known fact. "This way, we will get you sorted out in a jiffy." As William was led into a small side room, he looked over his shoulder to see the wooden name plaque in front of the beautiful face . . . Jess.

It took a while for William to get used to working out his budgets and not simply spend the money coming in. It was amazing how his new cash just disappeared, it wasn't so long since he had nothing but pocket money to survive on, yet now he had in comparison, untold wealth and it was all gone before the end of the month. What William did like about the whole process were his trips to the bank. He would walk by a try to see if Jess was on the counter, and if not he would come back later or another day. The only way to get cash from the bank was to take in a cheque made out for cash, so he would get little and often to maximize his trips. It was lucky that his lunch hour was twelve until one, which coincided with when Jess would cover on duty. It was always a game, trying to get served by her, if it were obvious he wouldn't be, he would often break out of the queue and pretend to write something else in his cheque book as if he were stupid enough to have made a mistake. Sometimes he was lucky, sometimes not, but he always tried to smile or hold eye contact with Jess. She always smiled back but he feared it was pure professionalism. He so desperately wanted to ask her out, but the risk was so high in his mind. If he embarrassed himself by asking and she was offended how could he set foot in the bank again? What would he look like in front of all the people waiting? Each time he reached the counter his heart raced, he could barely talk to her yet always managed to crack a joke or make some light hearted comment that would provoke her smile . . . or was it just customer service . . . ? One day he might find a way, the more he couldn't bring himself to ask, the more he desired her, he was like a moth to a flame.

His work was excellent, and his results from college on his day release course for his apprenticeship were outstanding. His father of course knew all this through keeping his ear to the ground, but never interfered, he let William cut his own path, fight his own battles. The manual labour, heavy lifting coupled with his continued activities with sport and the Cadets were turning his body into a powerful and toned human machine that was yet to reach its prime, he was turning into a man physically and in his mind he was already there. He would find the courage to ask out Jess, and resign himself to a career as an engineer like his eldest brother (which pleased his brother greatly and after recent world events his mother too).

With steady resolve, he walked into the bank and took his place in the queue. He looked over at Jess who was serving another customer, she quickly acknowledged him with a smile before turning back and smiling at her own customer. She was such a breath of fresh air, such a pretty and bright person, maybe she was just like that to everyone and William was going to make a fool of himself? He didn't care, he had heard nothing back from the Navy about his application, he refused to let that get him down but he needed to take charge of his life, he was going to ask her. It was his turn in the queue and Jess wasn't free, he turned behind him and ushered the next person through, and again . . . people were looking at him strangely and his heart rate was climbing but he was committed. Jess too had noticed and was thrilled at the same time as horrified at what she thought might be happening, she was going very red indeed. As she became free, with legs like Jelly William walked to her window. They were both tongue tied as he passed through his cheque made out to cash, then a note which simple said "will you go out with me?" As Jess read the note she could have kissed him there and then had the glass partition not been in the way. She almost loved him already for both wanting her and for not embarrassing her with the verbal question. As she counted his cash she looked at him and nodded with a hesitant smile as if the whole world were looking at her, but William could see she was genuinely happy and his heart soared. He was about to leave, as she said "Hold on Mr Dole . . ." she passed a paying in slip through the window and for a brief moment their fingers touched, it felt like electricity passing between them, it took a while for William to realize that the four digits she had written on the slip were her phone number.

That night he pedalled home so hard that he must have set a record time. The excitement he felt and the adrenaline in his system pushing him on and on, he was bursting with happiness at the thought of ringing Jess. As he slammed through the back door, out of breath but recovering quickly, sweaty and smelly from the factory, it was clear to William that the family had been arguing. As he put his things down, they all looked at him and his heart sank.

His eldest brother, his mother and his father were sat round the kitchen table. His brother had left work earlier than William and having a car had made it home quicker despite Williams sprint. Between them on the table was a brown envelope with the letters OHMS clearly prominent at the top. William's eyes dropped to the letter, it had been opened, it was addressed to the parent or guardian of William James Dole. His father's voice cleared up the confusion "You got in son!"

The reality thumped William in the stomach like a medicine ball. He had written this moment off.

"You join on the 7ᵗʰ February 1983 if you accept, you have to reply within 10 days, and you got in as a Weapons Engineer, well done son." This was one of the few times William had ever heard that phrase from his father and his head was spinning, what a day . . .

"Where do I sign?" William scrapped for the letter.

"Hold on, hold on, we have to sign to say you can, you are only sixteen!" It was his mother's outburst and it pushed her over the edge as she burst into tears, the memories of a war so fresh, less than three months ago haunted her every thought, all she could see was her boy's face burned like those poor men.

"It's a lot to think about Will," his brother Simon said, "you are doing really well, they are thinking about putting you on the fast track route to become a foreman after your apprenticeship. I really think you should stay here."

William respected Simon almost as much as his father, Simon had been the discipline in the house when his father was away and was fourteen years older than William, he had always been a man in Williams eyes not just a brother.

"There is nothing to think about, he's not going!" His mother wailed through more tears.

William was confused and scared, could his dream come so close and get snatched away? Would this also put the mockers on Jess? Would he really be a foreman in five years? (he hadn't considered that one).

"It's William's decision!" his father's voice took charge, as the objections started he asserted his authority talking about William as if he wasn't even in the room, but William loved him for it at that moment. "Listen, if we make this decision for him he will resent us for the rest of his life! He has to decide for himself and all we can do is help him make that decision. Now I suggest we all think about it for a couple of days."

William was still shaking after lying on his bed for an hour, his eyes continually scanning the Naval memorabilia in his room. His brain whizzing from place to place, touching down at the various facets of his life while it looked for solutions to problems that he didn't even understand. He suddenly sat bolt upright and whispered out loud "Jess!"

"Can I use the phone Dad?" He shouted from the cold hallway where the telephone table with its stool attached on one side and shelf for the directory under the table top where the telephone itself sat.

He didn't get a reply and took that as a yes. He fumbled for the slip of paper with her number and put his finger in the rotating dial, dialled the four digits and waited a second for the click, followed by the dialling noise. It rang four times, a man's voice answered by repeating the number he had just dialled.

"Could I speak to Jess please?"

"Who is calling?" the voice was immediately defensive and had to be that of her father.

"It's William!"

He heard the phone muffle as if the man had put his hand over the speaker, "Jessica, it's someone called William for you . . . you do? Well don't be long!"

It was a few moments before William heard another muffle and Jess's voice saying "Dad, please!!" then her wonderful voice suddenly clear "Hello?"

"Hello Jess its Will, Will Dole!"

She giggled, it was a lovely sound "I know, Dad said! Listen I can't be long he will be trying to earwig!"

"OK, can we meet up?"

"Yes meet me after work on Friday, you can walk me home if you like?"

"What time?"

"5 O'Clock, out the back of the bank, you know down the passage?"

"I'll be there! I have some big news too."

"OK, listen I've got to go, Dad is hovering, I nearly died today when you kept waiting for me, but I am so glad you did!"

"Me too!" William was beaming and she could almost hear it over the phone.

"OK, see you Friday, don't be late!"

"I won't!"

"Bye"

"Bye" As the receiver went down, William felt more lonely than he had ever felt before in his life, Friday was three days away and between now and then he had a decision to make, quite a big one.

Not surprisingly Simon and his mother had been campaigning him with all the compelling reasons he should stay at home, including working the angle of his latest love interest implying that long distance relationships couldn't work and that she was such a lovely girl, everyone knew her from the bank. It was having some effect and William was beginning to have doubts for the first time in his short life about a career in uniform.

The Navy wanted him. His father had spoken to the commanding officer of the Sea Cadet unit who had informed him that the careers office had marked him out as one of the best candidates they had seen to date. William was not to know this and his father didn't want him to, in case it influenced his decision in a biased way. It was time for the chat!

"What do you recon then son?"

"I don't know Dad, Simon recons I could be foreman in five years and what with Mum and everything, I just don't know how to make my mind up."

"Want to know what I think?"

"Yes please Dad, tell me what to do!"

His father laughed, "Oh no, I'm not telling you what to do on this one, but I'll give you this to think about. If you go in and hate it, you will have to serve a minimum of five years, now that might sound a long time right now, in fact it will be the best part of a quarter of your life, but you will still only be twenty one, that's no age and you can pick up pretty much where you left off only you will already have a trade and qualifications. If you go in and love it you have a career for life and you will see the world. Yes there is a risk that you might have to go to war, if you are the man I think you are you will put up with that if and when it comes. If you don't go in, you will do well and have a good life but you will always wonder what you missed."

The last few words hit home. How could he live his life wondering what might have been?

He was about to start his adult life by adopting an attitude that would drive him for the rest of his days . . .

"Better to regret something you have done, that something you didn't!"

A mother's tears were to fall upon the railway station platform, while a father's chest swelled with pride. Jess would have to watch her dream sail away and simply hope he would one day find her again . . .

Playlist

"Pretty Baby" - Blondie—Parallel lines, 1978—side one track five

"Rat Trap" - Boom Town Rats, 1978

"Hopelessly Devoted" - Olivia Newton John—Grease Album, 1978, side one track three

"These Boots are made for walking" - Nancy Sinatra 1966

"Blue Eyes" - Elton John—Jump Up, 1982—side one track six

"The Prince" - Madness—1979

"Baggy Trousers" - Madness—1981—Complete Madness—side one track four

"Just like starting over" - John Lennon—1981

"Being with you" - Smokey Robinson—1981

"Keep on loving you" - REO Speedwagon—1981

"Don't you want me?" - Human League—Christmas No 1 1981

<u>Quotations</u>

"Tough times don't last, but tough people do!"—Robert H. Schuller

"It's better to regret something you have done, than something you have not!"—Anon

"Life is not measured by the number of breaths we take, but by the moments that take our breath away"—Anon

"No-one has the power to affect your state of mind without your personal consent" Eleanor Roosevelt

"The hell I am . . ." John Wayne

"Stress—The state which occurs when the mind overrides the bodies basic desire to punch the living crap out of some arsehole that desperately needs it." Royal Naval ratings unwritten rule book

"Houston, we've had a problem here"—Jack Swiggert, Apollo 13 Astronaut

Lightning Source UK Ltd.
Milton Keynes UK
UKOW042111010413

208509UK00001B/20/P